D0341690

I SAY A LITTLE PRAYER

DOUBLEDAY

New York London Toronto

Sydney Auckland

I Say a Little Prayer

E. LYNN HARRIS

PUBLISHED BY DOUBLEDAY

Copyright © 2006 by E. Lynn Harris

All Rights Reserved

Published in the United States by Doubleday, an imprint of
The Doubleday Broadway Publishing Group, a division of
Random House, Inc., New York.
www.doubleday.com

DOUBLEDAY and the portrayal of an anchor with a dolphin
are registered trademarks of Random House, Inc.

Lyrics by Gordon Chambers

Book design by Gretchen Achilles

Cataloging-in-Publication Data is on file with
the Library of Congress

ISBN-13: 978-0-385-51272-5
ISBN-10: 0-385-51272-4

PRINTED IN THE UNITED STATES OF AMERICA

1 3 5 7 9 10 8 6 4 2

First Edition

In Memory of

JOHN H. JOHNSON
1/19/1918–8/8/2005

Thank you for being such a marvelous example
and inspiring another (colored) boy from Arkansas
to dream big.

ACKNOWLEDGMENTS

This author thanks God for the gift of creativity and for two careers that I am passionate about. I'm thankful once again for the life lesson that "tough times don't always last but tough people do."

I'm thankful for my mother, Etta W. Harris, and my aunt, Gee (Jessie L. Phillips), for a love that sustains me during difficult times. I'm grateful to my sisters, cousins, uncles, aunts, nieces, nephews, and godchildren (Gabby, Lamark) for the love and pride they show me every day.

It has been a while since I've had the opportunity to talk to you, my cherished readers. I've missed you so much, but trust me: I needed the time away. I want to thank each and every one of you who wrote me just to make sure I was okay. I can't tell you how much your deep concern meant to me.

I'm especially grateful to have a publisher and editor who understand the creative process and offered unconditional support and friendship even when they didn't have a new book to sell. So I give a billion thanks to the afore-mentioned Stephen Rubin and the amazing Janet Hill. I must also thank Michael Palgon, Bill Thomas, Alison Rich, Meredith McGinnis, Clarence Haynes, Rebecca Holland, John Fontana, Emma Bolton, Jackie Everly, Judy Jacoby, Jen Marshall, LuAnn Walter, and Anne Messitte for their much-needed support and talent.

I send out a special bouquet of gratitude to Pauline James and Gerry Triano for the extra effort they always give.

I must thank my good friend Gordon Chambers for allowing me to use lyrics from his fantastic debut CD *Introducing Gordon Chambers*. His music gave the perfect voice to my character Chauncey and was the one of my favorite CDs to listen to as I wrote this novel.

Thanks so much to Chris Fortunato and his staff.

I'm blessed to have friends who've been there for me over two decades. They know who they are and don't need mention here. But I'm so proud of them and the special bond we have that is just as strong as family. They are: Vanessa Gilmore, Lencola Sullivan, Robin Walters, Troy Donato, Cindy and Steve Barnes, Pam Frazier, Ken Hatten, Chris Martin, David and Tracy Huntley, Anthony Bell, Reggie Van Lee, Sanya and Derrick Gragg, Brenda and Tony Van Putten, Dyanna Williams, Yolanda Starks, Sybil Wilkes, and Blanche Richardson.

I would like to thank African American Radio, *The Early Show* on CBS , and publications like *Ebony*, *Essence*, *The Advocate*, and *Black Issues Book Review* for their faithful support and for ensuring that my voice is heard.

For a moment I felt I'd lost my writing mojo, but two special young ladies helped me to break out of my funk and served as unofficial line editors and idea bouncers. Victoria Christopher Murray and Celia Anderson are both wonderful writers in their own right, and I will never be able to thank them for all their support and encouragement. I must make a special mention of thanks to my friend and former editor Charles Flowers for always being only a keystroke away.

I have the best agents in the business. John Hawkins and Moses Cardona are not only at the top of their game but wonderful humans whom I'm proud to call friends. I also have a great attorney and accountant in Amy Goldson and Bob Braunschweig.

There are several special people whom I drive crazy with last-minute decisions and my frenzied life. Some might call them assistants, but to me they're miracle workers, so I must offer my gratitude to Anthony Bell, Laura Gilmore, Sanya Whittaker Gragg, Kem Watkins, C. J. McClain, and Angel Beasley.

During my unofficial writing sabbatical, I discovered a new passion: teaching. For the last three years, I've had the privilege and honor of returning home to teach at my alma mater, the University of Arkansas–Fayetteville. U of A made me feel so welcome; it's a place that will always mean the world to me. I thank Dean Don Bobbitt of the Fulbright College of Arts and Sciences, and Chancellor John White and Bob Brinkmeyer for giving me the opportunity of a lifetime. I have also been blessed with wonderful graduate assistants in Elizabeth Bryer, Maya Sloan, and Celia Anderson. Remember these names, because all of these ladies are talented writers whom the world will soon discover.

I would also like to thank all my students (each and every one of them) for opening their hearts and minds to me. I will never be able to voice what you all mean to me.

While at U of A, I've been able to also work with the Razorback Spirit Squads. These extraordinary young men and women have been a gift to me that is beyond measure. So I offer a heartfelt thanks to every Razorback cheerleader, pom-pom squad, mascot, and coach from 2003 to 2006.

I was able to enjoy this bounty of blessings thanks to a remarkable lady whose love and friendship have made a tremendous impact on my life. Jean Nail, spirit coordinator at U of A, gave me a precious gift that allowed me to erase a few not-so-great memories and replace them with new ones that are beautiful and amazing. Thank you, Jean, for being so special and loving the Razorbacks as much as I do.

Finally, I must thank the men in my life. These men have given me unconditional love and bring a smile to my face at the mere thought of them. To one, who due to his place in the world shall remain nameless: I could not enjoy life without the love and support he gives when I need it the most. My son, Brandon Hammons, for teaching me that being a parent is the most difficult (but rewarding) job in the world. I give special thanks to the Hammons family of Plummerville, Arkansas, for allowing me to be such a huge part of Brandon's life.

And finally I thank my two Seans, Lil' Sean (Sean Harrison Gilmore) and Big Sean (Sean Lewis James), for being two of the most special people God has seen fit to put in my life. The Seans shower me with a love I treasure.

For me it all begins and ends with God. So I offer to all who read these words His blessings and love.

E. Lynn Harris
Atlanta, Georgia
February 1, 2006

I SAY A LITTLE PRAYER

There are times when I think that I, Chauncey Dion Greer, am passing through this life on my way to the life God really planned for me. Then, at other times, I think that God must have a wicked sense of humor. Who knew? How else could you explain me sitting here in the green room at CNN on Election Eve, sweating like a fat man in a sauna wearing a warm-up suit, and staring at a tray of sliced melons? I don't know if I'm about to do something noble or if I'm about to get P-I-M-P-E-D.

It's not like my life has been without its good moments. Whenever I'm stressed out, I think back to the days when I went fishing with my daddy, and I begin to smile inside. We'd stop at Reverend Nick's Bait and Tackle with our fishing gear, purchase our supplies, and then pack it all together with the peanut butter and homemade strawberry jam sandwiches that my mother would make for our lunch. All the way to Blue Lake, we'd brag about the fish we were going to catch. I also remember when I won my first songwriting contest when I was sixteen. And, of course, I'll never forget when I met *him*.

Still, something happens to your soul when the expiration date on your love life comes and goes before you turn twenty-five. Was I getting ready to share that love life with the world because I thought it mattered, or because I wanted to finally get revenge? Was I trying to do the right thing, or just wanting to settle the score with the person I had once loved the most but I now despised?

I stood up, glanced at the mirror on the wall, and straightened my tie. I stared at my reflection, checking to see if the makeup artist hadn't applied too much powder to my mink-colored skin and if it would really prevent me from shining once the studio lights hit my face.

Just as I picked up a small paper plate and headed for some melon, a high, annoying voice whispered into my ear.

"Mr. Greer, we have a small problem."

I turned and faced the tall, thin, pale woman with freckles dominating her oval face. Her strawberry-blond hair was pulled back in a cheerleader's ponytail.

"Excuse me," I said.

"I'm Lauren Masterson, the executive producer of *Larry King Live*. Thank you for coming," she said as she extended her ringless hand.

"What happened to Mr. Gains?" I asked.

"He's coming down in a few, but I need to explain something." She motioned toward the red leather couch, and we sat down. Lowering her voice so the other guests in the green room couldn't hear her, she continued. "I think you spoke with one of our associate producers, Dana Wynn, and she agreed to interview you with your face in shadow and your voice disguised," she said.

I nodded. "Yes, both she and Mr. Gains promised me that we'd do it that way. That's the only reason I agreed to do the interview."

"Yes, Mr. Greer, and I know this is a very private matter for you, but I just don't think the interview will have the punch we need if you're not willing to reveal your identity. These are very serious charges that you are alleging against a man who could be elected U.S. senator within the next twenty-four hours and tip the scales as to who controls the Senate. The repercussions could be far-reaching."

"I understand that, but I only agreed to do the interview one way," I said firmly.

She shook her head, unwavering. "I'm sorry about what you were promised, but we simply can't do it that way." She paused. "Mr. Greer, this is live television, and I need to know if you're going to go on and tell your story just as you are."

For what seemed like an exceedingly long moment, we sat face-to-face in total silence. I pondered my choices. Either decision would change my life as I knew it.

What should I do?

What would I do?

CHAPTER ONE

Oh, hell naw were the only three words that came to mind, and I found myself saying them out loud.

"Oh, hell naw," I said.

"Hold up," Jayshawn whispered as he held his finger to his lips.

"Oh, hell naw," I repeated.

He got up from the bed with his cell phone glued to his ear and walked into my bathroom. I could hear him saying, "I'm sorry, babygirl, I don't like it when you get upset like this. Give me five minutes and I'll call you back."

I sat up in my king-size sleigh bed and wondered how I got myself into situations like this. I had just enjoyed a quiet evening with great Chinese takeout from my favorite restaurant, P. F. Chang's, a bottle of Merlot, a blunt, and ended the evening with head-banging sex. I'd fallen asleep wrapped up with a handsome redbone PTB (pretty tall brother) and was having sweet dreams until they were interrupted by the sound of his cell phone.

I ignored the first call, and didn't mind when Jayshawn

jumped out of bed and took the call in the adjacent bathroom. But then it happened again, and again. Every time I tried to go back to sleep, that fucking cell phone, playing rap music like we were in a club, woke me up. I'd had enough of this shit. I was even willing to give up the promised wake-up sex session with Jayshawn. It served me right for dealing with another so-called DL brother like Jayshawn. That nigga just wasn't in the closet, he *was* the closet—all three walls and the double-lock door, too. But what choice did I have, since I didn't date sissies or men who defined themselves strictly by their sexuality.

"I'm sorry, Chaunce," Jayshawn said as he walked back into the bedroom, completely nude with a semi-erect penis swinging from side to side.

"What's going on?" I demanded. It was going to take more than a fat dick to calm me down.

"My girl, you know she be bugging," he said.

"About what?"

"Thinks I am up here cheating with another girl," he said as he sat at the edge of the bed and turned toward me as if he was trying to gauge my anger.

"I thought you told her you were working."

"I did, but you know bitches—they always think they know something. Trying to catch a nigga in some shit," he said. "I think I need to catch the first flight out. I think there's one at seven A.M."

I looked at the digital clock on my DVD player and the time flashed 4:12 A.M. I turned back to Jayshawn and was getting ready to tell him that he needed to catch a taxi because I was not about to get out of my bed at this hour and take his tired ass to the airport, when the damn cell phone rang again!

"Don't answer that," I demanded, this time not trying to keep the anger out of my voice.

"I got to, Chauncey," he said. "I'll be downstairs trying to get her to chill."

"Listen, Jayshawn, you need to leave. I don't care where you go, but you need to get your ass up outta here. I'm going to church in a few hours, and I need some sleep." I tossed the covers to the floor and got up to take a leak, shaking my head in disgust.

While I was in the bathroom, I thought about all the conversations and e-mails that had led to this evening. Several years ago, I met Jayshawn as I was walking through the lobby of the Ritz-Carlton in Washington, D.C. I was there on a business trip and Jayshawn was having a drink in the bar. We gave each other *the look*, and before you could say, "Brothers gonna work it out," we had exchanged business cards. A couple of days later, I got an e-mail from Jayshawn with a nude picture attached. From that moment, it was on. We agreed to drive and meet each other halfway, which meant I had to drive from Atlanta to Raleigh, North Carolina.

I liked Jayshawn Ward because he was handsome, smart, and like me he wasn't a card-carrying member of the gay community. He was honest, telling me that he was the father of a six-year-old boy and a two-year-old girl. Jayshawn told me he was no longer involved with his baby's mama but had lady friends he dated occasionally. Neither one of us was looking for a relationship, or as I call it, a relation-shit; we both just wanted some regular hookup sex with another cool brother.

Everything was fine for about two years. We would get together every two months, and the sex was off the chain. Jayshawn knew how to use every part of his six-foot-five-inch frame—he was a former college basketball player who still knew how to dunk.

Last year Jayshawn called me and told me he'd met a special young lady, and he wanted to pursue a relationship with her. He told me we had to end our sessions. I don't know why, even though it was just sex, I was a little hurt. But then I thought about it and realized that my sex was so good, he'd be back. It might be a couple of months or even a year or two, but they always come back.

I was right.

Right after Memorial Day, after months of noncommunication, I got an e-mail from Jayshawn supposedly just checking on me. I started not to respond to his simple "Sup" message, but I did. His next e-mail said, "I been missin' my nigga and I got a few new things I need to show you."

I started to make him wait, but since I hadn't found a replacement for him, my plans to make him beg went out the window just like dirty dishwater. Now, only three weeks later, he and his loud-ass cell phone had to go.

I stomped back into my bedroom and saw Jayshawn in baggy jeans, a black wife-beater T-shirt, and a white do-rag on his head, stuffing a pair of boxers into the small black bag he'd brought. He grabbed his blue shirt the color of jeans, put it on, and began to button it.

"I'm real sorry 'bout this, fam, but I need to get on. I can't believe this bitch is trippin' like this. But she's asking me all kinds of questions, like what kind of work I'm doing and what hotel I'm staying at. Why she can't call me at the hotel and shit."

I didn't respond because I didn't want to curse his ass out, but this girl was smarter than the average sister who dealt with down-low bisexual brothers. And if he was so in love with her, why did he keep referring to her as a bitch? Didn't she have a name? But I knew this was just Jayshawn's way of hanging on to the street-boy credibility that he so cherished. Every time we'd finish banging, he always had that guilty *I'm not gonna do this no more* look.

"Are you gonna run me to the airport?" he asked.

"No," I said without looking in his direction or missing a beat. I picked up the covers from the floor and climbed back into bed.

"How am I going to get there?" he asked, dumbfounded.

"You can take MARTA—the station is a couple blocks away—or you can use your loud-ass cell phone and call a cab. I'm done. See ya." I pulled the covers over my head, welcomed the darkness, and wished someone would create a "no more dumb mofo" vaccine. And quickly, before someone got hurt.

A few minutes later, I heard my front door slam shut.

*   *   *

If someone asked me who Chauncey Greer was, and I wanted to be really honest, what would I say? I'd start by telling them that due to a previous, painful experience my personal theme song is "Love Don't Love Nobody. Believe That Shit!" So I'm not with the hardhead dude love/relationship program.

I would tell them that I'm a reformed heartbreaker trying to do the right thing when it comes to dealing with other people. There was a time in my twenties when I broke a lot of hearts and didn't give a damn about how the person felt when I told them to hit the road or when I stopped returning their phone calls. This one dude, Greg, claimed he was so in love with me that he was going to kill himself if I left him. At that time in my life I was so cold-blooded, I slammed the door in his face and silently waited for a gunshot or broken window. I ignored him when I saw him a year later with another guy I'd slept with. I started to warn the other brotha that he was dealing with a psycho but felt they deserved one another—at that point in my life I would just go along to get along.

I'm a good-looking brotha (not bragging, just a simple fact) and I've had more than my share of equally good-looking brothers and maybe a half-dozen great-looking women. I have my weaknesses like any other man. I guess you could say I'm a LSC (light skin chaser). I prefer my men (and women) to be on the yellow side. Not the light bright and damn near white yellow, but that real nice golden brown. Good hair and light eyes doesn't hurt. I'm not prejudiced or anything—I have mad respect for my darker-skinned brothers and sisters, since I'm chocolate myself—but my tastes tend to lighter.

I'm not confused about my sexuality. I'm basically bi with a gay leaning. You could say that my sexual tastes are similar to my love for gumbo. You feel what I'm saying? Sometimes I like a little sausage, other times a bit of shrimp. And every now and then, I get a taste for fish. But today, with so many people talking about *down-low this* and *down-low that*, it's too much of a hassle dating women, because they ask too many damn questions. I still find myself attracted to women, but I don't like to lie. I can save that sin for something else—like cussing out Jayshawn. The only thing brothas are interested in is your HIV status (like a brother gonna tell the truth) and how much you're pack-ing. Which also adds to my reputation when word got out that my stuff could extend a couple zip codes. And sisters, even though they don't want to admit it, like that shit, too. Size does matter—to both sexes.

Lately, though, I've been thinking about my own mor-tality, and since I already got a point against me for the sleeping-with-dudes thing, I've been trying very hard to be nicer and not lead on women and fat ugly brothas unless they're exceptional. If statistics are right about the life span of a black man, then I'm approaching the halfway point. Maybe God won't hold my having been a whorish asshole the early part of my life against me. Now, when I meet somebody I want to hook up with on a sex tip, I tell them right up front that I will only go out (or, let's be honest, fuck) with them up to three times. When they ask me if

I'm kidding, I look them dead in the eye and say when a person tells you who they are, believe them. It's the one thing I got from watching *Oprah* every now and then.

Still, these days I treat people the way I want to be treated, which means being honest and saying what's what. Some people seem to appreciate that, while others think they can change me. But I know me, and I ain't about to change for anyone. Been there, done that, got the heart-break.

For me, love came calling the first time during the summer of 1982. My hometown—Greenwood, Mississippi—was as humid and sweaty as it always was when the extremely good-looking young outsider moved to town. I was strolling near an old dusty pink brick building known as Greenwood Junior High after a day of summer-school algebra. I hadn't flunked the tough math course, but I'd made a D and my parents made me attend summer school "voluntarily," forcing me to give up my annual trip to Chicago and my chance to play baseball. That made me mad, because I was just getting good at hitting the ball out of the park.

I looked toward the basketball court, where six young men ran up and down the court so fast, I wished I had the coordination and height to play with them. I heard the rhythmic sound of the basketball hitting the pavement. Then the clinging of the metal nets as the basketball swooshed through. I closed my eyes and imagined that I was in the middle of Harlem, witnessing a game of New York street ball like I had seen on television. But when I opened my eyes, that's when I saw him. He was wearing a nondescript white T-shirt and baggy shorts. He looked like a midget among a forest of tall trees. I found myself gazing at only him, and when he looked in my direction, an aggressively bright sun stung his golden brown face. His eyes sparkled like a cold glass of ginger ale. From a distance his body looked compact, without an ounce of fat.

One of his teammates shouted for him to shoot, and the ball flew from his hand and arched high in the air before hitting nothing but net.

I heard a guy say, "I guess you can play, D. I heard they can shoot some hoops down in Georgia."

Another echoed, "Your shot is so sweet, from now on we gonna call you Sweet D."

After a few more laps up and down the court, Sweet D stopped his stride and looked at me. He smiled as he twirled the burnt-orange ball on the tip of his finger, and I knew that somehow he would become an important part of my life. The way his eyes seemed to pierce through me cemented my feelings.

That summer I made a B in algebra. I prepared myself for geometry and high school, and my sexual confusion began taking shape.

CHAPTER TWO

The rain pattering against my bedroom window and Jayshawn's early exit several hours before almost caused me to miss church. I had decided against the early 7:30 A.M. service, and when I finally woke up around 9:30 A.M., I really didn't have a good excuse not to go to the 11:00 service.

I crawled out of bed and slowly moved toward the bathroom. Inside, I turned on the shower, and as I waited for the water to warm, I began to stretch, trying to release the fatigue out of me.

As the steam from the shower misted the full-length mirror, I turned my 6'1", 193-pound frame to check out my body. I stared at my reflection and had to smile a little. My body was still as tight as a teenage boy's. I was two years from forty, but my stomach was as flat as a biscuit without yeast. I worked hard on my body, and building a home gym was the best money I ever spent. I was determined to ease slowly, but magnificently, into middle age.

I jumped into the shower and soon was patting myself

dry with a leaf-green beach-sized towel. I spent more shower and mirror time than I planned, so I avoided my razor, dressed quickly, and then dashed off to the Abundant Joy Baptist Church in midtown Atlanta, off Peachtree Street near Grant Park.

When I walked into the tiny church with a growing congregation of over five hundred, the praise service was in full force, with tambourines banging and melodic voices singing loudly. I had joined Abundant Joy over two years ago because it felt like a real church and didn't have the businesslike attitude of Atlanta's megachurches. At Abundant Joy, no one was concerned with my tax return, what type of car I drove, and more important, who I slept with.

It had taken me almost seven years to get over my last church trauma. When Shiloh Baptist turned from a friendly and supportive congregation of 1,000 to a 15,000-member cultlike organization, it didn't seem like anything God wanted to be a part of. It was more like a business where the mission was to put on a show every Sunday. I mean, who ever heard of a church where you had to send in an audition tape to even try out for the choir or where the minister talked about his new house and Rolls-Royce as much as he talked about Jesus? To me it felt as though God had left me and the church I loved. That made me mad, and for years I used my Sundays to sleep off my Saturday-night hangovers.

But I was smart enough to know I needed God in my life every day and that the right church could fill that need. It's not like I came to church in search of perfection. Perfection is dangerous, and I am nowhere near perfect. I'm a sinner, and I continue to sin. I like to get my drink on every now and then, and have been known to use the N and F words. Okay. I like to cuss. Especially when I get upset. And Lord knows I love sex. Lots of sex. With men as stupid as Jayshawn, with women as beautiful and spiritual as Giselle, a woman I met at church and whom I lost to the cult formerly known as Shiloh Baptist. I fell in love with Giselle because she was such a kind woman and I thought maybe God had sent her to change my desires for men. It worked for a while—until one day I walked into a gym and was smiled at by a tall, well-built man with a swinging dick. All he had to do was give me the look and I was ready to switch teams again. I've come to know that no matter what I do and how many times I do it, forgiveness and God's love are always there. I just have to find them. Nevertheless, Giselle was not so forgiving after my confession.

Abundant Joy Baptist Church was headed by Pastor Kenneth Davis and his wife, Vivian, two dynamic people in their early thirties who used secular references in teaching the scriptures. It was not unusual to hear Nelly and Jay-Z mentioned right along with some of Jesus' favorite disciples. In some ways, though, Abundant Joy was like an old-time country Baptist church where weekly announcements were read aloud, visitors were asked to stand and were welcomed warmly, and hymns like "Sweet Hour of Prayer" and "Just How Much We Can Bear" (my favorite) were sung.

I loved the fact that the church had no dress code and both male and female members often wore jeans or, on occasion, a hip-hop designer sweat suit. The only people who wore anything close to traditional garb were the praise team, who wore all black each week.

I took a seat on the last row of the left side of the church and said a little prayer, asking for the forgiveness of my sins of the night before. Then I glanced around. Almost all the seats in the pews were filled. There was a rumor going around that Pastor Kenneth was looking for a larger space. It looked like our little church was growing, and that had me concerned. Atlanta didn't need another black megachurch. A few minutes later, it was time for the offering. I pulled out the check I had written the night before and placed it in the tithing envelope that I got from the rack attached to the back of the pew in front of me.

Pastor Kenneth took the pulpit and began his service with his usual jokes. He brilliantly used examples of dumb mistakes he made in his youth. We had so many young members, many of whom attended local colleges like Clark University and Morehouse, so Pastor Kenneth was always able to reel folks in and get their attention.

Pastor was a tall, greyhound-slim, chocolate-brown man with a bald head and dazzling smile. He talked about when he had pledged a fraternity in college and how he almost had not finished the process because he was afraid of what might happen before initiation. Even though I was older than most of my classmates when I attended college and didn't have time for fraternities, I'd heard tales of hazing that made me wonder why anyone would ever want to join such a club. Wearing a T-shirt or a certain color and disfiguring your body didn't seem to make sense to me.

Pastor cited a couple of scriptures and then started shouting like he was talking directly to me.

"Fear will keep you from accomplishing greatness," he said as the sun's rays beamed through the stained-glass window behind the altar. "Nobody cares if the only party you want to attend is a pity party." He talked about how his fear could have kept him from the brotherhood of his fraternity and some of the best friendships of his life. He mentioned how he was afraid to approach his wife when he first saw her at a college football game because of her personality and beauty. But he told himself he could do it.

Members of the congregation stood and clapped. I sat transfixed as Pastor Kenneth jumped up and down like he was on a pogo stick, shouting, "Whatever it is you're afraid of, you must tell yourself, 'I can do it! I can do it! I can do it!' Y'all don't hear me, church!" The congregation continued to shout and cheer. "What are you afraid of, church? What dreams are you going to let go unfulfilled because of fear? Where there is fear, faith cannot exist. God has not given us the spirit of fear! You can do it! Look at your neighbor and tell him or her that 'I can do it.'"

I turned to a beautiful woman with a blindingly white smile and said confidently, "I can do it." And for the first time in a long time, I believed I could. It was time to dust off that dream that had been delayed for almost two decades. Even if it came wrapped up in a whole lot of bad memories, I had to do it, I had to make my dream come true.

*   *   *

That night, right before I went to bed, I took out the black-and-white journal I kept in my nightstand. I used it as a prayer journal and for the occasional brilliant insights God granted me. I wrote:

Memories and loneliness look backward
Fear looks around
But Faith always looks forward.

CHAPTER THREE

Monday morning, I walked from my car to my office excited that maybe I had reached a turning point, and I was going to make the most of it. Still high from the pastor's message, I needed to act quickly before somebody reminded me of what I couldn't do.

The sky was so clear and blue that I wanted to take a huge spoon and eat it like a bowl of ice cream. Instead, I would have my usual fried egg, cheese, and bacon on a sesame seed bagel, and coffee with one sugar and a dash of cream that I picked up from the local deli.

Once I reached my office, the first thing I noticed was my vice president, Celia, talking on the phone. A tide of hair, part weave and part real, covered half of her face, and she pulled it back with her left hand before she smiled and waved at me. Since I wore my head clean-shaven, I didn't understand why women wanted someone else's hair on their head, especially in the summer. I smiled back and opened the door to my conference room, where I normally ate my breakfast and reviewed my to-do list for the day.

After I'd taken a couple of bites of my breakfast sandwich, Celia walked in with a yellow legal pad, pen, and a mug and sat down at the conference table directly in front of me.

"How was your weekend, boss man?" she asked.

"Good. How was yours?"

"Just fabulous. I went to the outlet mall and the movies. Then last night I went to the club and met this phine-ass man named Lamar who just moved to Atlanta from Miami. I think he might be the one to make me dump you-know-who," she said with the supreme confidence I heard every time she met a new man. She had recently broken up with Marvin, her deadbeat college boyfriend, for the umpteenth time, but I was afraid she still had strong feelings for him.

"You think so?" I quizzed as I took the final bite of my breakfast. This was our drill for a Monday morning: She would tell me about her weekend, where she'd gone, who she'd met, and how he was going to be the love of her life. I wondered who had a tougher time when it came to dating: single, straight women or an almost forty-year-old gay man.

Celia Grace Ledbetter was more than a coworker. During the five years she had worked for me, I'd come to consider her a little sister. I felt a rush of protectiveness when she talked about the various men she met; I always wanted to call them and warn them to treat Celia right.

I met Celia at a job fair at Clark AU, where she was getting her MBA. Like me, she had attended the now-closed Morris Brown College and didn't start until her early twenties. Even though I attended Georgia Tech for my grad studies, I kept in contact with one of my professors from

MBC, Dr. Thomas Rainey. After an impressive interview with Celia, I called him, and he was excited. He told me that Celia was a hard worker and mentioned that she had grown up in public housing in Macon, Georgia. I knew I needed to hire her when I found out that she had paid her way through Morris Brown with scholarships and by working as a teller at Bank of America. All the while, she maintained a 3.68 grade-point average. She was a little more of an around-the-way girl (aka ghetto) than I preferred, but I had the polish she needed to become a diamond in the business world.

Celia was a cute girl, sturdy at 5'10", 170 pounds, and peppy with cinnamon-brown eyes that were gentle, but there was a touch of sadness about her. She had a full mouth with lips that were a little too big for her face. Sometimes she dressed like she was going hiking in the Colorado Mountains (think butch), and then there were days (like today) when she dressed like she was going to the club—a skirt too short and a blouse too small.

I glanced at Celia and noticed her earrings, which looked like teaspoons. Her print jersey dress was scooped so low at the neck, in a material so sheer, you didn't have to use your imagination to see the shape of her nipples. I wanted to call my good friend Skylar to do an emergency extreme makeover.

Despite her minor faults, I couldn't imagine my life or business without Celia Ledbetter.

"Take a look at this," Celia said as she pulled a sheet of white paper from inside her legal pad.

"What's this?"

"It's the monthly sales report. May was great. We got fifty more stores to carry the new line of cards. Just think what will happen if we can get into Wal-Mart," Celia said.

I looked over the report. Business was good. This might make it easier to take some time off to follow my delayed dream.

About ten years earlier, I had started a small card company out of my bedroom. CBCC (Cute Boy Card Company) started when I could never find a card with black men that didn't show their dicks and asses. I wanted cards that showed handsome men, not pretty-boy model types, and I wanted messages I could relate to. I hated sending cards that proclaimed love when in fact it was simply a strong "I think I might like you."

I had since expanded the line with mugs, journals, and T-shirts. The line also included cards and calendars with beautiful African American women of all different shapes and colors. I had several cards with young models wearing T-shirts with Greek symbols, which were a big hit at the black colleges and universities. My products were carried in every state except Idaho, Utah, and Montana. A few years ago, Celia designed an Internet site that increased business by almost 35 percent.

"Do you think we have a shot at Wal-Mart?" I asked.

"Yep, I do. Their card buyer is this beautiful Hispanic girl named Christy. We really hit it off, and she's working with her boss to bring me to Arkansas to do a card-buyer presentation to Wal-Mart. You can retire in your early forties if we get this account," Celia said with a wink.

"We'll both be able to retire," I agreed as I looked over the report and started humming, "Money, money, money," as Celia drank from her mug and bounced her head from side to side to my tune.

* * *

"What is that I smell?" I asked as I walked into my outer office. It was a little after ten o'clock.

"I got up early this morning and made these just for you. That's why I was running a little late," Ms. Gladys said. Gladys Singleton was the office manager and mother figure to both Celia and me. A sixty-four-year-old widow who looked forty and still dressed like she was running for campus queen, Gladys started working for me when I stole her away from Douglas High School. I was there giving a presentation on how I started my business, and I was impressed with the way she carried herself and how a single look from her cowed a rowdy male student into sudden silence. I could tell she was a "don't start nothing, it won't be nothing" kind of teacher.

After my presentation, we talked for over an hour about how she had reentered the teaching profession at age fifty-five after her husband died suddenly. Gladys had met her husband her freshman year at Tuskegee Institute in Alabama and had two adult sons whom she was estranged from because of their ongoing drug problems. I could see the pain in her eyes when she told me how her sons had stolen her wedding rings and pawned them for drugs. A week before her husband died, he had planned to use his retirement savings to get the rings back.

I gave her my card and told her if she was ever in the market for a new job, I would love to hire her. I was happy and surprised when, a month later, Gladys walked into my office and announced, "I'm not about to allow those little bastards to make my last years miserable." I hired her on the spot.

"Now, Ms. Gladys, I told you, you don't have to do that," I said as I peeked into a wicker basket full of blueberry muffins. I smiled and inhaled deeply.

"I know you already had one of them bagels with all that fattenin' stuff on it. You know you shouldn't eat eggs unless they come straight from the farm," she said. "Taste one of these muffins. I put in some walnuts I cracked myself."

I took a bite and said, "This is the best blueberry muffin I ever had."

"I thought you said your mama could cook."

"Yea, but not muffins like these."

"Little Miss Celia wanted to take one, but I told her we had to wait until you had one first." She shook her head. "I tell you, I don't know what to say about these young girls today. Don't she know menfolks get first shot at the food?" Ms. Gladys said.

"And I'm sure you reminded her of that." I smiled as I picked up another muffin. This would cause me to run an extra twenty minutes on the treadmill, but it was worth every step.

"I have to remind Celia every chance I get. Did you see

that dress she has on? Of course you did, you a man. Can I get you some coffee to go with your muffins?"

"Sure, with lots of cream."

"Now, Chauncey, baby, I know how you like your coffee. You just go on into your office and get busy making up new cards or whatever it is you do in there. I'll be in there in two shakes."

"Thank you, Ms. Gladys."

"No problem, baby."

When he opened up his mouth to sing, all the girls (and a few guys) pinched each other and giggled. They weren't laughing because he couldn't sing. They were simply doing what girls do when they see a cute boy. I heard one girl whisper, "He's so fine, he's bound to be a pimp or a preacher when he grows up."

Sweet D was a boy of many talents. Before he arrived in town, I never had competition when it came to being the choir director's favorite. But it looked like I did now. D seemed to have everything.

"In my home, over the-re. Where my Lord he did prepare," he sang in a tenor voice as clear as a spring day.

"In my home," he continued, and I began to worry about what song I could sing the next time I did a solo to outshine my new rival.

After practice, I watched him mesmerize Taylor Dillard and her running buddies with banter about living in the big city of Atlanta. To look at them, you would have thought he was commenting on their beauty, the way all three of them were batting their eyelashes and covering their mouths like they were white southern belles at a debutante ball flirting with the black wait-staff. He caught me staring at him again as I had on the basketball court, and as I had a few days after that while he drank a Coca-Cola with salted peanuts at the bottom of the bottle, shirtless (six-pack clear and present) at the Texaco service station. All I needed to do was go over to him, use my postpuberty deep voice, ask what was happening, and give him the black-

power soul shake. But I didn't have to do that. After Taylor and her crew left the church, he walked over toward the organ where I was sitting, pretending to study the keys.

"So I hear you sing, too," he said.

"Yeah. I sing a little," I said without looking at him.

"Do you play, too?"

"Play?"

"Yeah, the organ."

"A little."

"Play something for me," he said. It wasn't a command but rather a request.

"I can't do that," I said.

"Why not?"

"Dr. Owens, the minister of music, don't like us kids playing with his stuff."

"Who's gonna tell?" he quizzed. I looked at him, and he smiled and said, "Not me."

My stomach started grumbling and I jumped up from the bench. "I better not."

"Okay, some other time."

"Sure. We have a piano at home. Maybe I can play for you there sometime. Can you play?" I said.

"No, but maybe you can teach me," he said with a smirk. "What's your name?"

"Chauncey. Chauncey Greer."

"Nice to meet you, Chauncey. They call me Sweet D. I just moved here from Atlanta."

"Why did you move?"

"It wasn't my plan. My pops left town years ago and my

mama wasn't working, so one of her cousins told her we could come live with her until my mama got on her feet," D said.

"Oh," I said, wondering where his father had gone.

"Who do you live with?"

"My mama, daddy, and I have a sister and a baby brother."

Sweet D was quiet for a moment, and then he said, "Sounds like a real family. Like Leave It to Beaver."

"Naw, we're not like them, but maybe you can come see for yourself."

"Are you inviting me over?" he asked, sounding surprised. "Man, that's cool. Most of the dudes have been really shady except for the guys I play ball with, and they don't invite me over because they 'shamed they live in government housing," D said.

"Let me check with my parents, but I'm pretty sure it will be okay," I said as I started out of the church.

"Cool. Just let me know."

"I will," I said, waving good-bye and wondering why my heart was pounding and sweat was dripping down the center of my chest.

CHAPTER FOUR

I poured some pale pink sautéed shrimp over a plate of hot pasta, and the phone from the downstairs concierge rang. My dinner guest was on time.

"Hello," I said.

"Mr. Greer, this is Tad from the desk. I have a Sir Skylar here. May I send him up?"

"Sir Skylar?" I laughed. "Yeah, send him up."

I pulled a bottle of Merlot from the bar, opened it up to breathe, and then pulled out two wineglasses from the cabinet and set them on the granite countertop.

I took the Caesar salad I had made earlier from the refrigerator, looked around the kitchen-dining area, and declared myself ready for entertaining one of my best friends, Skylar Demond Roberts.

I'd met Skylar after I started my company and did an appearance on the local *Good Morning A-T-L* show. He was the makeup artist. Even though I have never been the type of person to walk up to someone and say, "Hello there, I'm Chauncey and I sleep with men," Skylar immediately clocked me by quipping, "So, how many young boys' hearts have you broken, Mr. Tall, Chocolate, and Handsome?" We've been friends ever since.

We're quite different. Skylar embraces everything about being gay and hasn't missed a black-gay-circuit party in years. Every year he treks to Washington, D.C., Los Angeles, Chicago, and Miami, where he tells me the finest black gay men in the country converge for a weekend of nonstop partying. He lives to fall in love, if only for a week or two. I live to avoid it. He laughs out loud every time I invite him to join me for church and teases me that I'm on the GL (the God Low). Meaning that the way I curse and love sex, he was certain that God didn't even know my name. I wasn't ashamed of my faith, but I did get tired of trying to explain to people how I could have sex with men, still believe in God, and consider myself a good Christian or at least a work in progress.

The doorbell rang, and I checked on the brownness of the bread in the oven before I rushed to the foyer.

"Chauncey, darling, darling," Skylar said as he swept in wearing a tight knit pullover with a fake fur collar and a large black leather bag thrown over his shoulder.

"Let me take your wrap." I inspected the dark brown fur and wondered why Skylar was wearing something like this in the summer—in Atlanta, in early July.

"What did you whip up? It smells great, like garlic," Skylar said.

"Just some shrimp scampi. I hope you're hungry."

"I'm always hungry, and you know I love to eat, despite

what my schoolgirl figure will tell you." Skylar twirled around the room. He was about 5'7" and slim, with sharp features and the small waist of a high school twirler.

"Come on, let's eat. Would you like some wine?"

"Do you have any beer?"

"I think I have a couple of Coronas," I said.

"Oh, no—on second thought, that's way too butch. Just give me a little white wine," Skylar said quickly.

"How was your weekend?" I asked as I grabbed a half-bottle of Riesling from the back of the fridge.

"Fabulous. I had a date with another horse-dick boy I met on the Net. We spent the entire weekend together, but of course he has a lover—wife or something. I forget. I just know I most likely won't see him again," Skylar said as he took a seat at the counter.

"Are you still doing that online stuff?" I asked.

"Don't try to *high-hat* me, Chauncey Dion Greer. Need I remind you that you tried it, too?" Skylar said.

"But I didn't meet anybody," I said, recalling how excited I was when I got my first response to my Internet ad. But I became quickly disenchanted when my date didn't look anything like his picture.

"Your standards are too high, but you'll get lonely one night and you'll be pulling out that computer for comfort," Skylar said, and laughed.

Maybe he was right. I didn't consider myself lonely, and with my growing business, the gym, and church, I led a full life. The guys I communicated with over the Internet all seemed like such losers—they regularly used fake pictures or listed themselves as tops but sounded like California Valley Girls over the phone. Besides, I saw enough half-naked boys every day in photos of models and wannabes who submitted pictures to be the next discovery of CBCC.

"Earth to Chauncey," Skylar yelled.

"What?"

"Didn't you hear me? I asked you how was your weekend?"

"The usual, nothing special," I said.

During dinner, Skylar chatted about some guy he was writing in prison (when it came to keeping a man, Skylar left no stone unturned) while I thought about what I had to tell him.

After dinner, I made tea and Skylar and I moved to the patio to enjoy the view of downtown Atlanta. A couple glasses of wine convinced me I was ready to share with Skylar my recovered dream to sing. I hoped he'd be supportive.

"So what are you working on?" I asked as I placed a berry-brown leather scrapbook under my chair.

"Another fucking makeover show, and trust me when I tell you I am sick and tired of trying to convince some short, nappy-haired, overpermed ghetto bitch that she doesn't need a weave," Skylar said. He was now an executive producer for *Good Morning A-T-L* and had a staff of five working for him. The only time he did makeup was when one of his favorites, like Patti Labelle or Jill Scott, was on the show.

"But aren't those shows popular?" I asked.

"Yes, and they pay the bills." Skylar took a sip of his tea and eyed the scrapbook I had brought out to the patio.

"Then I guess now is not the time to ask you to consider doing an executive makeover on Celia. We have a big presentation at Wal-Mart, and I want her to have a more professional look," I said.

"Can I get rid of the weave and those microbraids?"

"That's up to you two, but she got rid of the braids. "

"And the too-short blue jean skirt." Skylar laughed and then asked, "What's that?" as he pointed to the scrapbook.

"Something I wanted to show you. It's a little secret from my past," I said as I picked up the heavy book and handed it to Skylar. He opened it and looked at the first few pages, and his eyes grew big.

"I knew it."

"Knew what?"

"I noticed how you're always talking about how models bore you, and yada, yada. You used to be one of them."

"You think I used to be a model? Get real," I said.

"Oh, now, don't be so modest. Look at that face, those eyes. Honey, you could put Tyson what's-his-name on a boat back to the Islands selling fruit if you decided to strut the runway. Maybe I should suggest to the general manager that we do a show like Miss Tyra Banks, but for men. You could be my first winner and we both could make millions, since I would be your agent."

"Stop talkin' shit and finish looking at the book." I got up and walked through the sliding glass door to put on some music.

A few minutes later, Skylar's laugh and shouts blended

with Luther Vandross's soulful voice. I stuck my head outside the door and asked what was funny.

"You were in a group? And you were the star? Look at you on the cover of *Right On* magazine and *JET*!" Skylar said.

"I wasn't the star, but we were quite popular," I said as I sat down next to Skylar. I glanced at some of the yellowed newspaper clippings about the group, photos with me smiling and sporting a high-top fade like the other group members.

"All of you guys were fine. I would have had to give you all some. Who is that?" Skylar asked, pointing to one of the guys as we sat on a sofa in the lobby of some fancy hotel in Chicago.

"That's Barron," I said.

"And him?" Skylar asked as he pointed to the guy in the middle.

"Darron."

"Were they related?"

"Twins."

"And my, my, who is this cutie? I bet you two didn't like each other because you were both trying to be the best-looking one. What's his name and where do I find this rump shaker sho' 'nuff baby maker?" Skylar asked.

I looked at the photograph and a flood of memories covered me. I was speechless for a moment.

"Chauncey, honey, who is he?"

I took a deep breath, looked at the photograph and then at Skylar. "That's Sweet D."

"Hmmph . . . I bet he was," Skylar said.

I got up from my chair and stood close to the railing in silence, studying the city like it was a map that had come to life.

"So why the big secret?" Skylar asked.

I continued my survey, turning my attention to the cars, which looked like Matchbox toys from twenty-two floors up.

"Chauncey!" Skylar shouted.

"What?" I said as I turned quickly to face him.

"Why did you keep this a secret? This is fantastic. I remember the remake of *Since I Lost My Baby*," he said.

"It's not a big secret. It's just a part of my life that's over," I said.

"So why did you show me tonight? Are you guys getting back together? Can I be a part of the group?"

"Can you sing?" I asked, trying to lighten the mood, already knowing full well that Skylar couldn't carry a tune in even his most expensive leather bag.

"You know I can't sing, but I can shake my tail feather," Skylar said as he stood, did a little dip, and then did a Beyoncé-inspired booty shake as he slapped his left cheek.

"You're crazy."

"Yeah, I might be crazy, but you still haven't told me why you made me take a trip down memory lane. Did somebody die?" Skylar asked.

"What?"

"Where are these guys? What are they doing? Are they gay or straight?"

I hesitated for a moment. "They were straight and I haven't talked to them in almost twenty years. Our last performance was at the Regal Theatre in Chicago in 1988. I haven't seen them since," I said.

"Oh, honey, we need to get another bottle of wine, because I know there is a story here," Skylar said as he sat back down on the metal chair.

"There is no story and no more wine," I said as I picked up the scrapbook. "I just showed you this because I want to sing again and I'm going to need your support."

"You don't have to ask me that, baby. You know I got your back. What do you need me to do?"

"Right now all I want you to do is to be honest with me when you listen to my songs," I said. "Then I want you to tell me what you think."

"Are you going to listen to me? Because you know I'm going to tell the truth."

"Of course."

"Good, 'cause the Lord knows if a certain female singer had listened to me, we never would have had to find out that all that glitters ain't gold," Skylar said.

I simply smiled and took in one more look at the city.

* * *

After Skylar left, I went back out to the terrace. A dark sky with a handful of stars covered Atlanta. I was wondering if I'd lost my mind. Would pursuing a career I had given up in my youth really be possible? Would words and melodies come back and clutter my head with ease?

Fear, is that you? I thought as I strolled back into my house and did something I hadn't done in years. The piano that dominated the living area and that I rarely touched glowed under the subdued ceiling light, and I felt drawn to it.

I played a few chords of Stevie Wonder's "Overjoyed." My fingers danced across the keys as if I played that song every day. Minutes later, I played and sang one of my favorite Richard Smallwood tunes, "The Center of My Joy," a song that managed to bring tears to my eyes every time I heard it. Tonight was no different. The quiet of the night settled around me, but my voice filled the living room as if I were performing on the main stage at Carnegie Hall.

Sometimes the heart recalls things better than the head. While singing, I remembered how too much joy could sometimes lead to sorrow. I began to play a melody I was hearing in my head. Then I started to sing.

"It was an ordinary morning,
I should have seen the warning,
The air was clear, the sky not as blue."

I hummed to myself as I waited for the words to emerge painfully, yet powerfully.

"There was a coldness to your kisses."

I felt an excitement as chords continued to come to me and flow through my body, to my fingers as they caressed the piano keys.

"Was it my imagination?" I sang.

Hours later and in the wee hours of the morning, I had done something I hadn't done in years. I had written a song.

Wednesday came and I was on a roll with my songwriting, having completed three songs. I was sitting at my desk studying the lyrics of my latest song when Ms. Gladys walked into my office.

"I'm getting ready to leave and I wanted to check and make sure you didn't need anything," she said.

"What time is it?" I asked.

"A little before seven."

"It is? I need to get out of here and get home and get something to eat," I said as I stood up and stretched my body.

"What's been going on in here?" Ms. Gladys asked as she looked around my office with a suspicious look on her face.

"What do you mean?" I asked.

"Well, you have been holed up in the office all day, and Celia and I were wondering if you were okay. I even came and listened at the door to make sure you were in here and I knew you was because I heard you humming so loud it sounded like sanging," Ms. Gladys said.

"It did?"

"Indeed. What you making, some sanging cards now?"

"Oh no, but I've been busy working on some things and sometimes I hum to myself. It's a habit I've had since I was a little boy," I said, deciding against telling her I was writing songs again.

"So all you plan to do is fill that belly of yours this evening? Why don't you come and go to Bible Study with me at my church?" Ms. Gladys asked.

I knew she meant well and I knew Ms. Gladys attended one of Atlanta's colossal churches where the midweek Bible study was almost as well attended as Sunday service. I wasn't about to fall back into the trap of going to one of those big megachurches.

"Thanks for asking, Ms. Gladys, but I think I'm going to try and finish up my little project. Has Celia left?"

"Yeah, she and a friend left about an hour ago. I tried to get her to come with me, too, but I could tell by the shirt and high heels she changed into that she wasn't going to no church," she said as she raised her eyes in a way my own mother did when she was trying to prevent herself from saying something biting.

"Did she look nice?" I asked. I saw Celia earlier in the day, and she was dressed in a nice pantsuit.

"She changed out of that pantsuit and into something else. It might be some people's taste but it sho' ain't mine. I had to bite my tongue to keep from telling her something my beloved mother used to tell me."

"What was that?"

"If the shoes don't fit, then they ain't yours," Ms. Gladys said as she turned and walked out the door.

I shook my head and laughed heartily as I thought what a funny card Ms. Gladys's mother's saying would make.

CHAPTER FIVE

In a lot of ways I am a creature of habit. On most given days of the week, there is something that I always do, even if it's something like having sushi every Tuesday for lunch. Every Sunday night after supper, I call my family back in Greenwood. I start with my parents, Cleotis and Alma Greer, two proud African Americans who people refer to as the Ruby Dee and Ossie Davis of Mississippi due to their forty-plus years of marriage and deep, abiding love for each other. Not to mention Alma's role as choir mistress and lead soloist at the Bethel Baptist Church. You could say I get my singing genes from my mother and the ability to ignore what I see from my father.

My parents are both retired now and spend most of their time spoiling their grandkids and traveling to places like Canada, Florida, and nearby Biloxi, where my younger brother, Jonathan, lives with his wife, LaKeshia, and his four-year-old son, Canyon. Sometimes I pass on calling Jonathan, not because I don't enjoy talking to my knuckle-lehead brother, but because almost once a month his cell phone number changes or, shall I say, gets disconnected. Being the baby of the family left Jonathan without the responsibility gene, so I am never surprised to get a call from him asking if he can borrow a couple of dollars until payday. I always lecture him about keeping a budget, but in the end, I always acquiesce. It's gotten to the point that when I go to the service counter at my neighborhood Kroger, Jolene the manager smiles and just hands me the yellow Western Union form to fill out.

My older sister, Belinda, still lives in Greenwood, where she is married to the first and only man she slept with. She is the mother of twins, Hannah and Hudson, and is the principal of the Hattie McDaniel Middle School.

Belinda got Mama's singing genes as well, and she has sung for years with the Mississippi Mass Choir. She attended Jackson State and could have been the first black Miss Mississippi if she would have become more comfortable wearing four-inch heels while strutting her stuff in a swimsuit. She was second runner-up when she went to the state pageant in Vicksburg as an eighteen-year-old and everyone encouraged her to run again. But Belinda was not having it and was anxious to give up her virginity and marry Patrick Walker, the too-smart-for-his-own-good valedictorian of Greenwood High. Good thing she'd already run for Miss Mississippi, since she got pregnant after having sex for the first time. She lost that baby, but was doubly blessed years later.

Sometimes it's a little harder to get in touch with my parents due to their traveling, even in the age of cell phones. I still can't get over the sight of my father playing golf or fussing with my mother as she tries to get him to use an earpiece on his cell phone. I almost fell out of my chair when I got an e-mail from the "Traveling Grands." After I realized it was from my parents, they informed me of their travel schedule for the month.

When I picked up the phone tonight, I dialed Belinda's number instead of my parents'. Every now and then, I try to break out of one of my habits and do something different, even though I know I'll return to my old ways a week or two later.

After a couple of rings, Belinda picked up the phone and in her usual cheerful voice said, "What it be like, baby brotha?"

"I'm fine—and how are you?" I said as I wondered how people had ever lived without caller ID. No more mystery when the phone rang.

"You know, doing what I do. Picking up after my kids at school and at home. Trying to get my husband to realize that being married don't mean you can't still do things outside the box," Belinda said.

"How are my niece and nephew?"

"Growing like weeds."

"And Patrick?"

"In love with his newest computer gadget." Belinda laughed.

"I haven't called Mama and them. Did you see them at church today?"

"Honey, they are on a cruise in the Bahamas. Didn't you get the latest e-mail?"

"Oh yeah, I forgot," I said.

My sister was the only one in my family who accepted the fact that I would never add any grandkids to the Greer family brood, but even she had a hard time asking for specific details about my dating life. She just wanted me to be happy, even if it meant spending my life with a man. My parents, especially my father, just didn't talk about my preference for men.

On the rare occasion when my parents visited me or I took someone home, they were cordial, like the good Christian folks they are, but ignored the elephant in the room—my orientation toward men. But I didn't let that bother me, because I knew that no matter what, my parents loved me and my siblings dearly.

"Have you met anybody new lately?" Belinda asked.

"I'm too busy with my business. Have you talked to Jonathan?"

"He called me the other day and left me a message asking for a couple of dollars. I haven't called his begging ass back yet."

"You can call him. He hit me up the other day, so his money should be all right," I said.

"You know we got to stop doing that. He's never going to grow up if we don't stop bailing him out," Belinda said.

"Yeah, I know, but I don't want Canyon to suffer or to look up one day and see him on *America's Dumbest Criminals* trying to steal an ATM out of the Piggly Wiggly." I laughed.

"I hear you, but if his lazy-ass wife, LaTakia, would get

a job he wouldn't be coming to us for money," Belinda said.

"It's LaKeshia, darling, but baby brother needs to break some of his bad habits," I said. There was a time we were worried that Jonathan was hooked on drugs or something, but I finally got him to admit what his addiction was. Strippers. My baby brother loved putting dollar bills into thongs and buying drinks for skank women, both black and white, at the casinos in Tunica near Memphis. He even took me there once when I was back home, and he assured me that it was just a hobby. He said he would never cheat on LaKeshia. I believed him, because he wasn't dumb enough to do that. LaKeshia was the kinda ghetto country girl who would kick his ass and any type of mistress she might find. People still talked about the time LaKeshia whipped the captain of the cheerleaders and the most popular girl at Greenwood High during halftime of a football game when she found out the girl had called Jonathan, who was not only good-looking but a star athlete in both football and basketball.

Belinda hated Jonathan's attraction to strippers, but it didn't bother me as much, since I'd been known to stick a dollar or two in a jockstrap a few times myself.

"Don't even get me started talking about those skanks," Belinda said.

"Don't worry, Jonathan will grow up one day," I said.

"He better, because I have warned him that I was going to tell Mama what he's been up to and he knows she will have his butt in church 24/7 on his knees praying," Belinda said, laughing.

"I know she will," I said as I joined in with Belinda's laughter, imagining Jonathan on his knees praying, not to God but to some Amazon stripper woman instead.

"I love you, Chauncey, but I need to find out what my babies are doing," Belinda said.

"I love you too, sis. Kiss the kids for me."

"Will do. Bye."

"Bye," I said. I hung up the phone for a few seconds and then picked it up to call and leave a message for the Traveling Grands.

*　*　*

On a beautiful Thursday afternoon I was reminded of why I loved living in Atlanta. I was at Starbucks on Peachtree Road, jotting down lyrics and waiting for Skylar, who was meeting me to show me some of the outfits he'd picked out for Celia.

I was sipping my caramel macchiato when I noticed a man with a traffic-stopping body ordering at the counter. He had a broad chest with a six-pack on display through a sheer black tank top and faded jeans that looked like they were molded only for his ass and thighs. Add to that a perfectly shaped bald head that Michael Jordan would envy and a face that would prompt the question, Boris who?

I was wearing sunglasses but I took them off so I could get a clearer view. He noticed me looking—okay, staring at him—and he smiled as he picked up his order. Damn! How long had it been since I'd kicked Jayshawn out of my bed? I looked away and saw Skylar getting out of his car carrying a couple of garment bags. I was going to go outside and help, but I noticed the stranger walking in my direction. I felt my stomach rumble, and I grabbed my cup, then quickly put it down when I thought that my breath must smell like coffee.

"Excuse me, but do we know each other?" the stranger asked.

"I don't think so," I said.

"Then I guess your staring at me indicates that you'd like to know me," he said confidently.

There was something about the arrogant way he spoke that turned me off and reminded me quickly what I hated about Atlanta: good-looking men with attitudes. So I said with equal confidence, "Oh, you must be mistaken. I was looking at the beautiful young lady standing in line behind you."

"Yeah, right," he huffed as he walked away. As he was walking out the door I saw him bump into Skylar, and they gave each other a look of recognition but didn't speak. Skylar came over to the table, laid down the garment bags, and sighed, "Where is a big, strong, *helpful* man when you really need one?"

"Do you know that guy you bumped into at the door?"

"Her? Yeah, I know that queen. I met him at one of those sex clubs a couple of months ago," Skylar said.

"I thought you told me you'd stopped going to those sex clubs."

"Actually, it was more like a private party that changed direction after the china was removed from the table," Skylar said with his patent laugh.

I told him about our brief chat and Skylar told me to be glad I hadn't wasted more time talking to him.

"First of all, he got a little bitty dick and he likes getting stuffed more than a Thanksgiving turkey," Skylar said, laughing.

"Everything that looks good ain't good for you," I said.

"That should be the motto for the kids in Atlanta," Skylar said. "Forget you ever met that child and let's pick out some outfits for our fair lady Celia."

"Sounds like a plan," I said as I sipped the last of my drink. Who cared if I had coffee breath? It looked like it was going to be a while until I got kissed again.

CHAPTER SIX

Sometimes I like to watch.

On a rainy Saturday evening I pulled my SUV into a tight spot against the side of the street and looked in the back seat for an umbrella. I suddenly remembered taking it into my house a couple days ago, and so I picked up the gold baseball cap stuck between the seats. I snapped the crumpled hat into place, put it on my head, got out, and headed toward a mini mansion atop a small hill.

As I walked up the hill toward the house, I wondered if I was doing the right thing. What if I saw somebody I knew, like Skylar, whom I was always criticizing about being such a barfly? It wasn't like I was going to a gay bar. This was different, I told myself. It was advertised as a private party with only fifty members invited and was offering the finest black men in Atlanta on the DL. It even included the disclaimer of "no queens allowed." A part of me was flattered when I got an invitation via e-mail after I submitted a picture of myself wearing a snug-fitting pair of white boxer briefs.

I did as the instructions told me. I knocked twice on the door, counted to ten, and then added a single knock. I heard a buzzer, pushed open the door, and found myself standing in a foyer of black-and-white marble that looked like a checkerboard.

"Drop your pants," a deep male voice commanded.

I looked around to find the source of the voice. When I saw nothing, I let my baggy faded jeans drop and tapped my half-erect penis for effect. A few seconds later, the voice said, "You're admitted." I heard another buzzer and walked into a dimly lit area where several well-built and well-hung black men strolled around butt-ass naked holding cocktails and chatting like they were fully dressed.

"Welcome to The Back Door," a handsome, light-skinned brother with grape-green eyes greeted me. "Fifty dollars, please, and that includes clothes check and one drink. You can check your clothes over there." He handed me a white plastic garbage bag and motioned toward a room that looked like a huge walk-in closet.

"What's this for?" I asked as I followed him inside.

"Your clothes."

"Oh, my bad," I said, slightly embarrassed, and happy I hadn't worn my Sunday best.

I took out my wallet and dropped my jeans again, kicked off my Timbs, and unbuttoned my black starched shirt. I took off my socks and balled them together and put them in the bag. I didn't wear underwear, because the invite specified that no clothing could be worn once you entered the club.

"Do you want to check that bling?" he asked as he pointed to the two-carat diamond studs I was wearing.

"Do I have to?" I asked.

"No, you don't, but it might attract the wrong element," he said.

This was supposed to be a classy joint, and you would hope the wrong element couldn't afford the fifty-dollar cover fee. Besides, I wasn't going to be punked for the studs I wore only on special occasions.

"Naw, I'm cool."

"Nice tattoo," he said, noticing the Chinese symbol I had on my left pec.

"Thanks," I replied.

"Does it mean anything?"

"Love."

"That works for me. Have a great evening."

"I'm going to give it my best shot," I said as I walked out of the closet area into a long hallway with dark carpet specked with red. I walked slowly with my head down, passing men as I moved, wishing I had my hat to prevent eye contact. I was going to need a drink before I could look at these men eye to eye.

I passed a room that looked like a library. I paused at the large window and took in the scene inside. Two men were kissing as they leaned against a bookshelf. Another guy sat in an oxford-colored leather chair, receiving head from a guy on his knees, while another guy stood over him rubbing his bald head with one hand and holding a drink in the other. As I stared, I suddenly felt the weight of my penis increase. I touched the head and precum slid to the tip of my ring finger. The guy holding the drink and resident head rubber made eye contact with me and motioned for me to join them, but I smiled and moved toward the neon lights and music. I passed several rooms, none filled with much furniture. But that didn't stop the participants. There were threesomes, foursomes, on the floor, on the occasional bed, in the chairs—it didn't seem to matter.

Finally, I walked into the bar, where I was greeted by a bartender wearing only a white bow tie, which looked sexy against his smooth ebony skin and a white jock.

"What can I get for you?" he asked.

"Tequila shot with a beer back," I said.

"I got some Patrón. Will that work?"

"No, give me some Jose Cuervo," I said as I sat my naked ass on a leather bar stool. It felt cold against my skin, and I wondered who had been sitting here before me. I twisted a bit in the seat and suddenly felt like I needed a shower. No, make that a bath.

"What's good?" a handsome brother with perfect teeth asked. I wondered if they were veneers or if he'd had them whitened. I guess the invitation had been right when it said only the best-looking black men in Atlanta would be admitted.

"What up," I said as I took a single swig of tequila and then bit into the lime slice to rid myself of the bitter taste.

"Just seeing what I can get into," he said. "Or who can get into me."

"That's wassup," I replied, trying to be cooler than cool.

"Charles Thompson." He extended his hand toward me. I was startled briefly, but then I shook his hand. "Chaun . . . I mean Dion Greer." I had never shaken a naked man's hand before.

"Nice meeting you, Dion. Do you come here often?"

"Naw, this is my first time," I said as I motioned to the bartender for another shot.

"Yeah, mine too, but I can say I'm impressed," he said as he glanced around the room. Leather stools surrounded the perimeter. Men stood with drinks in their hands as they talked. It appeared the bar was the only sex-free zone.

"How did you hear about The Back Door?" I asked.

"I'm just visiting Atlanta on business, but a friend got me an invite," Charles said.

"Where are you from?" I asked, wondering for a moment if Charles was his real name. If he was going to tell me the truth about himself, I wondered if I should, too.

"From Colorado."

"Denver?"

"No, right outside. You've heard of Boulder, haven't you?"

"Sure. The University of Colorado and where that little girl got killed."

"Yeah, everybody always asks me if I'd ever been by the house where she was killed."

"Have you?"

"I hate to admit it, but yes," he said as he took a drink from a beer can.

"It gets cold up there," I said, shivering a bit just thinking about it.

"Yeah, but it's great skiing. Do you ski?"

"I went to Vail once and took a couple of lessons."

"Don't sound like you were impressed," Charles said.

"It was aight," I said.

"So what do you like to do besides hanging out in joints like this?" he asked, leaning closer to me.

I shrugged. "Listening to music and you won't believe what else," I said, laughing to myself.

"What?"

"You might think I'm corny."

"Bowling?" He grinned.

"No. Well, sometimes, but that's not it."

"Then what?"

For a moment, I wondered if I should tell a total stranger one of my hidden passions. The liquor got to me and I said, "I love to fish."

"Did you say fuck or fish?"

"Well, that too." I laughed as I wiped my mouth with the back of my hand.

"Is there much fishing around here?"

I shook my head. "Not in Atlanta, but there are a couple places right outside of ATL."

Charles looked at me, smiled, and said, "Fishing, that's hot. I bet you're a big old country boy."

"No shame in my game."

"Where you from?"

"Mississippi."

"That's wild. The dude I work for is from Mississippi."

"That's wild. What do you do? And tell me the truth," I insisted.

"I'm a political consultant. And why would I lie to a good-looking guy like you?"

"I heard they do that in places like this," I said.

"So that's why you come here?"

"This is my first time."

"Oh yeah, you said that," Charles said with suspicion.

"You don't believe me?"

"I believe you, Dion. So tell me, what do you like besides fishing?"

"I like to cook and make music."

"A real Renaissance man." He smiled. "I like that. And what else?"

"Are you talking about sex?"

"Yeah."

"I don't like to put myself in a box. And yourself?"

"I like to be punished," he said as he smacked his ass and licked his lips. I felt the weight in my penis decrease.

"Very interesting," I said as I stood up and looked around at two more handsome hunks who had walked into the bar area.

"Those two look tasty," Charles said when he saw me looking away.

"They aight," I said.

"Want to see if they're into a little couples action?"

"When did we become a couple?" I asked as I turned back to face Charles.

"The moment I sat next to you."

"Thanks, but I think I'm going to pass," I said as I walked toward the hallway.

"It was cool talking to you. Holla before you leave," Charles said.

"Aight."

*   *   *

I moved through the throb of hallway traffic into a large, dimly lit room filled with a carnival of handsome men with perfect bodies. The air was warm and thick with the intoxicating scent of sex. There were tables against the wall covered with candles. Two king-size beds were in the middle of the floor, with a frenzied tangle of bodies pleasuring each other.

I surveyed the room. A man with his back to the wall looked at me and smiled as he stroked his piece, which looked long and fat. As I moved closer to him, I paid more attention to his bean-brown muscular face with the black eyes of a bald eagle. My eyes moved down from his face to the lean muscularity of his abs and the curvature of his thighs.

"What's good, fam?" he asked. The weight in my own penis had returned, and I found myself so close to him that I felt a whisper of breath passing between us.

"Looks like you," I said.

"I hear you talking, but I like to let this do the talking." He took my hand and placed it on his penis. I felt it for a few seconds, then pulled my hand back with the dampness of his sweat covering my palm.

He kissed me, and his lips were soft and warm.

"What's your name?" I asked.

"Palmer. And yours?"

"Dion."

"Would you like to find a private room?" he asked.

"Isn't that extra?"

"I'm a Platinum member. I get them for free," Palmer said.

Just as I was getting ready to answer him, I heard what sounded like a primal animal scream and I turned toward the futon on the floor. I saw a light-skinned man who looked almost too pretty to be a man. *What happened to the no-queens rule?* I thought. A roughly handsome, dark-skinned guy was hitting him from the back with a fierce pounding as he held him down with one hand pressed against his shoulder.

It was like watching a live porn movie. I found my own sex getting harder, and suddenly, I felt Palmer's hand surround it. He started stroking me so slowly, and then his pace quickened. I was going to explode. He took his lips and started sucking on my chest. I removed his hand from my sex and replaced it with my own until I stroked myself to climax. From the sounds of moaning that rained down on the room, I was not the only one who suddenly needed a towel.

*   *   *

There are times (like tonight when I got home from the sex club) when I think if I wasn't attracted to men I'd be a much better Christian. Almost perfect. It's not because I'm willing to admit that being gay or the act of sleeping with someone of the same sex could be a sin. I just don't think it's any greater sin than being a liar, committing adultery, having lust in your heart, or being a person claiming to be a Christian yet holding a hateful heart.

I remembered the first time I heard a minister preach that God didn't love me and my kind, and it was earth shattering. I wondered what I'd done to deserve this fate. My passion for life and love suddenly felt choked.

But I still believed in God.

God is fair, and I hope that I will be measured by the love I have in my heart and not by the lust I have in my head. Was my experience tonight any worse than a straight man who goes to the local strip club and succumbs to a lap dance? If he asks for forgiveness and expects it, then why can't I expect the same?

CHAPTER SEVEN

Sometimes God be trippin'! I walked into church and was met by a cyclone of joyful noise. The choir had the congregation rocking to "When We All Get to Heaven," one of my mother's favorite songs. As I took a seat in one of the back pews, I remembered the times I played it for her on the family piano and sometimes at church. I picked up a hymnal, joined in the song, and looked toward the pulpit.

A few minutes later, I noticed Pastor Kenneth walking from his office with a man who looked familiar. They were coming from the back, down the side aisle, when I realized who the man was. It was that guy Charles from the sex party. Even though there were hundreds of parishioners standing, his glance met mine and a faint smile came to his lips. He cast his eyes at me for a few seconds, then quickly looked away.

As the two of them moved toward the pulpit, I was unsure of where I could safely rest my eyes. I suddenly experienced a pang of shame and felt emotionally numb. I felt like Abundant Joy was the last place I wanted to be. I put the hymnal back in its rack. As the rest of the congregation was singing and swaying, I stood still for a moment, like I was about to give a public confession, but a few seconds later I found myself walking out of the sanctuary toward the vestibule.

I hated it when God made me feel guilty.

D came to visit my house after school several times, but he never asked me to play the piano. We would talk about sports and singing. I felt extremely comfortable around him. I liked the fact that he was so sure of himself. And I hoped that one day I could be that confident. My parents liked him too, and suggested that I invite him to spend the night. I did, and he quickly agreed.

The first time D spent the night at my house, I slept through the night without a dream. I awoke on a sunny crisp September morning and looked directly into his wide-open eyes. He smiled at me, and I felt my stomach flutter like it did the first time I saw him.

We slept on the screened back porch of my home in the pull-out queen-size sofa bed. I was so happy my mother didn't insist that we sleep in the room I shared with my little brother. No matter how scared Jonathan said he was, he'd be sleeping in the room by himself. Mama allowed him to sleep with the lamp glowing on the table that divided our twin beds. Besides, I was too old to be sharing a room.

The night before, Sweet D and I had stayed up way past midnight as we ate popcorn and drank red soda from the same bottle. We talked about girls until we fell sound asleep. D fell asleep first, and I spent about ten minutes just staring at his face, wanting to touch him but afraid to. He was so stunning that I imagined at some point in his life his looks would become a problem. No young man should look so perfect. Beautiful yet handsome. Soft-looking but masculine disposition. It took everything in me to stop my fingers from tracing the flawless lines across his face. I knew touching him in that way would be wrong.

"What's up, Chauncey?" he said. His voice was gentle and morning deep as he opened his eyes wider and rubbed them.

"Good morning. How'd you sleep?" I asked.

"Like a baby still in his mama's womb," he said.

"I guess that's good."

"It is."

D sat up and pushed his naked back against the coolness of the fake-leather sofa bed. The top sheet and quilt covered the lower half of his body, and I suspected he was wearing just his boxers.

His face was covered with a look of thoughtfulness when he turned toward me and said, "You know, we should start a singing group."

"You mean you and me?"

"I think it should be four, like the O'Jays."

"Who else would we get?"

"We could ask the twins. I've heard them blow, and they can carry a tune better than most," D said.

"You mean Barron and Darron?"

"Yeah, those two."

"Think they'd do it?"

"Yep. Especially when we tell them how famous we're gonna be and how it can get all of us out of this country-ass town," D said.

"You think we could be famous?"

"I know we'll both be famous," he said with more confidence than I had ever heard from a sixteen-year-old. When he spoke *he sounded very mature, but he was only eighteen months older than I was. Maybe he sounded that way because he said he'd been the man of the house ever since his father left when D was in the fifth grade.*

"If you say so."

"There's another thing," D said.

"What?"

"We need to get girlfriends," he said calmly.

I frowned. "We do?"

"Yeah, we're in high school and so we need girlfriends."

"Who?" I asked. I really wanted to ask him why, but he spoke as if I should already know that answer.

"I'll make the moves on Taylor, and you go after her running buddy, Rochelle Mack."

"Rochelle is pretty," I said as the face of the light-skinned girl with the big legs and long dark hair came to mind.

"Yeah, both her and Taylor will be cool for us," D said.

"When should we do this?"

"I'll ask Taylor to go with me tomorrow. You wait a week on Rochelle. She'll be lonely, since Taylor will be spending her time with me," he said with a smile.

"You think of everything, D."

"Just stick with me, boy, and I'll introduce you to some things you don't even know exist."

I smiled and didn't say anything, although my heart pounded at the thought of all that Sweet D could teach me.

CHAPTER EIGHT

Something told me my day had been going too well.

Celia walked into the office with a look that spelled trouble.

"What's wrong?" I asked as she plopped down in one of the chairs in front of my desk and her body slumped.

"You're not going to believe this."

"What, Celia?" I said slowly, already feeling that I didn't want to hear this news.

"You know the new supplier I convinced you to use?"

"Which one?"

"Mercury Printing Press."

I thought for a moment and remembered the aggressive young black man in the navy-blue suit with off-white tailored shirt and sky-blue tie. It was not something I would have worn, but the brother looked good and confident. He'd walked into my office, smelling very hetero with a smile and firm handshake, and, twenty minutes later, walked out with a contract for over $50,000 to print a new

line of cards and the new female calendar we were introducing.

"Oh yeah, Phillip. That brother has his stuff together,"
I said.

"Yeah, that's what I thought, but he just called me with
some bad news," Celia said.

"What kind of bad news?" I frowned.

"He can't get us the calendars and cards on time, and
we have orders to fill."

"How late will he be?"

"At least three weeks, maybe longer," Celia said calmly.

I jumped up from my chair. "What the fuck? Doesn't
that asshole know we have customers waiting for our new
line?"

"I told him."

"Did he say why he was going to be late?"

"Something about a white guy who was actually doing
the printing screwed him around. Said something about he
got a bigger job and he put Phillip's job on backlog."

"So it's the white man's fault. I get so sick and tired of
niggas and their bullshit. Why doesn't he take responsibility and say he fucked up? He should have found another
printer, and why in the fuck does he wait until a week
before we're expecting our stuff to tell us this shit? Got
dammit. This pisses me the fuck off. You see, that's why I
don't want to do business with the brothas," I said as I
banged my balled fist against my desk. My eyes were bugging, my body warming, and the veins in my head expanding. I had gone against my better judgment. I should have

stayed with the known commodity, the printer I normally used. Instead, I was trying to give a small black business a chance, and this is what happened.

"I take the blame, since I'm the one who introduced you to him. I checked his references and everyone raved about him," Celia said, still calm even as I raged.

"I bet his references were his so-called brothas," I said sarcastically. "What are we going to do?"

"We could call Paragon," Celia suggested, bringing up the company who had done our printing for more than five years, never missing a deadline.

"Shit." I fell back into my chair. "We got to crawl back with our heads between our legs, begging the white man to help us out since the brothas fucked us over. I can't believe this shit."

"I'm sorry," Celia said.

I put my hand up in the air like it could protect me from Celia's response. I knew it wasn't her fault, but since Phillip wasn't sitting here I needed someone to blame.

"Where did you say you met him?"

"At Twist," Celia said.

I groaned. Twist was a popular spot in Phipps Plaza where black wannabes and nevergonnabes met for drinks on Friday evenings.

"Celia, what have I told you about mixing business with pleasure? Did you bring him to meet me because you were interested in him socially?" I asked.

"Chauncey, come on, now. Yeah, the brother looked good, but you said yourself how impressive he was, and I just made the introduction. You made the decision to give him the business," Celia said.

She was right, but it still wasn't going to solve our problem. That's what my ass gets for giving business to a good-looking man just so I could find out if he was on Celia's team or mine.

"Who was your contact over at Paragon?" I asked.

"Kristen Polk, the plant manager."

"Do you still have a relationship with her?"

"She's in my breakfast club," Celia said.

"Breakfast club?"

"Yeah, a group of women from small businesses who get together and talk about some of the problems and successes we face running small concerns. I usually sit next to her," Celia said.

"Do you think she can help us out?"

"I can give her a call."

"Do it now, and call my lawyer and get the contract with Mercury voided immediately. How much did we give him up front?"

"I think fifty percent."

"Got damn. That hurts," I said as I pulled out Phillip's card.

Celia stood. "I'll get on this right away."

I looked at the card in my hand. While Celia was going to be on the phone begging Paragon, I was going to be on the phone cussing Phillip out. Not that it was right, but it was going to ease my anger for a minute or two.

Sweet D touched me. He had spent the night again. It was just before sunrise, around the time the birds started their morning chorus.

I had just woken up when I felt D's toes and knees touch mine. I closed my eyes and felt strangely energized by the touch of his body and the warmth radiating through my body.

My penis carried extra weight, but I didn't know if it was from D's touch or my usual morning hard-on. All I knew was that I was afraid to open my eyes for fear that he would be staring at me, smiling. I kept my eyes closed for about ten more minutes and didn't open them until I felt him move away. His feet pattered across the floor, and then I heard the flush of the toilet.

I lay on the sofa, staring at the ceiling, wondering what I would do when he came out of the bathroom. Would I smile or frown? Would I say something or just stay quiet? I didn't know. But the one thing I did know was that I couldn't wait until D spent the night again.

$\mathcal{I}$ said a silent prayer of thanks for my 20/20 eyesight when this ferociously handsome man with a captivating smile walked into my office.

Every first Tuesday, Celia conducted open casting calls for both male and female models who weren't represented by agencies and who felt they had what it took to grace one of our cards or calendars. Since Celia was a tough gatekeeper, she rarely interrupted me to see anyone personally, but today she came into my office with a cat-who-ate-the- canary smile, sighed deeply, and said, "You've got to see this guy. He's amazing. Oh, by the way, I just heard from Kristen at Paragon. They can have our order in forty-eight hours."

"You're the best," I said as I gave her the thumbs-up sign.

"I live to hear you say that." Celia smiled as she was walking out of the door. She suddenly turned back and said, "Did Ms. Gladys tell you that a lady was asking questions about you?"

"What lady?"

"Why don't you let her tell you."

A few moments later, Ms. Gladys walked into my office.

"Celia said you needed to see me?" she said.

"Yeah. What lady was asking about me?"

"Some high-siddity-looking lady with a he-man by her side."

"What did they want?"

"I got in a little early to make coffee and heat up these cinnamon rolls I made, and they were nosing round the door. I asked them if I could help them. Then they asked, 'Is this the business that Chauncey Greer owns?' I told them, 'Who's asking?' And she asked me who I was. And I said, 'I might be the Queen of England. Who are you?'"

"Then what happened?" I laughed.

"I guess she figured out I wasn't playing, and they went off in a huff."

"What did she look like?"

"Like one them black women trying to act white. Dressed like she ain't never worked a day in her life. Unless she was trying out to be one of them Ebony Fashion Fair models. Which reminds me—I need to see when that show's coming through Atlanta again. Mrs. Eunice Johnson know she know how to dress up some black women."

"Thanks for looking out for me." I smiled to myself. I loved how Ms. Gladys would sometimes speak her thoughts even if they were totally off the subject.

"You want me to send that man Celia was talking to in? He's sitting in my area. She was looking at him like he was an Easter ham decorated with pineapples and cherries."

"Oh, I forgot—yeah, send him in."

A few moments later, the wannabe model walked confidently into my office. His shoulders were almost as wide as the door. His commanding arms stretched his perfectly ironed yellow shirt to perfection, and he completed his ensemble with very tight, black, straight-legged slacks. His skin was the color of dark, roasted coffee beans and his eyes sparkled with danger and desire as he walked around my desk to shake my hand.

When I stood up, I was close enough to feel the breeze of his minty breath and smell the delicious aroma of masculinity and scented soap.

"Mr. Greer, thanks for seeing me. I'm Griffin, but folks call me G," he said as we exchanged firm handshakes. I couldn't help but notice the warmth and the smooth texture of his hands, followed by the army troop of goose bumps that covered my arms.

"Nice meeting you, G. Have a seat. Can I take a look at your body . . . I mean book?" I asked nervously. A sly smile crossed G's face as he passed me a black leather portfolio.

"So you don't have an agent?" I asked.

"No. I've been in Atlanta for only six months and I decided to see what I could do on my own. I mean, why give somebody a percentage of what you make when you don't have to?" G said.

"Where did you move from?"

"New York."

"Did you have an agent there?"

"Yes, I was with Ford Men," he said quickly.

"Ford Men. And you left them?"

"I left New York," he said.

I looked through his book and couldn't help but be impressed. Not only was the guy a vision in person, but he photographed beautifully. There were several black-and-white photographs with G dressed in all white, a couple of nudes, and one shot where he was lying across crumpled white sheets wearing white briefs. He was breathtaking, and I couldn't wait to get this man in front of one of my photographers and onto one of my cards. I was already searching for the words I would place in my next bestselling card message. Maybe I could move quickly enough to get his mug into the Wal-Mart presentation Celia was preparing.

"What do you think of Atlanta?"

"It's straight. Kinda slow, but I can hang," he said.

"Are you familiar with what we do here?"

"I've seen your cards, and your calendar is really popular with the kids," G said.

The kids? Was this dream boy possibly on my team, or one of those aggressive straight men willing to play the "gay for pay" role just to be on one of my cards or calendars? I mean, his pants were tight.

"So do you mind showing me what your upper body looks like?" I asked as I began to look through his photographs for a second time—something I never did in front of a potential model.

"No problem." He stood up and quickly ripped off his shirt. *Note to self,* I thought, *double up on the ab workout.* The white rim of his underwear crept up from his pants and gave me a few ideas on the direction of his debut card.

"Very nice," I said, trying not to stare.

"Is that all you want to see?" he asked suggestively.

"Yes, that's fine for now," I lied, knowing full well I wanted to see what the total package looked like: the legs, the ass, and even the toes; I knew I wouldn't be disappointed.

"So do I get the gig?"

"I think we can use you," I said. I didn't want to seem too eager, but I wanted to see this man butt-ass naked lying on his stomach against the 300-thread-count white sheets on my bed.

"All right then. Glad you like what you see," G said.

"We pay a fifteen-hundred-dollar day rate for the photo sessions and a very small percentage for the number of units we sell. We also pay seven hundred fifty for personal appearances at clubs, expos, and trade shows, plus expenses. Do you have a business manager or lawyer to look over the contract?"

"Right now I am doing everything myself. You look like an honest man. Where do I sign?"

"Celia will give you the contract on your way out. I strongly advise you get an attorney to review it. Once we have a signed contract, we'll arrange a photo session," I said.

"How long will that take?"

"It depends on how long it takes for you to get the contract back to us. We work with several photographers in the city, so I would say at the very minimum two weeks. How does that sound?"

G didn't respond right away, but then he looked at me with a sexy grin covering his face. "What if I wanted to see you before two weeks?"

"Excuse me?"

"It's Chauncey, right?"

"Yes," I said, not really believing that this young man was being so forward. Did my staring and my quick double review of his book lead him to believe that I was gay? When I smelled his scent, had he inhaled mine? I didn't know if I should be mad or flattered.

"Chauncey, I know this might be terribly unprofessional, but I have learned that life is too short for regrets. Is it possible for me to take you to dinner before we do the shoot?"

"Is this a business meeting?"

"You want the truth?"

"Yes."

"Then no, it's not business. I mean, from the looks of this place," he said as he glanced around my office, "you're a smart businessman and it would be foolish not to put me on one of your products. So my invitation is purely personal."

The goose bumps returned, and this time I felt them marching underneath my tight cotton T-shirt. But I mustered up the courage to respond, "I'm a terrific cook. Why don't I invite you to my house for dinner on Thursday?"

"Sounds even better," G said as he stood up and removed his portfolio from my hands, smiled at me, and walked slowly from my office so that I got a full view of what, as far as I was concerned, was the most perfect ass I'd seen in a long time.

CHAPTER TEN

I knocked gently on the slightly ajar door.

"Come in."

I turned the knob and walked into the small office. Pastor Kenneth closed his Bible as he stood up to greet me.

"Brother Chauncey, what a blessing it is to see you tonight. How did you enjoy prayer services?" he asked.

"It was good. It was my first since I joined the church," I said.

"I know," Pastor Kenneth said with a slight smile. Of course he knew it was my first time. Pastor Kenneth and his wife knew everything about everyone in Abundant Joy. I heard that the midweek sessions were becoming more and more popular, and I counted about a hundred people in attendance. Not like the packed houses at Ms. Gladys's church, but still a nice crowd for Abundant Joy. I was surprised when I walked in fifteen minutes late and saw so many familiar faces from Sunday services. Tonight, I enjoyed the service even though I attended for the sole purpose of getting a few minutes with Pastor. I hoped that it wouldn't be like Sundays, when countless church members would vie for his attention.

"Thank you for giving me some of your time," I said as I sat down in a black leather chair right next to his maple desk covered with papers, Bibles, and a book with a picture of Bishop T. D. Jakes on the cover.

"What did you need to talk to me about?" The pastor leaned back in his chair and stared, giving me his full attention.

"I really just wanted to thank you. I mean, your sermon a couple of Sundays ago spoke to me directly. I went home and wrote down some of the things you said and even created a card from your message," I said. I hoped he wouldn't bring up anything about the sermon I'd walked out on.

"Well, thank you, Brother Chauncey. I sure would like to see it. I heard you have a popular card company," Pastor Kenneth said. I smiled to myself. Now was maybe not the time to tell the pastor about some of my cards. He might be a little shocked by some of the covers. But I certainly could come up with something tame to show him.

"I will make sure you get a copy of the card when it comes out," I said.

"Great." He slammed his hand on a stack of papers.

"But there is something I'd like to discuss with you."

I took a few minutes and told the pastor about my previous career as a singer and how his sermon had given me the courage to give it another try. I was surprised when he told me he knew of my former group and had even bought a copy of one of our albums for Sister Vivian while they were dating.

"I didn't know I had a bona fide celebrity in my congregation. You guys were as big as Boyz II Men," he said.

"I'm not a celebrity," I said as I tried to keep from blushing.

"So why did you guys break up?"

I paused before I answered. I didn't want to use up a sin lying to my minister. Finally, I said, "It's a long and complicated story. Maybe one day we can speak about it."

"I understand. So what can I do to help?" Pastor Kenneth asked.

"I just wanted to thank you, and of course ask you to keep me in your prayers that I'm making the right decision," I said.

"I can certainly do that. Why don't we get on our knees right now and say a little prayer." He stood and walked around the desk, took my hand, and fell to his knees.

I was a little shocked but I followed suit and found myself kneeling in front of the desk like it was an altar. I closed my eyes, and a few seconds later I heard Pastor Kenneth's powerful voice, sounding just as he did in the pulpit.

"Father, we come to You tonight on bended knee, thanking You for the many blessings You've given us. We thank You for waking us up this morning. We thank You for getting us to Your house safely, and we ask that You watch over us as we return home. Father, we come to You tonight asking for Your direction as Brother Chauncey takes on this new direction in his life. We ask that this wonderful gift You have given him be used for Your will and that You will show him that nothing is impossible as long as he puts You first. We ask that You remove all the obstacles that will get in the way of his dreams and that he will give You the praise, the honor, and the glory. We thank You in advance, dear Lord, for answering our prayers. Amen."

"Amen," I said as I opened my eyes and stood up. I was face-to-face with the pastor. He patted me on my shoulders and told me everything would be just fine.

"Thank you," I said.

"Hey, I just came up with a great idea," Pastor Kenneth said.

"What?"

"Why don't you start your comeback debut at one of our Sunday services?"

"I don't know if I can do that," I said, shaking my head. I hadn't told the pastor that I wasn't going to sing Christian music, just secular. I had sung in the church choir when I was younger, but I stopped when I joined the group. The elders at my home church had been disappointed by my decision to sing secular music, but a few forgave me when I dropped my first tithing check in the offering plate.

"Oh, sure you can. You can sing a solo right before I get up to give the message," he said.

"I don't know if I have enough time. I mean, it has been years since I sang in public," I said. This was not what I had in mind for my first showcase, but it did make sense.

"You can do it. I'm certain."

"I'll need some time to prepare a proper song," I said.

"I guess that's fair. How's the first Sunday in September?" Pastor Kenneth asked as he thumbed through his planner.

"I'll try not to disappoint you, Pastor. Thanks for the opportunity."

"Thank you for letting me know how my sermon ministered directly to you. It's what every man and woman spreading the word of God hopes for. Sometimes we don't know if we're reaching anyone," Pastor Kenneth said.

"Thank you, and have a good evening, Pastor," I said as I extended my hand toward him. He didn't accept it, but instead reached for me and pulled me close to him in a powerful and comforting embrace. Right then, I believed that pursuing my singing was the right thing to do.

On a cool and breezy October evening in 1984, I became a member of a new singing group, Reunion.

The name of the group was actually decided by a toss of a quarter after Barron and Darron Pope wanted to call the group 4 P.M. When D and I looked at them like they'd lost their minds, they explained they weren't talking about the time but Four Pretty Mutherfuckas.

D smartly pointed out that album covers could be a problem with a name like that, and I agreed with him. So I voted for the name Reunion. After we finally decided on the name, I wondered if the Pope Brothers were gonna always vote the opposite of D and myself. If that were the case, we would spend our entire career flipping quarters in the air.

After practice, D and I went to see Eddie Murphy in Beverly Hills Cop and ended the evening on my parents' back porch talking about the group and girls.

"We sounded good, didn't we?" D asked, referring to our earlier rehearsal as he poured a bag of salty Spanish peanuts into his RC Cola.

"Yeah, we did. Our voices really blend together. Do you think we have a chance to get a record deal like those boys out of Boston?"

"Out of Boston? Who are you talking about?" D asked.

"New Edition. I was reading about them in Right On magazine. It said they were coming out with another album real soon and were going to be on Soul Train."

"We gonna be on Soul Train. No, man, American Bandstand. I can see our name in lights now," D said as he took his fingers and wrote out Reunion with an imaginary pen.

"Man, it would be cool to get out of Mississippi," I said.

"Yeah, maybe I could move my mama and sisters back to Atlanta," D said.

"Do you miss it?"

D took a long swig of his soft drink. "I don't miss the place we was living in, because it was a dump, but I do miss seeing so many black people doing so well—and not holding their heads down when they're around white people. It made me believe that one day I could be driving a Benz or something like it and living in a mansion, and having white folks working for me."

"I always thought I might end up living in Chicago or New York."

"Naw, you can't do that," D protested. "You have to come to Atlanta, where I'll be."

The thought made me smile inside, but then he said something about us getting married to a couple of girls and living on the same block. I knew what he was saying was what I should be thinking, but something about that situation didn't sound right to me. Still, I didn't say anything for a while.

"Do you think you'll marry Taylor?" I asked after D finished his soda.

"Man, Taylor is just local. When we become famous, we gonna meet all kinds of women. Maybe even somebody like Vanessa Williams," D said.

"You think so? D, she's fine. I still can't believe they let her win Miss America," I said. "She was the most beautiful, but they usually never let our girls win."

"You know why they did that, don't you?"

"No, why?" I asked, wondering what words of wisdom D had for me this time.

"'Cause they thought she was mixed. I bet their asses was shocked when they found out both her parents were black. She's just a redbone like me," D said as he moved his hand against my dark face. At first I was a little upset with him for doing that, but I knew he didn't mean anything by it. Despite the color of my skin, I still had my share of female admirers. I told myself it didn't matter if I wasn't light-skinned. But I knew although it didn't matter to me, it would matter to others. I figured if Reunion made it big, D would become the star, because he was lighter than the three of us and had dreamy hazel-brown eyes.

"So I think it's time," D said as he stood up and looked toward the sky.

"I thought you were going to spend the night," I said quickly. "Mama already made up the sleeper sofa."

"I'm staying, but I wasn't talking about that."

"Time for what, then?"

"For you to sleep with Rochelle."

"What?" I almost fell out of the chair, but I did my best to stay calm.

"Yeah, I think you need to convince her you can't finish your tenth-grade year a virgin. Especially since you're going to be a big singing star."

"You think she's gonna buy that?"

"She'll do it."

"You sound certain. Are you going to sleep with Taylor?"

"Already done that," he said with a sly smile.

"When?" I asked. I was both excited and disappointed, although I didn't quite understand why. I was thinking about the Taylor that I knew. The one with the long skirt and white stockings who had walked down the aisle at church and professed her love and dedication for Christ. I remembered how she had cried the day she was baptized. I had even heard her mother bragging to my mama about how she was certain her precious daughter was saving herself for marriage like the Good Book prescribed.

"Two nights ago," D said, finally answering my question.

"Where?"

"In her bedroom."

"Where were her parents?"

"'Sleep."

"Man, you're wild. You snuck in?"

"She let me in. Two times." He smiled.

"How did it feel?"

"I can't tell you everything. You need to find out some things for yourself."

"Was that your first time?"

"Chauncey, come on, now. This is Sweet D you talking to. You know a nigga as fine as me had to beat the girls off in Atlanta. Man, I can tell you a story about me and a twenty-two-year-old girl."

"For real?" I asked. Sweet D was really my hero now.

"For sho'."

"So you think I'm ready?"

He nodded. "Better get some practice with these country girls here in Greenwood before you meet some city girls who know plenty of tricks."

"What if I don't know what to do?" I asked, so unsure. Although I'd thought a lot about sex, I wasn't sure I was ready. I certainly didn't want to be embarrassed.

"Think of it like a bike. You remember the first time you rode a bike, don't you?"

"Yeah, I do."

"It's just like that. Just get on and ride," D said with a satisfied smile.

Sweet D was just being my friend and trying to reassure me. But although I was excited, I was just as hesitant, a little scared even. One thing for sure—I didn't want to let Sweet D down. Now all I had to do was convince Rochelle.

CHAPTER ELEVEN

Griffin struck me as a man who could appreciate a down-home southern meal, so I prepared smothered chicken, collard greens, mac and cheese, and Mexican corn bread. I admitted to myself that I was a little nervous about the evening, so I sipped on a little white wine while I cooked.

It had been almost two years since I'd had a date-date. Even though I still found women attractive, it wasn't easy to get through a first date without questions about the whole down-low thing. Since I didn't like to lie, recently I'd passed on women who came on to me. I missed the days when women wouldn't even think that a man who looked like me might be hooking up with another dude.

Most of my encounters now consisted of hookups like Jayshawn, which wasn't a date at all but was usually a couple of drinks, a video game, and then straight to the mattress Olympics. Men who messed around with other men on the down low were not interested in romance. I had convinced myself I felt the same way because I didn't want to be disappointed. And I really didn't believe I deserved it, because in my heyday I'd messed over so many guys who wanted to get serious with me. From the conversations I'd had with Griffin over the past couple of days, I could tell that he not only wanted romance, he expected it.

Once the meal was ready, I went to my bedroom suite, showered, clipped my fingernails and toenails, and got dressed. I went to the kitchen and poured myself a glass of wine.

The concierge called a little after seven and told me Griffin was downstairs. As I waited for him to come up, I savored the sweet, buttery taste of chardonnay as it slid down my throat. Maybe I should go rinse my mouth just in case there'd be some kissing going on. I raced to the bathroom near the kitchen and poured the green liquid into the bottle top and then did a quick swoosh-and-spit. I was ready for my date.

When the bell rang, I opened the door and there was Griffin with a huge smile, holding a bottle of wine.

"How you doing, son?" he asked as he walked in. He stepped toward me, and I couldn't help but stare at his tight-fitting, off-white denim jeans that he wore with a cobalt-blue knit polo shirt, tucked slightly in his pants.

"I'm doing fine. Did you have any trouble finding parking?" I asked.

"Naw, I don't have a car, so I took MARTA and then a taxi," he said.

"You should have told me. I could have at least picked you up from the station."

"No problem. Don't want to seem like I can't get around on my own. Nice place," Griffin said as he looked around my kitchen-dining area. The space was glowing with candlelight, and the scent of just-delivered fresh azaleas filled my home.

"Thanks."

"I brought this for you." He handed me the bottle of white wine. Not only was he thoughtful, but he knew what I liked to drink.

"That's very considerate, Griffin. Thank you," I said.

"Call me G."

"Okay, G. Would you like a glass of wine?"

"Not now, but maybe with dinner—which, by the way, smells wonderful."

"Thanks. What can I get you to drink?"

"Got orange juice?"

"Sure, have a seat." I nodded toward the chocolate-brown suede sectional sofa.

Inside the kitchen, I did a little dance step because of the excitement I was feeling. Finally, I'd met someone who knew how to treat a man.

I poured a large glass of orange juice for Griffin and another glass of wine for me. I popped in my favorite CD, *Introducing Gordon Chambers*, and headed back to the living area.

"Here you go," I said as I handed G the glass of juice.

"Do you have a coaster?"

"Don't worry about it," I said as I sat next to him. He moved closer to me, and he smelled like the alluring scent of sexual promise. A film of perspiration began to form under my beige-and-brown plaid, cotton button-down shirt as he stared at me like I was the only person in the world. I looked away, because I didn't want to stare back into his dark eyes.

Griffin drained his glass of orange juice, put the glass on the table, and asked what was for dinner.

"I hope you like smothered chicken," I said.

"Dude, I love smothered chicken. It's been almost a year since I had some. Who catered this for you tonight?"

"I didn't use a caterer. I cooked myself," I said proudly.

"Damn! Good-looking, and you can cook, too. Where have you been all my life?"

I stood up and brushed away the wrinkles in my black linen slacks. "Can I get you some more orange juice?"

"No, I'm fine. Sit back down. Tell me what's up in your world." Griffin patted the empty cushion where I'd been sitting. I sat and tried to concentrate on Gordon's words as the soulful strains drifted from the speakers.

"What do you want to talk about?" I asked.

"We can start with why a handsome, successful brother like yourself doesn't have somebody sharing all this with him."

"I haven't really been looking," I said as I leaned back and settled into the sofa. "I got a question for you."

"Let me have it."

"How did you know that I would be open to something like this?"

"Let's just say I am always optimistic when I meet a good-looking man," Griffin replied.

"But you were on a job interview."

"When I saw you, I didn't give a damn if I got the job. Besides, the name of your company and the calendars doesn't really scream straight man. I mean, if you had a bunch of titties on your cards and calendars, then I might have done a little research," G said.

"I have a line of women's cards," I said defensively.

"Yeah, but come on. Cute Boy Card Company?"

"I think it's kinda catchy."

"And kinda gay." G laughed.

"So I guess you're out," I said.

"Depends on the situation I'm in. I don't consider myself bi or DL, but if I need to be straight to get a job from one of these evil, high-power bitches or a homophobic man, then I've had enough acting classes to get what I want."

"Are you hungry?"

"For you? Or haven't I made that clear?" G said as he inched closer to me.

"I meant for food," I said, trying to move away. I wanted to take this further, but we were less than a half hour into our date and I didn't want to give the wrong impression. Sure, most guys, including myself, had a little dick slut in them. But this was my home, not a bathhouse.

I got up from the sofa and started for the kitchen. After I had walked a few steps, I looked back. Griffin was still sitting on the sofa with a sexy grin on his face.

"Are you going to join me?"

"I was just sitting here enjoying the view." He smiled.

*   *   *

After dinner, Griffin and I had a glass of wine on the terrace. The wind was blowing a cool yet soothing breeze, and he had that *I hope I get some* look in his eyes.

"Now, tell me again why you don't have a lover, partner, or boyfriend?" he asked as he leaned back against the rail and fondled the top of his large brass belt buckle seductively.

"Too busy running a business. Don't know if I really still believe in love," I said.

"Have you ever been in love?" G asked.

"Once."

"Do you still love him?"

"Can't love someone if you don't even know where he lives," I responded.

"So you just want to be selfish and have all of this to yourself?" Griffin waved his large arms in a circle as though he was encompassing my entire condo.

"You think I'm being selfish?"

"I'm just kidding. Maybe you've been waiting for the right one to come along." He moved closer to me. He eased his shirt out of his pants like he was getting ready to undress.

"People can see up here," I said nervously.

"Then let's give them a show." He pulled me closer and then kissed me. His lips were soft and tasted like wine. When he started to move his tongue down my throat, I pulled away.

"Are you sure you're ready for this?" I asked.

"I am."

"Just like that?"

"What are you talking about?"

"Griffin, I think you're a nice guy, but I must tell you something about myself."

"I'm listening."

I paused a moment. Should I share what I was about to with someone who really was a stranger?

"I'm waiting." Griffin kicked off his shoes and undid his buckle.

"Why don't we go inside?"

"Lead the way," Griffin said as he picked up his shoes and moved closer to me. As I walked into the condo, his body pressed against my back and his arms rested around my waist. Once inside, I moved swiftly toward the sofa and sat down.

"Is this where we gonna make it pop off?" Griffin asked as he stood over me.

"Sit down."

Griffin sat and looked at me with a sadness I'd seen on the faces of jilted lovers before.

"Don't you think I'm attractive?" he asked.

"Come on, Griffin. You know I think you're attractive. You know you're a good-looking man. I just wanna ask you why you don't have a lover."

"I just haven't met the right person. I was hopeful when I moved down here. I thought that I'd find me a good ole southern boy and settle down. But these guys in Atlanta have more games than an arcade."

"So what makes you think I don't have game?"

"You just seem more settled, more mature."

"That might be true, but I'm going to share with you

something that I rarely tell anyone. You're a very nice guy, and I want to get to know you to see what happens."

"I'd like that, too. Are you going to tell me you're HIV-positive? Because if that's it, I'm cool. I'm negative myself, but we can use protection."

"That's mighty open of you, but that's not it," I said. As far as I knew, that was the truth. I had stopped taking the test twice a year and now only went every two years. I practiced safe sex. I knew oral sex might still be a risk, but I just saw no point to having oral sex with latex involved. I mean, come on, let's not take all the fun out of the art.

"Then what is it?"

I took a deep breath. "Okay, here goes. I guess you could say I have commitment issues. And when a guy is easy—I mean, if I get lucky the first or second date—then, for some reason I can't explain, I lose interest. I don't care how good-looking or great in bed he is, I just lose it. Whatever *it* is," I said.

"So you're saying you like a challenge. I'm cool with that, but believe me when I say you won't lose interest in me once you get some of this." Griffin leaned back into the sofa, and his body language said, *Take a look at me.* And from what I had seen in Griffin's book and the little peek I got in the office, there was definitely something to see. Something that might make me break my "once, twice, three times, I am through" way of life.

"It's not a challenge thing. At least, I don't think so," I said.

"So you're telling me you've never been in love or in a long-term relationship?"

"I didn't say that," I said defensively.

"So you are capable of love?"

"We all want love in our life," I said.

"Sure we do, but to me love also means a satisfying intimate life as well."

"Agreed."

"But you're telling me if we kickit tonight that would end any chances we might have."

I thought for a moment and then looked at Griffin. "Most likely."

Griffin stood up and looked down at me. He unzipped his pants and let them slowly slide down his muscular thighs like he was a male stripper. He was wearing a canary-yellow thong that looked marvelous against his chocolate-brown skin. As he pulled off his shirt with one hand, he rubbed his semi-erect penis with the other.

When he was standing in front of me wearing only the thong and a sexy smile, he said, "This is a chance I'm willing to take. Where is your bedroom?"

I bounced from the sofa and took his hand. "Come this way."

With Sweet D's advice and direction, I became a man. It was one of the last sun-drenched days of autumn and both Rochelle's and my parents were at the PTA meeting planning the annual homecoming talent show. This was the perfect time to do something we knew we shouldn't be doing, because the planning meeting was usually the longest one of the year, with parents trying to make sure their children had a spot in the popular show.

The evening before, D had given me a few pointers on how girls liked for you to feel on them before you actually stuck it in. He told me to whisper in her ear and tell her how pretty she was. He gave me explicit instructions. He told me to slowly open her blouse, button by button, and then unhook her bra. He told me to suck on her breasts like I was sucking on a pickle with a peppermint stick stuck in the middle of it. He said to palm her booty like it was a basketball.

I remembered all of D's instructions as I leaned into Rochelle. She closed her eyes and moaned as I sucked on her lemon-sized breasts. I took off my jeans, but D told me to keep my underwear on just in case her mother got home early. Less than an hour later, I went to the basketball court to let D know that I was now a man just like him.

"So, did she bleed?" D asked as he continued to shoot baskets.

"I don't think so," I said. I would have remembered blood. All I remembered was the feeling I had the first time the creamy juice sprayed from the tip of my penis into the air like a bottle *of champagne being opened. The liquid spread on my thighs up to my navel. I took my finger and touched it. I wanted to examine it closer and smell it, but I didn't. The feeling was incredible. I felt like I was falling off a cliff. The harder I pressed into Rochelle, the faster my heart beat, and I felt like I was plunging into the air. I remembered the intoxicating scent of sex and how I felt a little dirty, but I didn't feel the need to shower.*

"Are you sure she was a virgin?" D asked. I couldn't tell if he was really happy for me or upset about something.

"She said it was her first time," I said.

D stopped shooting and walked slowly toward me. He looked dead into my eyes and said, "Bitches lie. Don't ever believe anything they say."

I was shocked by his words. I'd never heard him use the B word before, so I just said, "Okay."

"So do you feel different?" he asked, returning to his normal tone.

"I know I want to do it again," I said, smiling.

"And you will, my friend. You will."

CHAPTER TWELVE

Sometimes I hate being a member of the group of *Homo sapiens* called men. Are we men the dumbest group of human beings, or what? If I were a female, I am certain I would be a lesbian so I wouldn't have to deal with niggas and their dumb shit.

Let me prove my point. I was in a meeting with one of the top photographers in the city, who wanted to work with me on my cards, and who was offering me a better deal than the current people I was using. Almost every five minutes, I heard my cell phone ringing inside my briefcase. I was embarrassed, because I was always getting on Celia about how unprofessional it was to have your cell phone going off during a business meeting. I apologized before I reached in and put it on silent.

After the photographer left, I looked at the screen on my cell phone and saw that I had thirteen missed messages. I wondered who was trying so hard to get in touch with me. I thought it had to be some sort of emergency. The first message I listened to was from my brother asking for a few dollars. And the next twelve were from Jayshawn. I thought I had made it clear that I didn't want to see him and his dumb ass again. But he still called and left a message that was so stupid, I had to listen to it three times to make sure I'd heard the message correctly.

"Yo, Chaunce, this is yo boy, J. I'm back in town, I know you still might be mad at me and shit . . . but you need to call your boy so we can hook up sometime this week. It's a new month, time for our monthly. I need to make up for what happened the last time. I would love to do this week, but I need you to call me between twelve and two, because you know how bitches are, and I am sure my girl will be checking my messages and shit. So, holla back, and I'll be checking my messages every fifteen minutes."

I had to shake my head after I heard that message. I thought if these dumb mofos didn't use simple passwords like their birthdays and IQs, nobody would be able to figure out their passwords.

I was so mad, I wanted to call his girlfriend and tell her how she should check Jayshawn's messages every five, instead of fifteen, minutes. She was probably somebody without a real job and had time to play Christie Love all day.

*　　*　　*

After a couple of weeks, I reached my three-date limit with Griffin, and to be honest, I wanted a fourth. We had amazing sex and surprisingly revealing conversations. Still, I was afraid that a long-term relationship with a man would

interfere with my return to my music career while I was running my card business. And I was a bit concerned because
Griffin seemed to have too much time on his hands. Whenever I called, he would call right back like he was sitting
by his telephone waiting for me to call. When I asked what
he was doing, he'd reply, "Thinking about you." *Please,
nigga,* I thought. If I didn't call, he left messages all day long.
I hoped I didn't have a stalker on my hands, because I'd
already had one of those and it wasn't as glamorous as it
sounds.

It had happened when I first started the business and
was interviewing a lot of models for my cards. One day, a
handsome man walked into my office and I almost fell to
the floor at the sight of him. He was mixed, his mother from
Senegal and his father Greek, and he seemed to have gotten the best traits from both—striking features, unbelievable coloring, dark curly hair, and the body of a god. In fact,
his name was Adonis.

We went out a couple of times, and when we came
to date three, I pulled back. I didn't return his calls, and so
he started just showing up at my apartment building. When
I stopped answering the intercom, he started calling my
cell phone and leaving so many desperate messages that I
couldn't receive calls from my friends or business associates.
I wasn't physically afraid of him, because from our bedroom
wrestling matches I knew I could kick his ass in a heartbeat. I thought I could handle him until he sent me a dead
black cat via overnight mail. That's when I went to the
police. When I filed the restraining order, I discovered he

was in the country illegally, and his ass was sent packing back to Africa faster than you could say "Eddie Murphy in *Coming to America*."

But so far Griffin hadn't made any stalker moves.

When I came home, I went through the lobby to pick up my mail rather than take the elevator from the garage. As I was flipping through my mail, a familiar voice called out my name. I turned around, and there was Griffin standing a few feet from me.

"Griffin, what are you doing here?" I asked, obviously startled.

"I need to talk to you," he said.

"Sure, but you could have called," I said, slightly annoyed. I pushed back the memory of Adonis that came to mind.

"Can we go upstairs?"

I paused for a moment and looked him over. He was wearing tight-fitting clothes, as usual, and didn't seem to have on anything that I should fear, and so I said yes.

Once we reached my home, I didn't know if I should offer G something to drink. That could easily turn this into a date, and I had other plans. I was going to cook something light and quick and then spend time writing some songs for a demo CD. I wanted to make it an early night.

As a compromise, I offered him a bottle of water, and he declined. G seemed nervous as he walked over to the terrace, looked out, and then moved back toward me, wringing his hands like they were covered with something he wanted off.

"G, what's up, dude? You're making me nervous," I said.

"Chauncey, you're a real cool dude and I have enjoyed every minute we've spent together, and I mean that. But I haven't been totally honest with you."

"How so?" I frowned.

"First, my name isn't G. I mean, it could be, but actually Griffin is my middle name. My first name is Willis."

"What's your last name?" I asked, wondering why I was still so calm.

"That's not really important."

"Then why are you here?"

"To warn you."

"Warn me about what?"

"You shouldn't let people in your life so easy. Everybody don't mean you good," he said nervously.

It took me a moment to digest his words.

"What are you saying? Come on, now, I don't have any enemies." I laughed. That was true as far as I knew. I mean, Adonis might have been pissed, but he was halfway around the world. I thought about the couple Ms. Gladys said had been asking about me, but we hadn't heard another peep from them.

"Trust me," he said strongly, as if he was trying to convince me with his tone. "I don't know the full connection, and I could get in big trouble if they knew I was doing this, but you seem like such a nice guy, and you've treated me real cool and with mad respect. I did this because I needed the money."

"Did what?"

"Met you. Found out where you lived and how you were living here. Who's in your life. Just basic information."

I looked at G, or whatever his name was, to see if this was some kind of sick joke. I still expected him to burst out laughing, but after a few minutes of silence, I knew he was dead serious.

"So you're saying someone hired you to find out stuff about me?"

"You could say that."

"Who hired you?" I demanded.

"I can't say."

"What do they want with me?"

"Look, I'm sorry. Like I said, you a cool dude. But you need to watch your back," G said, and then he dashed out of my apartment and was gone like a vampire at daylight.

CHAPTER THIRTEEN

After a marathon day at work, I came home, kicked off my loafers, and made myself a bacon, avocado, and egg sandwich. I finished the sandwich and was planning to go into my office and write a song or some inserts for future cards. Even though I was exhausted, I felt the creative juices flowing through my body, or maybe it was the glass of wine I'd had with my meal. Either way, I was ready to create something brilliant.

I'd had a good day. I reviewed Celia's proposal for the upcoming presentation for Wal-Mart and was pleased with what she had pulled together, and I had my first rehearsal for my solo. I had decided to sing "I Need You," a song I had fallen in love with from Smokie Norful's popular gospel CD.

The church's musical director, Vince, seemed blown away when I opened my mouth to sing, and afterward I actually blushed when he said, "Baby, you can sang!" He even flirted with me by telling me he had seen me several times in the audience but it never dawned on him that someone as good-looking as me could sing. I thanked him, and he responded by saying, "No, thank you, baby, because I just got me a new soloist and I don't have to put up with that prima donna Patrick Morse anymore." I didn't really know who Patrick was, but I assumed he was the heavyset guy who had a great voice and sang a solo almost every Sunday, and, faithful to his Holy Ghost routine, waved his handkerchief every week when he took the microphone.

I picked up a white legal pad and pen and was heading to my office when my phone rang. I looked at the caller ID and saw Celia's number flash across the screen, so I picked up.

"What are you doing up this late?" I asked.

"Chauncey, can you pick me up in the morning and drive me to work?" Celia asked. Her voice seemed distressed to me.

"Sure. Is everything all right?" I asked.

There was a pause, and then Celia said, "No," and I suddenly heard tears on the other end of the phone.

"Celia, what's the matter?"

The tears continued, and finally, Celia told me that someone had smashed all the windows and slashed the tires on her car.

"Did you call the police? Do you know who did it?" I asked.

"I think so," she said as I heard her blowing her nose.

"Who would do something like that?"

"I'm pretty certain it was Marvin," she said.

"Marvin? Are you sure? Why would he do that?"

"He's trying to get back together with me. One of my

girls, Donita, told him how I had this great job and had bought my own car and condo, so he's been blowing up my cell. She even told him where I lived. A couple of weeks ago, I was getting out of my car and there he was sitting on his piece-of-shit car, smiling at me like I should be glad to see him," Celia said.

"Did you tell him that you weren't interested?"

"Not really. I told him I was too busy with my job to have a boyfriend. That I just wanted to play the field," Celia said.

"So why do you think he's the one who slashed your tires?"

"Oh, I know he did it. When I wouldn't go out with him, he made some snide remarks saying all the material possessions I had could be gone as quickly as I had gotten them. Then he said, 'If you ain't careful, you could be riding on rims.'"

"Yes, Celia, I'll pick you up in the morning, but we're going to stop at the police station, file a report, and get a restraining order," I said.

"I don't know if I want to do that," Celia said.

"What? Celia, have you lost your mind? This guy sounds dangerous," I said, remembering my strange meeting with Griffin. Was I in any real danger myself? Maybe it was Marvin who was after me. A lot of people sometimes thought that Celia and I were dating because of our close relationship. Maybe this dummy had seen us out at lunch or picking out ties at Saks Fifth Avenue at Phipps Plaza, which we did often.

"He's just trying to scare me," she said, trying to sound casual.

"Duh," I said.

"Don't worry. As soon as I get off the phone, I'm going to call his parents and he won't bother me again," Celia said.

"Are you sure?"

"I'm sure. I'll see you in the morning."

"Celia, please be careful. Lock your doors," I said.

"Don't worry. They're double-locked."

*   *   *

I woke up sweating like a bricklayer in the middle of July. I'd had a nightmare. I dreamed that somebody with no face was chasing Celia and me with a knife. Griffin was in the distance, trying to tell us which way to go, and I could feel the faceless body coming closer just as I woke up.

I got up from my bed, went to the kitchen, and downed an entire bottle of water in two gulps. The water cooled my body, and as I was getting ready to return to bed, I looked at the phone, picked it up, and dialed Griffin's number. It was strange that I remembered the number after knowing him for only a few weeks.

A few seconds later I heard, "The number you have reached, 555-369-1228, has been disconnected."

Now I knew it was going to be hard for me to go back to sleep. I thought about taking an Excedrin PM, but instead I put on Luther Vandross's *Dance with My Father* CD, slipped back into bed, and hoped that Luther's voice could soothe me back to sleep.

"Promise me you will never sit like that," D whispered to me.

"Like what?" I asked.

"Like him," D said as he moved his eyes toward the corner, where Mr. Charles sat with his legs crossed like a pretzel, drinking a Coca-Cola and wiping his brow with the red handkerchief he always seemed to carry.

Mr. Charles was from Jackson, Mississippi, where he owned a dance studio and made up routines for the Jackson State Jaycettes. He had come to Greenwood to teach us steps for an upcoming performance we were doing for the Deltas in Biloxi. Mr. Charles was a wiry man, about 5'5" and 125 pounds. His hair fell in Jheri curls that ended at his neck. Today, his hair hung to his shoulders, but sometimes he wore it in a ponytail. His voice was high-pitched and soft, but Mr. Charles knew some steps.

"I would never sit like that," I said.

"I hope not," D said in relief.

"You don't like Mr. Charles?" I asked.

"It has nothing to do with liking him. We don't have to like him. All we have to do is just learn the steps. When we make it big, I'm sure he will be the first person we get rid of."

I wanted to ask why, because besides being a little feminine, Mr. Charles was a nice man, always kind to us. Sometimes he brought us fried-chicken sandwiches and pound cake his roommate made. He always complimented D and me when we did our steps, telling us we were going to be big stars one day like

Sammy Davis Jr., whom he said he once danced with in a stage show in *Las Vegas*.

"I think Mr. Charles does a good job," I said.

D shrugged. "He does okay, but I think we should get a female to teach us steps. I mean, she would know what the ladies want to see us do."

"I guess you're right," I said as I watched Mr. Charles finish off his soda and put his dance shoes back on. He looked rested, like he didn't have a care in the world.

Then I looked over at D, who was still staring at Mr. Charles. D's face was filled with disgust, and again I wondered what he had against the man. I knew D wouldn't tell me what was bothering him then, but I made a point to ask him about it later.

CHAPTER FOURTEEN

"*So* are you nervous?" Skylar asked me.

"I'm trying not to think about it," I said as I took my seat on one of the dark maple wooden stools at Skylar's bar. He had invited me over to dinner on Saturday evening to show me photographs he had taken of his latest "boyfriend." I was happy, because I was too nervous worrying about my debut at church the next day to cook.

Dinner at Skylar's meant takeout, not a home-cooked meal, but that didn't stop him from bringing out his favorite Versace china to serve the fried chicken wings and mac and cheese from Gladys and Ron's Chicken & Waffles in midtown Atlanta. "So why did you pick church for your comeback debut?" Skylar asked.

"My minister asked me, and I used to love singing in church. It was the first place I ever sang," I said.

"Oh, that's so precious. What did you sing?" Skylar asked as he tapped me on my arm like I was a little boy.

"I remember it like it was yesterday. I was eight years

old, and at our Easter pageant, I sang 'Yes Jesus Loves Me,'"
I said, smiling at the memory from my childhood.

"So what do I have to wear to this church? I hope you
don't expect me to wear a suit or something stiff like that,"
Skylar said. He moved over to his liquor cabinet and pulled
out a bottle of cognac. He came back over to his place at
the bar and poured a capful of the golden liquor into his
glass of lemonade.

"Would you like a little taste?" he asked as he tilted the
bottle toward my half-empty glass of cola.

"No, I'm fine. I'm in training. Got to protect the voice,"
I said, clearing my throat.

"Whatever. How's the chicken?"

"Greasy but good," I said as I dipped the wing into a
vat of blue cheese salad dressing Skylar had poured into a
Versace gravy bowl.

"It's fried chicken, darling. It's supposed to be greasy. It's
not some of that fancy stuff you make." Skylar laughed.

"So where are the pictures?" I asked.

"In my office. Finish your vittles and I'll let you see."

I ate my chicken and walked through the dining room
to Skylar's office on the other end of his Victorian-style
house about two blocks from Piedmont Park. Skylar had
decorated it himself in bright colors like lime green, yel-
lows, and rose reds. His office had a faux leather covering
on the wall and a beautiful Queen Anne desk and chair.

I looked on the desk covered with photographs and
comp cards. Meeting models on a regular basis was some-

thing Skylar and I had in common. Sometimes he would give me a call and say, "I just saw the most beautiful boy, but I can't use him over here. I am going to send him your way."

I could hear footsteps and the barking of Skylar's miniature poodle, Diva Delight. I was getting ready to turn toward the doorway to greet Diva when I spotted a comp card of Griffin on the edge of the desk. I picked it up and inspected it. I didn't know Sky knew him.

"What are you doing?" Skylar asked as he sauntered into the room in a matching robe and pajamas.

"This is the guy I've been dealing with," I said as I held up the comp card. "The one I actually considered going out with more than three times."

Skylar frowned. "Please tell me you're kidding."

"Why? He's beautiful," I said.

"Yes he is, but honey, he's a pain in the ass. And I don't mean the good kind," Skylar said, shaking his head in dismay.

"Yeah, you're probably right. A few days ago, he came over and told me some bogus story about being hired to find out information about me. Told me to watch my back."

"Well, believe him, honey. A friend of mine who was a flight attendant based in Denver told me that Ms. Griffin is a real switchblade-carrying sissy," Skylar said.

"I didn't know Griffin lived in Denver, and why would he come after me?"

"Because he probably thinks you got more money than you have. I heard his family had money but he got disinherited, probably for being so ghetto. He's just bad news. Tear that number up."

"Don't have to do that. He's already changed his number," I said.

"Good. Save your pennies for somebody bringing some throw-you-against-the-wall sex," Skylar advised.

CHAPTER FIFTEEN

It was such a stunningly beautiful morning that I was
tempted to keep walking past the church. I took a deep
breath and inhaled one final smell of the fading scent
of summer. It was hard to believe it was the beginning of
September.

Moments later, I found myself more nervous than a five-
year-old child getting ready for his first Easter speech as I
noticed the sunshine stream through the stained-glass windows. I shifted a bit in my seat, straightening the legs of my
new navy-blue pinstriped Italian suit. I wanted to make
sure I looked sharp the first time I sang in church in more
than twenty years. If something went wrong and I didn't
sound my best, at least church members could say, "*Well,
he looked good.*"

I turned my attention to Sister Maria Lawson as she
extended a welcome to the visitors with a huge smile painted
on her face. She was wearing a pale pink jersey dress that
camouflaged the fullness of her figure, and her long dark-
brown hair fell in a sweet order of tight curls. I looked nerv-

ously around the church; it seemed filled with more than the usual five hundred worshipers. I knew that if Skylar made it on time there would be one more than normal.

The offering was taken and the time for my debut was getting closer. When Vincent nodded for me to take my place just a few feet from the pulpit, a sudden flush of excitement passed through my body, but my nervousness remained. I straightened my lemon yellow tie, trying to loosen it against my ivory white shirt.

I felt like I was walking in slow motion as I moved toward the microphone. At that moment, I said a little silent prayer. Everything was so still you could hear a tear drop, and then there was a bristling energy in the church as members started whispering. I wondered what they were saying, and then I caught Skylar prancing into the back of the church. He winked at me and waved. I returned him a fragile smile like my mother used to give me when I sang back home.

I suddenly wished I was among those supportive people back at Bethel Baptist, but the members of Abundant Joy loved me just the same, or at least I hoped they did.

I looked at Vincent, and he began playing the overture. I opened my mouth and I felt my heart beating as I sang the first three notes. *"Not a second,"* spilled from me in a clear, tenor voice that sounded rich and solemn. *"Or another minute . . . not an hour or another day."*

That was when the first "Hallelujah" rang through the church.

Halfway through the song, I felt like I had been singing

in front of this church my entire life. I unclenched my fists and reached toward the heavens with my eyes closed tightly, and continued to sing.

I could hear applause and a female voice shout, "Sing, baby." Just as I was singing the last stanza, I heard a familiar voice shout, "Sing, bitch. You ain't sanging. You better just sang, Chauncey Greer. Sang!"

I opened my eyes and saw Skylar almost prancing down the aisle waving a white lace handkerchief, encouraging me. Some of the members turned toward him with disapproving glances. Skylar put his hand over his mouth and sought refuge in the closest pew.

"*O Lord . . . O Lord,*" I sang.

As I finished the song, I didn't know if I should shake my head in shame at Skylar's antics or break out laughing. Instead, I listened to the crescendo of applause and more shouts of "Hallelujah" from the congregation. A feeling of calm warmth radiated through my body as I almost stumbled back to my seat in the first row. I was surprised when warm tears streamed down my face, and I felt a hand tap my knee. Sister Maria passed me a perfectly starched white handkerchief. I smiled toward her and mouthed, "Thank you."

Pastor Kenneth took the pulpit with a huge smile on his face.

"Can the church say Amen?" he said as he looked toward me and started clapping. Suddenly, the entire church was standing and applauding as my tears continued.

"Stand up and take a bow, Brother Chauncey," Pastor Kenneth said.

I stood up meekly and half waved through my blurred vision of smiling faces. Then I sat down quickly.

Pastor Kenneth continued his applause, and when he stopped, he looked at me. "Brother Chauncey, the Lord has blessed you with a tremendous gift. Can the church say Amen?"

"Amen," the congregation said in unison.

"You know, in a couple of months, our church and city is hosting a revival with one of this country's most promising young ministers. The host committee was trying to work out a contract to bring Donnie McClurkin to do the opening song. Now, you members know me and my wife love us some Donnie McClurkin, but after what I just heard, I think Donnie just lost a job. Will you sing that same song at the opening, Brother Chauncey?"

I didn't know what revival Pastor Kenneth was talking about, but it sounded important. I nodded my head in an affirmative motion as I wrapped my arms around my chest and rocked myself as though I was in my mother's arms.

* * *

"Why can't I be your manager?" Skylar asked.

"What do you know about managing a music career?" I asked as I removed the remains of the standing rib roast I had prepared for Sunday dinner, along with scalloped potatoes and asparagus. I was still on a high from my performance at church, and now I felt even more confident about regaining my singing career.

I made up my mind to look into moving to either New York or Los Angeles, where it would be easier to get a record deal. Still, doing my own CD had its advantages, like singing my music my way. If I wanted to sing about loving a *him* rather than a *her*, then I could do that. If I had a song that talked about my faith and love for the Lord, then why shouldn't I be able to sing that? I didn't want to be put in a musical box.

I walked back into the living area, where Skylar was sitting on the sofa with his legs crossed tightly and sipping a glass of cognac.

"So you didn't answer my question," Skylar said.

I opened a bottle of water. "You don't know anything about managing a music career."

"I didn't know anything about dressing tacky bitches either, but that didn't stop me from becoming one of the top stylists in the country. You can sing, baby. I mean, I was blown away by you this morning. If I had known singing like that was going on in church, I would have taken my ass to church long before. Did you see all those church girls looking at me all cross-eyed when I had my slight slip of the tongue?"

"Skylar, you did use a curse word in church," I said, not being able to keep the smile from my face.

"*Bitch* is the name for a female dog. I just got kinda carried away because I didn't know you could sing like that."

"Didn't you listen to the copy of the CD I gave you from the group?"

"Yeah, I listened to it, but I just figured they had fixed y'all voices with one of those mixing machines."

"So why do you want to manage me?"

"'Cause you gonna be a rich bitch, and I am tired of picking out skirts and blouses for women who don't know how to dress. I am sick of smelling their perfume and hair spray and listening to them talk about their boring-ass husbands, or boyfriends who won't marry them. I want to be on the road meeting people like Usher, Ashanti, and Little John," Skylar said.

"That's not the kind of music and crowd I am trying to go after. I want to write and sing songs like Stevie Wonder and Luther Vandross," I said.

"Those two are old school. Only people who want to listen to them are old folks. We need to reach the masses. The young people. See what a good manager I would be? I think big!" Skylar said as he snapped his fingers in the air. Before I could respond, the phone rang. I looked at the caller ID and saw *private caller* displayed across the screen. I started not to answer, but then I picked up the phone.

"Hello," I said.

"May I speak to Chauncey?" The voice sounded familiar, but I couldn't quickly identify it.

"This is Chauncey," I said.

"Chauncey, this is Vincent, the minister of music from Abundant Joy."

"Oh yeah, Vincent."

"I hope you don't mind, but I got your number from the church secretary," he said.

"That's not a problem, and please forgive me," I said.

"For what?"

"I got caught up in the moment and didn't thank you properly. First for working with me on my solo, and second for playing so beautifully today," I said.

"You don't have to thank me. It's my job, and it was a joy to play with somebody who sings so beautifully and has such a warm spirit."

"Thanks. That's so nice of you to say," I said. I was getting ready to ask him what I could do for him when I heard the call-waiting beep sound.

"I'll hold on," Vincent said before I could even ask him.

I clicked over to the other line. "Hello."

"Hey, baby. Just called to tell you that your daddy and me made it back from the Bahamas. You won't believe this, but both of us got sunburned and we went snorkeling," my mother said.

"That's great, Mama. Can I call you right back? I'm talking with the minister of music from my church," I said.

"Are you back to singing in the church? Because me and your daddy would love to hear you sing in a church again. I would be ready to meet my maker if I could just hear my baby sing the Lord's praises one more time. Please tell me I didn't miss it," Mama pleaded.

"I sang today and it went wonderfully. It went so well, I've been asked to sing at this big revival in Atlanta," I said.

"Praise the Lord. Praise Him. Then I don't plan to miss that. When is it?"

"I'll call you back, Mama," I said, remembering that I still had Vincent on the other line.

"Now, don't forget. Have you talked to Jonathan?"

"About a week ago."

"I think he took some of those bonds I've been saving for my grandkids and cashed them in. I don't know what's going on with him, but you can bet the butter on your toast that I'm gonna find out. Something is rotten in Mississippi, if you ask me," Mama said.

Sometimes when my mother got on a roll with her conversation, it was hard to get her to stop talking without sounding disrespectful or rude. "Don't spend a lot of time worrying, Mama. Jonathan is a grown man," I said.

"But he is still my baby, and you and I both know he doesn't act like a grown man."

"Okay, Mama, you know what's best. I'll call you back," I said.

"And don't forget to get those revival dates for me. I have to make sure it doesn't conflict with any of your daddy's and my travel plans. Can't let any dust gather under these old feet," Mama said.

"I don't think you have to worry about that." I laughed. "'Bye, Mama."

"'Bye, baby, and don't make me have to call you back for that information. The Good Lord has answered my prayers. My baby is singing again. Praise Him."

"I love you, Mama."

"I love you too, baby."

I clicked the phone over and apologized to Vincent.

"That's cool. Look, I'm not going to hold you long, but I want to talk to you about singing at the revival."

"Oh, I'm really excited about that. I can't believe Pastor Kenneth is going to have me replace Donnie McClurkin!"

"Do you know the bishop who's doing the revival?" Vincent asked.

"No, I don't. Should I?"

"He's a guy from Denver, Colorado, and he is no friend to the black community or, more specifically, to black gay people. I'm thinking about trying to organize a boycott during his revival, and though I'm not trying to dip into your business, I thought you should know about this guy before you agreed to sing," Vincent said. "I also have to tell you that if you do decide to sing, you'll have to find another musician, because I won't play for this man."

"What's his name?" I asked, surprised at the passion I heard in Vincent's voice.

"Bishop Upchurch," Vincent said.

"Upchurch," I repeated, thinking I hadn't heard that last name in a long time.

"Yeah, Bishop Upchurch and his wife, Grayson. Both of them are some real pieces of work. They led a march to the state capitol in Denver against gay marriage, and are heading a drive to get a very anti-gay amendment on the ballot in November. Also, he's running for the Senate as a Republican," Vincent said.

"Is he white?"

"White? I know you don't know me that well, Chauncey,

but I never worried about what no white man thought of me, my religion, or my bedroom practices. This is a black man with a black Barbie doll wife. They have a television show, and he spends more than fifty percent of his time bashing gay people. We have to take a stand," Vincent said.

"Is there any way I can find some information on this guy?" I asked.

"I'm going on the Internet tonight to get some info from his campaign Web site. Then I'm going to organize some of the church members who are either gay or pro-gay, and ask them to meet with Pastor Kenneth. We need to get him to reconsider bringing this fool to our church."

"Thanks for giving me the heads-up. If I give you my e-mail address, will you send me the link to anything you find?" I asked.

"Sure. What's your e-mail address?"

"Send it to my office. It's cgreer@cuteboy.com," I said.

"I will. I'll give you a call or e-mail when we decide when we're going to meet," Vincent said.

"Do that."

"Thanks for listening," Vincent said.

"No problem," I said.

As I walked back toward the living room, I mouthed, "Upchurch," and thought, *Naw, couldn't be.*

*   *   *

Early the next morning, my phone rang. I started to let the machine pick it up, but my curiosity got the best of me and I ignored the caller ID.

"Hello."

There was silence over the line.

"Hello," I repeated.

"Stay away from my husband, you fucking faggot," a female voice said firmly.

I suddenly heard a click, then the dial tone. Must have been a wrong number, since I had a strict no-husbands policy. I hoped Jayshawn or Griffin hadn't got married and forgotten to tell me.

My eighteenth birthday was a special one. The group had our first big gig outside of the South. We were the opening act for DeBarge at the Indiana Black Expo in Indianapolis before a crowd of over 30,000, mostly women, screaming our names.

We wore suits Darron and Barron's mother had made, and at the time we thought we were cleaner than a hospital operating room. Looking back, we were a hot country mess in polyester suits with huge lapels and wide-legged pants. D and I wore egg-yellow suits, while Darron and his brother wore light blue. It was his mother's idea that we wear different colors, because she felt like it would make us stand out.

But we turned it out with our fancy dance steps and harmonizing, D on one end and me on the other, stealing glances at each other as we worked up a sweat. D had started this little game of seeing who could wink at each other the most without anyone seeing us. It was a game he always won, because just one of his sexy winks was all that it took to knock me off my game.

After the show, four contestants from the Miss Black America pageant, which was also going on, came to our dressing room for pictures and autographs. Three of them left. One, Miss Nevada, a leggy young lady with an impressive head of hair, took to D and didn't seem like she was ever going to leave. D did his thing, flirting with her and still winking at me whenever he got the chance. Just when I was certain she had convinced him to go back to her hotel room on my birthday, fate intervened.

There was a knock on the door and in walked Mr. Charles

with skintight black pants and a white sweater hanging from his back. There was a well-dressed black man with him who didn't seem like he was on Mr. Charles's program.

"Boys, this is Terry Butler and he's the former manager for the O'Jays, and he wants to talk to you about a record deal."

"What?" Barron asked. "This is what we've been waiting for!"

The four of us hugged each other as the beauty queen looked on. D and I shared a hug, and he whispered, "Stick with me, boy, and I'll take you places."

A few minutes later I heard Mr. Charles say, "Honey, we got some business to take care of. You don't have to go home, but you got to leave here."

She grabbed her purse and stormed out of the dressing room. D didn't even notice.

*   *   *

Two weeks later, we signed a three-record deal with legendary Motown Records, and very soon after we were in the recording studio singing our lungs out. We signed with Mr. Butler's management company, which gave us each a ten-thousand-dollar signing bonus. Barron and Darron bought matching silver Datsun 280-Z's. I wanted a Mustang, but D convinced me to save my money because he wanted us to invest in real estate. I hoped he meant a town house or even a house with a pool in Memphis or Atlanta. I was a little surprised when D bought a motorcycle, but even more shocked when I found a helmet for me sitting on the bed in my hotel room.

The next day, after leaving the studio, D took me on a ride down a dusty country road that ended with the two of us throwing rocks into the Mississippi River as a shimmering moon glowed down.

When we got back to the hotel, I felt dusty from the ride. I took a shower while D ordered room service. When I stepped out of the shower, there stood D. He slowly toweled my body dry and touched me in places I didn't know could be touched by another man. A sudden burst of warmth wrapped around my body.

He whispered, "I think it's time. You're legal now."

In his own nakedness, D looked good, smelled better, and felt best. I found myself falling into him helplessly, not trying to stop myself. D made love to me with a certain caution, as if I were fragile and might break. We made love for hours, and then we slept holding each other like we were protecting each other from the outside world.

When I woke up, I thought that if I had become a man with Rochelle, what was I now?

"Do you think we will always feel like this?" I asked.

"Why not? Just a long as we keep it to ourselves," D said.

It had been almost two years since I'd met D and my life was changed. I was happy, and he loved me in a way that I never could have dreamed possible.

"What do you think would happen if someone found out?"

"Don't even think about shit like that. Besides, we're too smart to get caught," D said. His voice was masculine and musical, exuding the strength I so admired in him. It was like he had the world in the palm of his hands and I was the center.

*   *   *

The next day moved fast and smoothly. We practiced, met with potential publicists, and had fittings. I was just going through the motions, because all I could do was think of D and the previous evening.

It was late, 2 A.M. We'd finished a show around midnight and signed autographs until a little after one. When Barron and Darron asked if we wanted to go get something to eat at the IHOP, D told them he had a late date with a groupie, and I said I was tired.

We used those excuses often, and would then go to our separate hotel rooms and wait until we were certain everybody in the group or working with the tour was sound asleep. Then we would get together, meeting in one of our rooms, and talk (and do other things) until just before sunrise.

On this particular night, we sat on the concrete balcony of a downtown Detroit hotel watching the night do absolutely nothing as we ate thick deli sandwiches and drank ginger ale.

When D finished his sandwich, he lay back against the brick wall, his hands locked over his chest.

"When I was growing up in Atlanta, watching my mother work two jobs to keep food on the table, I never thought my life could be this good. I mean, fancy hotels, nice clothes, money in the bank," D said as if he were remembering his past.

"You didn't know your voice could make you successful?"

D shrugged. "There were a lot of dudes who could sing on my block. But most of them ended up singing in the joint."

"The joint?" I quizzed.

"Yeah, you know, the state pen."

"Oh."

"So in a lot of ways it was my destiny to move to Green-wood and meet you," he said as he gave me an engagingly boyish smile.

Whenever he looked at me that way, I fell in love again. "You make me very happy," I said softly.

"Not as happy as I am, my special friend. Not nearly as happy as me," he said as he gently touched my face.

I shuddered at his touch, and at that moment I hoped we would always be this way.

CHAPTER SIXTEEN

"I think you're ready, Celia. You've done a great job," I said after Celia finished showing me the PowerPoint presentation she had prepared for Wal-Mart.

"I really worked hard on this, and I'm so glad you like it." Celia nodded gratefully toward me.

"Girl, you're smarter than a whip when you ain't trying to find a no-'count man," Ms. Gladys said as she left my office. I had invited her to view the presentation to get Celia ready for being in front of more than just me.

"Thank you, Ms. Gladys," Celia said as Ms. Gladys left my office.

"You want to go have a drink to celebrate?" I asked.

"I wish I could, but I got something I need to handle," Celia said mournfully.

"Is everything all right?"

"It will be. My mother is insisting that I take out a restraining order on Marvin."

"Is he still bothering you?" I asked, wondering why she didn't get the restraining order when I suggested it.

"I just keep getting phone calls late at night and early in the morning," Celia said.

"What does he say?" I asked. My mind wandered back to the strange call I'd received.

"Nothing."

"I agree with your mother. You should be proactive," I said. "Would you like me to go down to the police station with you?"

"No, I'll be fine. I'm going to get it done and then go home and get packed for my trip to Bentonville. I'll be styling with all the outfits Skylar picked out for me. Did I tell you he was even able to get a jewelry store to loan me real pearls to wear?"

"No, but that's cool," I said, realizing Celia didn't want to talk about Marvin and his threats. She was a tough girl, but I hoped she wasn't taking this fool lightly.

I spent the rest of the day looking up numbers for local producers. I wished that someone had taped my performance on Sunday, but I realized that even if I'd had a tape, I was still going to find myself in a producer's office, standing in front of a desk, singing a cappella like I was auditioning for *American Idol*.

I then began to imagine what a customer like Wal-Mart would do for my business and my bank account. I might even be able to hire some smart MBA person to run the day-to-day business so I would have more time for my music.

Just as I was getting ready to go home, a sudden storm washed over the evening sky. I watched the rain pour from the heavens and decided to stay in my office a little longer and answer my e-mails.

I scrolled through my in-box. There were a couple of e-mails asking how to order my cards and a few pictures of guys who obviously had liars in their life who told them they were good-looking enough to be models.

There was an e-mail from the Traveling Grands with suggested flight times from Jackson, Mississippi, to Atlanta, and a message telling me to call them so that we could talk about what song I should sing at the revival.

The last e-mail was from Vincent, with a short note thanking me again for listening to him and advising me to check out the attached link. I put the mouse on the blue line and, a few seconds later, I was face-to-screen with my past.

There he was, staring at me. Damien Lee Upchurch. But he was not alone in the photo; sitting next to him was a beautiful woman identified as Grayson Upchurch, and each had a child in their lap. Damien held a little girl with too many ribbons and bows on her tiny head, and his wife was holding a little boy who obviously had been visited recently by the tooth fairy.

As I read about Bishop Damien Upchurch—who was still unforgivably handsome and looked like he was still just in his twenties—and his Restore Ministries, headquartered in Denver, Colorado, anxiety clenched my stomach. It felt like Damien was in my office sitting across from me, and I could smell the musky citrus fragrance he'd favored in his youth.

I continued to read that the mission of Restore was to bring moral values back to the family and to take the battle against gay marriage to the desk of the President of the United States. There was a link to sign an amendment against same-sex marriage in Colorado, and a place to make contributions to Restore Ministries and to Damien's campaign for the Senate.

I learned from the site that his wife of over ten years was the former Grayson Cunningham, the daughter of the late Theodore Cunningham, the first black oil millionaire in Colorado. Cunningham had served as the state chairman of the Republican National Committee and was a golf partner of the first President Bush. On the Web site, there was a picture of Grayson and her father when she was presented as the first African American debutante at the Denver Country Club just before she entered Harvard. It stated that she had transferred to the University of Miami after her freshman year. How odd it was, I thought, for someone to leave Harvard to transfer to Miami.

I scrolled through the Web site, and memories that were forever tangled in my mind were now front and center. I noticed there was no mention of Damien's humble beginnings in Atlanta or my hometown of Greenwood, Mississippi, where he and his siblings had lived in a section of town known as GP, for government property. His mother, Merlene, had been a cook at the Crystal Grill, a local restaurant where black people could only order and pick up food, not eat inside, even in the late 1970s.

Of course, there was no mention of Reunion and how

we had a No. 1 R & B hit and a multiplatinum album. And since Damien was now trying to instill moral values into people in his new community, there was certainly no mention of me and the time D sat across from me in a booth at the IHOP in Kansas City after a show, sipping chocolate milk shakes and whispering the words that I'd never forgotten: "You are the first person in my life I feel like I can love forever."

CHAPTER SEVENTEEN

It had been a week since I looked at Damien's Web site. Now I was pulling up behind a candy-apple-red BMW 500 series with a bumper sticker that read, "I'm Gay and I Vote," and I wondered what had I gotten myself into. Vincent had called and asked me to attend a meeting he and some other church members were having to discuss the upcoming revival with Damien. It couldn't hurt to attend. I pulled out the piece of paper with the address of the choir member who was hosting the meeting and realized that it was a couple of doors down from where I had parked my car.

It was the first time I had been in Stone Mountain in about two years. I'd told my mother and father that I was going to a dinner party, and they told me that when I was a little boy I had participated in a march against the Klan in Stone Mountain with members of my church. I didn't remember, since I was only four years old at the time, but I thought it was ironic that I would find myself in Stone

Mountain again fighting against another form of discrimination: straight churchgoers versus gay ones.

I reached the rose colored front door of a traditional brown-and-white brick town house and rang the doorbell. A few seconds later, a portly black man with a bald head answered the door with a plastic cup in his hand and a bright smile covering his face.

"Oh, it's the singing star. Baby, you turned it out when you sang a couple of Sundays ago. My name is Bruce Maxwell. Come on in," he said as he extended his ringed hand. "Come on in."

"Chauncey Greer," I said as I shook Bruce's hand and followed him into a marble foyer.

"Come on into the kitchen and get something to drink. I think Vincent is in there," Bruce said.

We walked through the living room, tastefully decorated in black and white, with two matching black leather love seats and a few white ottomans scattered about. There was a high vaulted ceiling that gave the room extra light. *I bet Bruce gives some awesome parties in this house*, I thought as I followed him into a large kitchen with beautiful maple floors and matching cabinets. There was a long island in the middle of the room. There were about fifteen people drinking and eating as I glanced around the room searching for Vincent.

I was happy that the crowd looked evenly divided between men and women, and equally pleased that I couldn't tell anyone's sexual orientation by just looking at them. I recognized a few of the faces from church, but most of them were not familiar.

I spotted Vincent placing some chicken wings on a paper plate, and our eyes met before I reached him.

He put the plate down, moved toward me, and we engaged in a brief but awkward hug. He whispered in my ear, "Thanks for coming."

"No problem," I said.

"Come on, get something to eat. We're going to be starting in a few minutes, because it looks like everyone is here," Vincent said.

I got a few wings, some vegetables and dip, and then moved toward the large great room, where folding chairs were set up. I took a seat in the back row but suddenly wanted something to drink, so I returned to the kitchen and got a bottle of water from an open ice cooler.

When I walked back into the room, a couple of young ladies had taken seats in the back row as well.

"Are you ladies trying to take my row?" I said as I sat back down.

"Yeah, we figured if we sat back here we wouldn't get called on. You know, like in school," one of the girls, a beautiful young lady with a short haircut, said. "My name is Lisa, and this is my girlfriend, Paula."

"Chauncey Greer. Nice meeting you, Lisa and Paula," I said. I wondered if she meant sistergirl girlfriend or sleeps-in-my-bed girlfriend, but I would find out soon enough.

"You're the guy who sang at church. You were amazing. I didn't know you were family," Paula said.

"Thank you," I said, noting that Paula had used the insider word "family" that referred to the community of gay folks.

A few minutes later, Bruce stood in front of the room and thanked everyone for coming. Then he turned the floor over to Vincent.

"Why don't we give Brother Bruce here a round of applause for allowing us to use his house, and for whipping up some vittles," Vincent said as he started clapping. Bruce stood up, bowed, sat back down, and then stood back up and said, "There's plenty of food in the kitchen, so please eat as much as you want and take some home if you want. I'm watching my weight, so I am eating like a supermodel." Bruce laughed.

"Plus size or Tyra Banks?" Vincent joked.

"You know me and Tyra are like this," Bruce said as he crossed his fingers.

Vincent laughed before his face took on a serious expression.

"Again, thanks for coming," he began. "What we want to do is to come up with a plan that will let Pastor Kenneth know he can't let this Bishop Upchurch and his crew come down here and take over our church. I, for one, am tired of switching churches to avoid the hateful rhetoric from the prosperity pimps who think they are spreading the word of God. I am here to tell you they don't represent my God," Vincent said. "We can't let these people take another church from us."

"Amen, Brother Vincent," a few voices said in unison.

"So this is what I propose. Before the good bishop arrives from Denver, we let Pastor Kenneth know how important we are to his congregation. I think that we should have a

Sunday of Absence when all of us who are gay, bi, transgender, and our supporters skip the church services when Bishop Upchurch and his cohorts come. Brother Bruce has once again offered his home, and we can have a service here. Let's see who's left at Abundant Joy to direct the choir, greet the guests, and, more importantly, fill up the tithing plate," Vincent said.

Someone close by moved, and I looked over and saw Paula standing up.

"May I make a suggestion?" she asked.

"Sure, but why don't you tell us your name, sister?" Vincent said.

"My name is Paula Minter. What I think might be more effective is if we pack the church in big numbers a few Sundays before Bishop "Upchuck" brings his traveling show to Atlanta. Each of us should put it upon ourselves to bring five friends to church and to make sure they put a little something in the offering plate," Paula said. "And while this is a beautiful home, I think we should consider renting a hotel space and including people from other churches."

"That's an excellent suggestion," Vincent said.

It was a good idea, but I didn't know where I was going to find five people to bring unless I asked Ms. Gladys, Skylar, and Celia to loan me a couple of their friends.

"May I say something?" I heard another female voice ask. I looked up and saw a short, middle-aged woman with beautiful gray hair standing up near the front of the room.

"Sure, Sister Esther," Vincent said.

She turned and faced the room, holding a dainty handkerchief. Sister Esther's face painted a picture of anguish, and I was certain that she was getting ready to tell us that our plans were wrong.

"I don't know how to say this," Sister Esther said, her voice breaking.

"Take your time, darling," Vincent said as he moved closer to her and placed his arm around her shoulders.

"I'll be all right. I just don't know what I would do without Vincent. Not only can he play the piano and organ, but he has been a good friend to me and my family. For those of you who don't know me, my name is Esther Mae Smith and I have been attending Abundant Joy for almost three years. I love the church and what Pastor Kenneth and Sista Vivian are doing. But something is bothering me. Vincent said that we can't let them take another church from us, and I want you to know that it's not just gay folk who feel that way," Esther said.

She paused for a moment, took her handkerchief, and dabbed the corners of her eyes. Then she placed the cloth over her mouth for a moment, paused, removed the handkerchief, and began speaking again.

"Me and my late husband, Herman, were founding members of Mount Olive Baptist Church out in Decatur, and we were proud members for over twenty-five years. Herman and me were married there, and my two children were baptized there. Our church was no bigger than a couple of large walk-in closets, but I felt the presence of the good Lord every time I stepped foot inside the sanctuary.

Well, many of you know Mount Olive is a lot bigger than any closet these days. Ever since our founding pastor, Ralph Sinclair, retired and turned the church over to his son, Ralph Sinclair the Third, the church has been expanding. You know, his services are now telecast on television not once, but twice a week, and they have outgrown their second sanctuary. They even have a school and credit union now. I ain't got no problem with the church expanding, especially when it's helping our people. But I left Mount Olive at least two years too late. I should have been out of there the moment that young man told me . . ." Sister Esther stopped talking, and this time she could not get the handkerchief up to her eyes to prevent the tears from flowing freely down her face.

"Take your time, Mrs. Esther," Bruce said.

"Yes, Mama, take your time," Vincent added. The room was suddenly silent. I glanced at Paula, who was holding Lisa's hand and gently stroking her hair.

"I just don't know if I can finish the story. Vincent, you know it. Please tell these young people what that church did to me," Esther said.

"Are you sure? We can wait," Vincent said.

"No, you go on, baby. I'm going to sit down, but before I do, I want to tell you young people that I am with you whatever you decide. But I also think we all need to go home tonight, get on our knees, and ask the Good Lord for direction," she said through her tears before she sat down.

Vincent looked eager to finish her story.

"The church wouldn't let this wonderful woman have

the funeral for her son, my best friend, Bennie, in the church he had been raised in. It was a scandal and an embarrassment, and that's why we can't let this happen at Abundant Joy," Vincent said.

Vincent went on to tell the crowd the situation. The minister had told Sister Esther that if she dared to bring her son's coffin there, he promised to stand at the door and block her entrance.

Vincent had to pause before he told the rest of the story. "That man actually told Sister Esther that he didn't want Bennie's kind in his church—dead or alive."

As Vincent continued, I could hear not only Sister Esther crying, but several others as well. He ended the story by sharing that Sister Esther had stayed at the church some two years after Bennie's death, but left the day after she buried her husband, Herman.

I found myself wondering why Sister Esther stayed at the church so long. But no matter what her reason, I had to do something. It was time to take a stand and not allow what had happened to Sister Esther and her son to ever happen anywhere again.

*　　*　　*

When I got back home, I went to my office computer, and looked again at Damien's site. I noticed a white pad where I had scribbled down a Denver phone number I'd found for a Damien Upchurch. I didn't know yet if it was Damien's number, but I decided I would give it a try and determine if he really had changed that much since our youth.

I jotted down numbers for Restore Ministries and his campaign headquarters. There was a place where you could send an e-mail to Damien, but I decided not to. I was certain he had a personal assistant or someone answering them.

I picked up the phone and dialed the number. After a few rings, an answering machine picked up. "Praise God from whom all blessings flow. This is Bishop Upchurch, and right now I am away from my office, out in the community doing God's work. Please leave a name and a number, even if you think I have it. Please know God wants you to have a blessed day, and so do I."

The voice sounded the same, and there was no doubt that it was Damien. My heart fluttered at a rapid rate, and I felt like a young boy making his first phone call to someone he intended to make his beloved. But instead of leaving a message, I simply hung up and let out a long sigh of disappointment.

CHAPTER EIGHTEEN

It was Friday, and I was looking forward to the weekend. I walked out of my office and saw Ms. Gladys taking off her heels and putting on her tennis shoes, a ritual that meant she was heading home.

"You got big plans this weekend?" I asked.

"Naw, baby. Just church and my club meeting on Saturday," she said.

"Is Celia still here?"

"Yeah, she in there with that girl," Ms. Gladys said, her face twisted with disgust.

"What girl?"

"You know, the one who looks like she trying to be in one of them BET videos," Ms. Gladys whispered. "Girl wear her skirts so short you can see the color of her underpants."

"Oh, Lontray," I said. Lontray, who, Celia had explained, was named after a combination of her father, Lonnie, and her mother, Tracy, was one of Celia's ghetto friends she had not been able to shake from her high school days. Celia referred to her as "hood rich" Lontray. When I asked her what that meant, Celia responded, "You know, when your car note is five times your rent."

"I guess they getting ready to go out to the club. Miss Celia just changed from that nice blouse she had on and put on a top that look like a Christmas tree decoration."

"So you think it's safe for me to go in there?" I laughed.

"Wear some sunglasses, baby. They are sparkling in there. I'm gone," Ms. Gladys said as she pulled her purse from under the desk and headed toward the door.

"Have a good weekend, Ms. Gladys. See you Monday."

"You too, baby," she said. "Be careful in there with those girls."

As I got closer to Celia's door, I heard laughter mixed with loud music. I guess the party had started early. I tapped on the door and opened it at the same time. The first thing I saw was Lontray swinging her arms above her head, dancing with a low-cut top, short skirt, and body glitter accenting her cleavage. They didn't notice me, since Celia was adjusting her makeup while facing the window.

"That's my cut, girl. TI is crunk."

"He is aight, but Fiddy still my man," Celia said. "Vivica Fox is crazy for letting that go."

"Hey, Celia, are you up for church on Sunday?" I asked.

She turned around with her lipstick still in her hand. "Let me get back to you on that. You remember my friend Lontray."

She smiled at me.

"Yes, I do. Hello, Lontray."

"Hey, Mr. Chauncey with your phine self." Her grin

covered her entire face. "How come you didn't ask me to go to church with you?" she asked, still moving her head as her blond-streaked weave ponytail bounced to the beat of the rap music that played from Celia's computer.

I started to tell her that she didn't strike me as the churchgoing type, but I said, "Do you want to go?"

"Is it going to be like a date? And are you paying?" she said with a roll of her neck. "Church expensive now 'days. Not to mention I'd have to get my hair and nails done."

I had to hold back my laughter. "Now, Lontray, you know I'm old enough to be your daddy," I said. This was not the first time she'd flirted openly with me.

"That's fine, 'cause I'm always looking for a daddy. A sugar daddy, that is. Hey, do you know any good lawyers? I'm trying to get my baby's daddy, Marcel, to give me more child support. He working two jobs now, but he still behind with his support payments," she complained.

"You know Chauncey don't know nothing about no child-support lawyers," Celia said, turning back to her reflection in the window.

"Why couldn't I meet someone like you?" Lontray asked as she moved closer to me. When her drugstore perfume reached my nose, I stepped toward the door.

"Must be looking in the wrong places," I said.

"Why don't you come to the club with us?" Lontray said.

"Yeah, come on, Chauncey," Celia encouraged. "You might meet somebody nice."

"Meet somebody nice? I got what he needs right here," Lontray said, her grin becoming even wider than I thought possible.

I ignored her and said to Celia, "I'm going to pass. Call me if you want me to pick you up for church."

"I will," Celia said.

"That bopper's ass ain't going to church. She gone be at the club or pushing up on that tired-ass Marvin," Lontray said.

"Bitch, didn't I tell your ghetto ass we don't cuss in the office," Celia said. "Yeah, Chauncey, I'll go to church with you, and I'm going to bring Ms. Need Some Jesus with me," she added, as she looked at Lontray and rolled her eyes.

I shook my head and smiled as I left the office.

CHAPTER NINETEEN

"*This* man must have really rocked your world, Chauncey," Skylar said.

I stirred a packet of sweetener in my glass of tea as the two of us sat in a booth at the Cheesecake Factory in the heart of Buckhead. It was a little before six, but there had still been a fifteen-minute wait at the popular restaurant, which was short considering it was Friday evening and the parking lot was packed.

While we waited for a table, I told Skylar the full story about my relationship with Damien. He already knew that he was now a minister and running for the Senate.

"I still can't believe what he did to me," I said as I looked at the colorful menu.

"Tell me, child. Was it a big scandal? Did he beat you?" Skylar asked, almost a little too eagerly.

"No, but he betrayed me like no one else has ever done. It still hurts to this day," I said, remembering the day it happened as if it were just twenty-four hours before.

"Did you catch him with another man or, heaven forbid, a *woman?*" Skylar said as he mockingly stuck his finger in his mouth.

"No, I didn't catch him with anyone, but someone caught us," I said. I told Skylar how our manager, Mr. Butler, called us into his suite after one of our performances and asked us what was going on. He wanted to know why we felt the need to spend so much time together after our shows. It seemed that someone on the security team had told him that almost every morning he saw Damien or me leaving the other's room. Before I could respond or deny the allegations, Damien spoke up. He told Mr. Butler that he was counseling me and holding prayer with me. When Mr. Butler asked for what, Damien said that he was working to rid me of my "homosexual demons."

Skylar's eyes were as wide as silver dollars. "No, he didn't call you out like that!"

I nodded sadly as I relived what I had felt that day. The sadness and disappointment overwhelmed me. "I stood there stunned while Mr. Butler told me how my being gay would ruin the group if any magazines or fans found out. He commended Damien for trying to help me. And then he turned to me and asked if the prayer thing was working."

"I hope you told him a thing or two."

"I was too stunned to say anything. There I was standing next to the man I loved, who told me that he loved me. And he had turned his back on not only me but our relationship."

"So you didn't say anything?" Skylar asked.

"Not a thing. When the tears started to roll down my face, I raced out of Mr. Butler's suite and went straight to my room. Later that day, someone slid a letter under my door. I still remember shaking as I read those words. The letter said that I was no longer a member of Reunion and, if I wanted to receive future royalties, I had to sign the attached statement stating that I would never talk about why I was leaving the group. They even had the nerve to tell me to never speak in public about Barron, Darron, or Damien."

"I cannot believe that," Skylar said.

I wanted to tell Skylar that to this day, I still couldn't believe it, either. I said, "What was so amazing was that there were so many things going on in that group but nothing else seemed to matter. Barron had a fourteen-year-old girl he was sleeping with. She hung around us so much, you would have thought she was a member of the group as well."

Skylar raised his eyebrows. "Isn't that against the law?"

"I guess not in Illinois," I said.

"So did Damien come back later for a little makeup love?"

I stared silently for a minute—Damien's face and the way he looked at me that day still smoldered in my mind. It was not the look of love that I'd come to know, but one of disgust.

"He did apologize, didn't he?" Skylar asked.

"I never saw him again," I said sadly.

Although I didn't know what I was going to do, I wanted Skylar's opinion. A part of me still had feelings for Damien even after all these years, but another part felt anger at the way our relationship had ended. Now his current stance against gay people fueled my rage even more. What would his wife and his political party say if they found out about his past, about me?

"Chauncey!" Skylar yelled, breaking me out of my tea-stirring trance.

"What?" I said as I laid down the long, thin spoon alongside the pink torn packets of sweetener.

"I thought you wanted to talk about this?" Skylar said.

"I'm just wondering what I should do."

"I think you should call a press conference right before he comes to town and tell the world in your best suit that 'this man was my lover.' You know, pull an Amber Frye on him," Skylar said with a laugh. He looked around the restaurant for the waiter.

"What do you want?" I asked.

"I need something stronger than this lemonade. I don't know what I was thinking. I need a drink. Oh, there he goes. Hey, you," Skylar said, waving at the waiter who had taken our order.

The waiter came over and Skylar ordered not one but two glasses of wine. When I looked at him with raised eyebrows, he leaned over and whispered, "Who are we kidding here, honey? We both know I'll be ordering another glass. So let's save some time."

I just shook my head. Maybe after a couple glasses of wine Skylar might have some advice I could use. I never really thought of "outing" Damien, because that simply wasn't my style and what purpose would it serve? I just wanted to talk to Damien so that I could understand what he was doing with his life. I wanted him to understand my life, too, and respect it.

"Have you seen all those billboards of 'your man' all over the city with that wife of his? I must say, he is something if you like the pretty-boy look," Skylar said.

"What billboards?" I asked.

"They're all up and down I-85 and, of course, all over I-20, you know, where most of your people live," Skylar laughed.

"I guess I need to take a trip down I-20 and see," I said.

The waiter delivered a plate of pasta for me and an appetizer portion of ribs for Skylar. The food silenced us for a few minutes.

"Well, at least you fell in love with a smart man," Skylar said as he placed a half-eaten rib on the saucer.

"How do you know he's smart?" I asked as I decided against another piece of garlic bread.

"Look at the career he picked. Preaching and politics are the world's greatest hustles," Skylar said.

"He could be serious about saving souls."

"Yeah right, just like I'm interested in starting a long-term relationship with every man I let in my bed."

I chuckled to myself. "Now that you know why I avoided love for all these years, tell me why you run from real love," I said.

"Chauncey, who said I run from love? True love runs from me. You gotta chase it. But most times love is wearing track shoes, and you know I don't like to sweat," Skylar said, and laughed.

"Have you ever really been in love?"

"Not really," Skylar said sadly.

"Not even when you were young?"

Skylar didn't answer; instead, he took a long gulp and finished his first glass of wine, then took a quick swig of his second glass. There was a look of sadness in his eyes, and melancholy seeped into our booth and took over.

After a few minutes of silence, I gently touched his hand. "I'm here if you ever want to talk about it."

More silence passed and Skylar finished his second glass of wine, then motioned toward the waiter and ordered a third. After one sip on glass number three, Skylar began to cautiously reveal his story of lost love.

"I was in love once, but it didn't work out," he said softly and slowly.

"How old were you?"

"Sixteen."

"What was his name?"

"Tank. Tank Malloy, and he was the best wrestler in Cleveland, and maybe the entire state of Ohio. His skin was as dark as chocolate and as smooth as a Dove bar. He was bowlegged, and had hair on his face before he was sixteen."

"Did he go to your high school?"

"No, he lived on the other side of town and went to Central West, which was our archrival. I met him when I was visiting some of my cousins and he rode past their house on a ten-speed bike with no shirt on. I was just mesmerized."

"What happened when you met him?"

"You mean the first or second time?" Skylar asked.

"What do you mean first or second?"

"I didn't really meet him the first time. I asked my cousin who he was, and she told me his name and that he was already having sex with some girl from the neighborhood who was going to Ohio State University. Since everybody in my family knew I was gay, it was no big deal for me to tell my cousin that I wanted to meet him. I'm glad I never really had any issues about what I wanted. The biggest choice I had to make when I was growing up was how tight I was going to wear my short-shorts. I knew what I wanted, and that was Tank Malloy. I was going to do whatever it took to get him."

"So did your cousin introduce you to him?"

"Not really. She told me he was all boy. She also said he rode his bike every evening and played baseball or something at the Little League field. So for about three days in a row, I went down to the field and watched him from the fence. He was always the last one to leave, and I would just stare at him like he was the only boy on the planet."

"Come on, Skylar, tell me how you met him," I said impatiently.

"I realized my tight jeans and Izod shirts were the wrong outfits. I went back home, and for about a week, I plotted out my plan. When I went back to visit my cousin, I waited until it was dark and I strutted down to the ball field in the tightest little poom-poom shorts, some white tennis shoes with matching socks, and a little white midriff blouse. You know, my skin was as flawless as it is now, and I had an apple-bum ass that had all the girls in my high school wanting to scratch my eyes out. I used one of my mother's nice silk scarves and her Dutch-boy wig, stole some makeup out of Kmart, and I was ready to claim my man."

I looked at Skylar with a puzzled look, wondering if I was hearing him right.

"You dressed in drag?"

"I don't know if you could call it drag. I was a naturally pretty boy and I just did a little enhancing. I guess you could say it was my first real makeover." Skylar smiled.

"I don't know what to say." Why did Skylar's confession make me nervous?

"Oh, baby, ain't no shame in my game. It turned out to be the best move I ever made."

"What happened? Did he know you were a guy?"

Skylar motioned to the waiter to bring the check, then looked over at me.

"I can't finish my story now, honey, I've got a hot date tonight. Drag-free, of course. I'll have to continue this story at a later date. But let me warn you, it's a trilogy."

"I can't wait," I said as I reached for my wallet and pulled out a credit card.

CHAPTER TWENTY

I took one last spoonful of raisin bran and picked up the ringing phone on the kitchen counter. Before I said hello, I put the Saturday edition of the *Morning Show* on mute. I usually didn't answer the kitchen phone, because it didn't have caller ID.

"Why didn't you tell me you were singing at a revival?" It was my sister Belinda.

"I thought I told you, but if I didn't, how did you find out?" I asked.

"Mama told me. And like her, I didn't think I would ever hear my brother's beautiful voice again. I'm thinking about coming with Mama and Daddy to the revival."

I thought for a moment before saying, "Well, I'm not certain I'm going to do the revival."

"What? That's all Mama has been talking about. She and Daddy are so excited. Why aren't you singing?"

"It's a very long story."

"I got time. Let me just shut the door to the kitchen," Belinda said.

As I waited, I wondered how much I should tell Belinda.

"Okay, I'm back. Now, tell me what's going on. I was going to check to see if I could take some time off and come down with Mama and Daddy and maybe stay a few days after they leave so we can visit."

"What about your husband and kids?"

"They won't even know I'm gone," Belinda said mournfully. "To tell you the truth, one morning I might just get in my car and keep driving, right out of my neighborhood, past the school, and out of this city to some place where nobody knows me."

"Are you all right?" I asked. I did not like the sound of my sister's voice.

"I'm okay." She sighed. "It's just one of those days when I'm feeling sorry for myself. Wondering if life is just passing me by."

"How long have you been feeling like this?" I was concerned about my sister, but at the same time, I was relieved to take the focus off of me.

"It comes and it goes," Belinda said. "I don't think I'm depressed or anything. Just disappointed by some of the opportunities I've let pass me by. That's why I was so excited when Mama told me you were singing again. I always thought it was a big mistake when you didn't go after a solo career when you left the group. Does your long story have something to do with that?"

"Not really," I said quickly, then added, "Well, maybe just a little."

"What?"

"Before I talk about that, I want to make sure you're all right. I haven't ever heard you sound so depressed."

"All I need is to see my brother and hear that marvelous voice of his. That will cure whatever's bothering me, and I know Mama will just die if you make them cancel the trip."

"So they're really excited, huh?" I already knew the answer to my question, but I'd done my best not to think about what my parents might say if I decided not to perform.

"It's like they were going to the White House for dinner and President Clinton was still the commander in chief." Belinda laughed.

"Have you registered to vote?" I asked, trying not to talk about me and the upcoming singing engagement.

"Are you kidding? I was raised by your parents, too. Even though I don't think it'll matter. This state is redder than the blood flowing through my body." My thoughts went back to my childhood when my parents took Belinda and me with them when they voted and told us how important it was.

"Well, you never know," I said as I looked at my watch. I lied and told Belinda that I had a meeting and that I would call her later on.

"You promise? I wanna hear about that long story."

"I promise, and please don't say anything to Mama and Daddy about me not singing. I'm praying on it, and I hope to get an answer soon," I said.

"I'm sure you'll get the right answer. Have a great day."

"You too, big sis," I said as I hung up the phone.

CHAPTER TWENTY-ONE

The word got out. That old game of tell-a-phone or tell-a-sissy still held true. On the first Sunday in October, Abundant Joy was packed like a pint of Ben and Jerry's Cherry Garcia. I couldn't believe it when I walked out into the choir stand and saw people standing against the wall and in the aisles. I looked out the window and saw what looked like hundreds of people milling around the parking lot because the doors to the church were locked. When I came in earlier like the rest of the choir, the number of cars in the lot looked normal for Sunday. I was certain if the fire chief knew about the crowd, services would have been halted.

When I stood at the microphone to sing my solo, Vincent smiled and winked at me. I smiled back nervously as I spotted Skylar grinning and waving a white handkerchief. He was sitting next to Celia and Lontray, who were dressed like they might stop at the club on their way home from church.

The choir stood up at Vincent's direction, and I sang

Edwin Hawkins's standard "Oh Happy Day" like it was the last song I was ever going to sing. The choir rocked with the chorus and several members got happy and passed out. The ushers rushed from the back of the church to fan them. It was like I was back home in Mississippi, where the pastor didn't mind if the Holy Ghost came in and took over service.

When I finished my solo, I was so happy that I found myself trembling, with my hands raised in the air, and I couldn't have brought them down if I wanted to. I found my way back to my seat and collapsed as another soloist took the microphone and kept the church and Holy Ghost going.

With his face beaming, Pastor Kenneth took to the pulpit. I could tell from the look on his face that he was surprised by the crowd.

"It looks like the Good Lord has spread the word about our little church. Can I get everybody to say 'Praise God from whom all blessings flow?'"

"Praise God from whom all blessings flow," the church repeated.

"Amen, amen," Pastor Kenneth said as he closed his Bible.

He paused for a moment as he surveyed the crowd. I wondered if he could tell that the majority of the visitors were gay men and women.

"I had prepared my sermon on Tuesday," he said. "But as I look out on the crowd and the way the Holy Spirit has anointed these wonderful singers, I feel like the Lord wants me to deliver a different message."

Vincent and I exchanged nervous glances, and I was praying that Pastor Kenneth wouldn't use this Sunday to preach his first "If you're gay you're going to hell" sermon.

"You know, in less than a month we will elect a new president of the United States, or reelect the current one. Now, I've heard that several churches in the area, our churches, are instructing their memberships on how to vote. When I hear this talk, I'm reminded of something on a poster I have in my office. It reads 'What Would Jesus Do?'" Pastor Kenneth said as he moved his right hand in the air as if he was pointing out the words on a blackboard to the congregation.

Oh, please don't go there, Pastor, I thought to myself. Don't have these kids turn on you.

"I tell you what Jesus would do, or at least what I think He would do. He would tell us that so many of our ancestors fought and died for our right to vote that we shouldn't take that right too lightly. He would also tell us that we shouldn't let the leaders of our churches take away that right. Telling us who to vote for essentially takes away our very precious right to vote. Can I get an Amen?" Pastor Kenneth shouted.

I don't know what got into me, but I found myself leaping from my church seat, pumping my fist in the air, and saying, "Amen. Tell 'em, Pastor." And I was not alone. The entire church broke into such a thunderous applause that I felt the church might crumble from the sound alone.

"Jesus would tell us that our votes were not for sale. That they couldn't be used to fill the offering plates so that the ministers could drive cars that cost more than many of the houses we live in."

One of the older members of the church, Sister Bertha, stood up with a fan in her left hand and shouted, "Preach, Pastor. You ain't tellin' nothin' but the truth."

Again the church joined in and erupted with "Amen" and "Preach, Pastor."

About ten minutes later, Pastor Kenneth ended his sermon by telling the crowd that while it was important to listen to the leadership of the church, he and the rest of them were mere mortals.

"Put your faith in God, because He will never let you down. Don't let man block your blessings. Can I get a witness?"

The church responded with a standing ovation, and Vincent eyed me and began playing "Oh Happy Day" again. I took that as my cue and returned to the microphone and began to sing once again.

*   *   *

After church, I was feeling so good I invited Skylar, Celia, and Lontray to join me at the over-the-top brunch at the Ritz-Carlton Buckhead. At fifty-five dollars a head, it was something I allowed myself to splurge on maybe twice a year to celebrate a birthday or a big month of sales.

Before I left church, I stopped in Pastor Kenneth's office to tell him how much I enjoyed the service. He was ecstatic. Not because the sermon had been so well received but because he said the Sunday offering was three times what it normally was.

"I wish we could have those worshipers here every Sunday," he said. I smiled to myself and whispered, "Me, too."

While Celia and Lontray filled their plates at the seafood station with boiled shrimp, crab legs, and oysters, I got a Mexican-style omelet. Despite the array of different food stations, like one that featured fruits and cheese, a roast beef carving one, and one with pasta, Skylar arrived back at the table with California rolls, shrimp dumplings, and caviar.

The four of us ordered mimosas after Skylar explained to Lontray what they were, and we began to enjoy the delicious food. After a few bites, Celia looked over at me and said, "There sure were a lot of good-looking men at your church. Why didn't you tell me that?"

"Tell you what?" I asked.

"About all the fine men who go to church. If I had known that, I would have gone to church instead of using Sundays to get my nails and toes done," Celia said.

"I know that's right," Lontray said as she gave Celia a high five. "But did you notice how a lot of the women looked like men?"

Skylar and I gave each other the eye, while Celia said she hadn't noticed because she was too busy looking at all the men.

"Maybe I got the wrong game plan, trying to find someone at the club to replace Marvin. Lontray, I'm going to get me some more of them shrimp with some of that white sauce. You want me to get you some?"

"Naw, girl, I've had enough seafood. You would think in a place this fancy a girl could get a fried chicken leg or some gravy," Lontray said.

"Why don't you try some of the caviar?" Skylar suggested.

"What's that?" Lontray asked.

"Caviar? Oh, girl, it's just divine. You must try it."

"But what is it?"

"Well, if you must know, they're fish eggs," Skylar said.

"Those little black thangs are fish eggs? You mean from real fishes?"

"Of course real fish, and honey, you know I don't do fish as a practice." Skylar laughed.

"You selling that program to the wrong girl, Skylar. I ain't even trying to eat no fish eggs. What else they got over there?"

"They have bacon and sausage over at the breakfast station. You can also get a fresh waffle made," I said.

"Now you talking," Lontray said as she got up and followed Celia.

A few seconds after the two left, Skylar shook his head and said, "Poor chile. You can take the bump fish out of the ghetto, but you can't take the ghetto out of the bump fish."

"Who are you talking about?"

"Lontray. She's bump fish if I ever saw one. What you want to bet she got a switchblade in her purse?" Skylar asked. "Bump fish" is what Skylar called females who were not only ghetto but reveled in being that way.

"She's harmless, and besides, Lontray is one of Celia's best friends," I said.

"And poor Celia. I mean, when will these so-called educated women learn that them men up in church don't want them? Chile, I ain't seen so many sissies since I was in Atlanta Airport on Labor Day weekend. I saw a few people up in there who needed to be throwing themselves on the altar," Skylar said, and laughed.

"I guess it is kinda sad that women can't tell when a man is gay or bi. I don't guess that's ever gonna change," I said.

"You right about that. Women will never learn the power of a little lips, hips, and fingertips," Skylar said. "But that's fine with me, because that certainly leaves them at a disadvantage. Makes it easier for me to come in and steal their husbands."

Skylar got up and headed toward the island of food, and I sat in silence. I wondered again why women as smart as Celia couldn't or weren't able to distinguish between a gay and a straight man. As someone who considered myself her friend, almost a big brother, would it be fair to tell Celia that the majority of men at the service were gay? Had I been deceptive when I asked her to come to church because we were having a special service to show how important gay people were to the black church?

Celia sat down at the table with a plate full of freshly cut meat and pasta.

"This is so good, Chauncey, thank you! I'm trying lamb for the first time," she said, beaming.

"Glad to do it. Thanks so much for coming to church with me," I said.

"Oh no, thank *you*. I don't know why, but I was moved by something. I mean, it's been a while since I went to church, but when I walked into your church this morning I felt a certain peace. It was like God knew I was coming and He was waiting there to greet me," Celia said.

I didn't say anything for a few moments as I savored Celia's words and fought back my tears. Finally, I said, "He was there waiting for you. And I'm pretty certain He'll be there if you ever go back."

CHAPTER TWENTY-TWO

Even with all the chaos in my life, I slept soundly and woke up earlier than usual with Damien on my mind. No, it wasn't one of those rock-hard sex fantasies, but how much I really wanted to have a conversation with him. It didn't matter if I spoke to him on the phone or face-to-face, although I believed that if I saw him, I'd be able to read his body language.

I got up from bed, brushed my teeth, and turned on the shower to let the water warm up. Then I walked into the little office off my bedroom. I checked my e-mail, looked at the news headlines, and was headed back to the bathroom for my shower when I noticed the pad with Damien's number.

I picked it up and then quickly dialed the number. I listened to his greeting, and this time when I heard the beep, I said, "Yo, Damien, or should I say Bishop Upchurch. This is a voice from your past that would really like to speak with you. Hopefully, my voice hasn't changed, so you know who this is. I can be reached at 404-555-3421 or 770-555-9834.

Both are Atlanta numbers. Hey, it would be nice to recon-
nect," I said before I ended the message, which I suddenly
feared sounded dumb and needy. Still, I was glad I made
the call.

As I showered, I wondered what it would be like to talk
with Damien or see him in person. Would he ignore my
calls, or would his curiosity about why I was calling him
prompt a call? There was no way for him to know that I
had been asked to sing on his opening night, or that I was
even a member of Abundant Joy, unless Pastor Kenneth had
said something. Would he set up a meeting with me? Would
he bring the wife and kids to prove to me that he was now
firmly on the other team?

When I stepped out of the shower, I grabbed a towel
and moved to my dressing area. My radio was on V-103
because I loved the Frank and Wanda morning show. Not
only could you hear good music, but they had witty conversation and jokes as well. Frank didn't shy away from
controversial topics, and he did a spiritual vitamin segment
where he read something inspirational and followed it with
a song from one of the more popular gospel artists. I loved
starting my day this way, and it didn't sound preachy or out
of place on the popular R & B station.

But this morning, something very strange happened. It
wasn't Frank's and Wanda's voices I heard but Pastor Kenneth and Damien. With just a towel wrapped around my
waist, I moved to my stereo system and turned up the vol-
ume. The two of them were telling Frank about the revival
and how they hoped all of Atlanta would show up. "We

hope to have so many people this year that next year we'll have to move from the church to the Georgia Dome," Pastor Kenneth said.

I sat on the edge of the bed and listened intently for Damien to say something hateful about gays, or about reclaiming our country, but all he talked about was how he and his wife were looking forward to visiting Atlanta and helping Pastor Kenneth make Abundant Joy one of the most powerful churches, not only in Atlanta but in the entire Southeast. Pastor Kenneth mentioned how the church had been packed the day before and if that kept happening he would be looking for larger space sooner.

The tone of his voice and the cadence of his words gave me goose bumps. I thought about Sister Esther and the testimony about her deceased son. Maybe it was time for me to start searching for a new church home.

CHAPTER TWENTY-THREE

Just as I hung up the phone from leaving my third message in several days for Damien, the telephone rang. I looked at the digital display and recognized the number as my parents'. I smiled to myself every time I realized the fact that they'd had the same number for almost forty years, even back in the days of rotary dials.

"Hello."

"Chauncey."

"Hey, Mama."

"I'm not bothering you, am I? I know how busy you are," she said.

"No, I'm fine, Mama. I was just making a few phone calls and trying to decide what to cook for dinner," I said, not mentioning that I was doing everything I could to keep my mind off Celia and the Wal-Mart presentation that had happened today.

"I bet you wish your mama was down there to fry you some chicken. You think you can cook, but I still make better fried chicken than you," she said, chuckling.

"That's because you won't give me the recipe. You're worse than the Colonel." I laughed.

"If I give you the secret, I may never see you again."

"Now, you know that's not true," I said.

"Well, I'm not giving it out today, so you'll have to get you some Church's or Popeye's," Mama said.

"I think I'll pass. How's Daddy?"

"Just fine. I don't know if he's out in his garden or tinkering with that truck. But let me tell you why I'm calling," Mama said.

"I'm listening."

"Did you get my e-mail with the attachment?"

"When did you send it?"

"Just a few minutes ago. Your baby brother finally installed my scanner, and I sent you a little diagram."

"I'm not near my computer right now, but what kind of diagram?" I asked. How was it that my mother was so computer savvy when she was slow to embrace other technology? Belinda and I had installed call waiting on our parents' phone without their knowledge, because both of us got sick of hearing a busy signal. Still, my parents rarely used the feature.

"It's a little sketch of the dress I am having Claudine Moore make me for when I come hear you sing. You remember her, don't you? She used to just make dresses and school uniforms out of her bedroom, but now she's big time. Claudine even opened a little shop downtown, and she has customers both black and white. Got herself a real nice business," Mama said.

I thought for a moment and tried to remember Claudine, and even though I couldn't picture her, I thought it best to say that I did, rather than have Mama give me her complete history.

"Oh yeah, I think I remember her. So she's making you a dress?" I quizzed.

"I don't know. That's why I want you to look at the sketch and tell me if it's good enough for your affair. If you don't like it, then I might have to go over to Jackson and see what they got in the stores. I still got my McRae's charge card, even though I haven't used it since Jonathan was in high school."

"I'll look at it, but I'm sure whatever you wear, you'll look beautiful." I still couldn't tell my mother that I was thinking about not doing the revival. Not only would it break her heart, but she'd start asking questions that I wasn't ready to answer.

"Chauncey. Chauncey!" Mama said loudly, interrupting my thoughts. "Look at the sketch and tell me what you think. Belinda loves it."

"Then I'm sure I will love it as well. I'll look at it and call you back," I said. Before my mother could respond, the call waiting signal beeped on my phone and Celia's cell phone number spread across the display.

"Mama, I need to take this call," I said, anxious to speak to Celia. This is the call I had been waiting for.

"I don't know why you and Belinda and them have to have all these gadgets on your phone. If someone else calls, people just need to wait until you get off the phone," Mama said.

"I know, Mama, but I'll call you back later tonight," I said, rushing my mother off the phone. "Love you."

"I love you, too, baby. I'm so happy that you're going to be singing in the Lord's house. I feel like I can go on to glory," Mama said.

I rolled my eyes in a good way and shook my head at my mother's going-to-glory talk. If I didn't sing at the revival, then I was going to have to find a church to sing in, or I'd never hear the end of it.

I clicked over to the other line, and without even saying hello I asked Celia how the presentation went.

"It was fabulous, if I do say so myself," Celia said. "I had them at 'Good morning.'"

"Where are you?"

"At the Embassy Suites in some place called Rogers."

"As in Roy Rogers," I teased.

"Yes, just like old Roy," Celia said. "But it's not as bad as I thought. It's a nice-size city."

"So did they place a large order?"

"Not yet, but I have no doubt they will, because the senior buyer asked me to stay over an extra night. They wanted to discuss doing some major business with us."

"That's great! This is what we've been working for." I couldn't hold back my grin. "How are you?"

"I'm fine. I'm going to dinner with the buyer and her assistants."

"Great. When you get back, we'll take ourselves out to celebrate," I said.

"That sounds like fun, but we gotta make it someplace fancy." Celia laughed.

"Wherever you want," I said.

"Okay. Well, sleep tight. I've got to get ready to go do my thang," Celia said.

"Have fun, but remember you got a deal to close tomorrow," I said.

"Don't worry. I got this! Good night."

"Celia," I called before she hung up.

"Yes."

"Thank you—I'm proud of you."

"No, thank you, for giving me the chance."

"You've earned it."

I hung up the phone and leaned back on the couch. Tomorrow at this time, I would officially be one of Wal-Mart's suppliers. Life was moving in the right direction. I still didn't have any music connections, but if my luck continued that would happen soon, too.

CHAPTER TWENTY-FOUR

"*Let's* just say Halle Berry wasn't the only high school beauty in Cleveland," Skylar said as he took one more bite of his beef stroganoff. "With my Naomi Sims Dutch-boy wig and some Fashion Fair makeup, I gave the most beautiful girls a run for their money," he added.

Friday had started with a spitting rain but ended as a dazzling sun-soaked day. Celia returned with the Wal-Mart deal signed and delivered. Skylar phoned me around midafternoon and asked me to make one of my best dishes and then he would give me the Skylar and Tank story, part two.

"And this guy didn't know you were a guy?" I asked.

"No. I knew all the tricks and had an answer for everything. When he wanted to go to public places, like the movies and the mall, I told him I had very strict parents who didn't allow me to date. So we had our secret places, and we would often skip school and hang out in his basement."

"So what happened when he'd pressure you for sex?"

"I had my ways." Skylar smirked. "I knew how to tuck my stuff where he could touch around it, and let's face it, no matter how much sex boys have at a young age, they're too young to know everything about the female body. Besides, I had no problem pleasing him." Skylar laughed.

"I bet you didn't. Where did you get the money to buy the outfits? From what I hear, makeup ain't cheap."

"I guess you could say I had a fairy godmother. There was a lady in my neighborhood who none of the other ladies liked because she was single, and most everybody called her a whore. Looking back, she probably was one, but even a whore doesn't like being called a slut. I used to run errands for her, and she worked at Dayton's department store as a manager, which was a big deal back then for a black woman, even if she was light-skinned with large breasts. I just loved her, and she is probably the only woman besides my mother who I had seen naked."

I raised my eyebrows. "How did that happen?"

"Well, let's just say Miss Angela was comfortable with herself and it wasn't anything for her to open the door naked. I used to love it when she wore sexy black underwear and she would reach into her bra to get money when she wanted me to go to the store for her," Skylar said before he paused and took a sip of Merlot.

"So did she know what you were doing? I mean, fooling Tank about being a girl?"

"I don't think so. I told her I needed the stuff for a project I was working on, and she knew I was interested in women's fashion and makeup. She told me that once I got out of high school and went to beauty school, she would introduce me to the Fashion Fair rep and help me get a job applying makeup at Dayton's. I was able to order new wigs by saving some of the money I made from Miss Angela and stealing a dollar or two from my mother. She was getting hip that someone was wearing her wigs but thought it was my sister."

Skylar went on to tell me that most of the time he and Tank met at the high school football stadium near his house or at the back parking lot of the Kmart after it was closed. Skylar convinced Tank that it was better this way, and while they met during the day, the two also often met after both of their families were sound asleep. One night they got caught making out at the stadium by two policemen, and Skylar thought they had realized that he wasn't a girl and were going to blow his cover. Instead, when the policemen separated the two and talked to them alone, the officer who took Skylar aside whispered that he was the most beautiful girl he'd ever seen. He told Skylar "she" should drop this high school punk and get herself a real man.

He laughed louder when he told me how black girls in Cleveland were spreading rumors that Tank Malloy was dating a white girl in Shaker Heights and that he had gotten her pregnant.

"He would get on that bike and trek halfway across the city to see me. Tank won the state championship in wrestling his senior year, and he gave me the letter jacket he earned. I still have it. He used to always bring me flowers and cheap perfume. Some of the stuff, like the cards and letters, I kept, but the other stuff I gave to Miss Angela, because if I gave them to my mother she would ask where I got them from."

"That's funny," I said with a muffled sigh as I tried to listen to Skylar attentively.

"What's funny?"

"That you would keep the letters and cards. I did the same thing with the stuff Damien gave me. Matter of fact, I still have them locked in a box I keep in a safe place in my house," I said. I could picture the dark wooden box where I kept the cards, notes, and cassette tapes that Damien had given me.

In many ways, Damien was responsible for my current career of making cards. The first card I ever made was a hand-painted card that had *Love Is* on the cover, and when you opened it there was a photograph of Damien sitting on the corner of a hotel bed, wearing a wife-beater T-shirt and jeans, smiling at me.

"So our first loves had a few similarities," Skylar said.

"Yeah, I guess they did. So what happened to him and the relationship? Did he ever find out you were Skylar, the guy, and not a girl?"

Skylar took the napkin and slowly wiped his lips, dragging out the silence before he answered my question.

"I've been eyeing that dessert over there," he said as he glanced at the cheesecake I made. "And no one makes cheesecake the way you do." He stood and sauntered to the counter where the dessert rested. "I'll have to answer that question when I tell you part three."

CHAPTER TWENTY-FIVE

"I guess you'll want your attorney to look this over, but can you get it back to us as soon as you can," Pastor Kenneth said.

I looked over the first page of the contract he'd given me for the upcoming revival. It was pretty straightforward, but I was surprised by the $7,500 honorarium they were paying me. It was more than I expected, even though I knew Donnie would have gotten four times what they were offering me. But that was cool. He was the Grammy Award–winning Donnie McClurkin, after all.

"I'll do that, but I'm sure it won't be a problem," I said, not looking at Pastor Kenneth. I still hadn't decided what I was going to do, since I hadn't yet spoken to Damien.

"We're so glad you're doing this for us, Brother Chauncey. Not only are we getting a great singer, but it's saving us a little money, and I tell you, we're going to need it. The bishop and his wife required first-class travel, and that means the Presidential Suite at the Ritz-Carlton. Do you know how much that bad boy goes for?"

"No, I don't," I said, thinking this didn't sound like the Damien I knew. When we were singing together, he didn't flinch when our manager suggested we use a tour bus to save money when we went on tour.

"It costs two thousand dollars a night. Can you believe that?" Pastor Kenneth said.

"Wow. That sounds like a Bobby and Whitney suite," I said. This might be the perfect time to ask Pastor how much he knew about Bishop Upchurch and why he was bringing such a controversial figure to the tiny but loving Abundant Joy.

"It's more like a George W. suite for real. I guess they don't call it the Presidential Suite for nothing," he said, and laughed.

"Pastor Kenneth, can I ask you something?"

"Sure, Brother Chauncey."

"How well do you know this Bishop Upchurch? The reason I ask is because I visited his Web site and he seems pretty politically conservative. Did you know he was running on the Republican ticket for Senate?"

"Yes, I know that, Brother Chauncey. I met the bishop at a pastors' conference in Seattle. Our wives hit it off, and even though I don't agree with all of his views, I think he is one of the most dynamic young ministers in the country. His wife, Grayson, is equally impressive. Why the concern? You know I try to bring different voices to this church, and I don't side with either," Pastor Kenneth replied.

"I know. It's just that Bishop Upchurch has some pretty conservative and discriminating views. I just hope he doesn't bring a divisive force to our church. I know most of the members just love Abundant Joy, and I would hate to see that end," I said tentatively, not wanting my words to sound like a threat.

"I appreciate your concern, Brother Chauncey, but trust me, I will keep the lid on everything. Abundant Joy will be just fine."

"I'm glad to hear that," I said. I'd said enough. I stood up and shook Pastor Kenneth's hand.

As I was walking out of his office, Pastor Kenneth called out my name.

"Yes?" I said as I turned around.

"How is the music career going?"

"I need to start looking for a producer, but as soon as I do, I have some great songs I've written, and I'll share them with you." I smiled, pleased that Pastor Kenneth would take the time to ask.

Pastor Kenneth opened his desk drawer and pulled out a business card and then walked over to me.

"Give this young lady a call. Lucy used to be our children's nanny, but now she's a television producer. She was at the service when you sang, and she talked about you for days. She might be able to help you. I'll give her a call also and tell her to look out for you."

I looked at the card: *Lucy Quinn, Executive Producer, Starting Over.* I pulled out my wallet and tucked it inside.

"Thank you, Pastor Kenneth. Good lookin' out," I said.

"No problem, Brother Chauncey. I hope it works out. I'll send up a little prayer for you this evening."

"Thanks, Pastor. It doesn't hurt when you got somebody working for God holding your name up in prayer."

Pastor Kenneth nodded his head. "No truer words have been spoken."

*　　*　　*

When I got home from church, Reggie, the evening concierge at my building, asked me if I'd been expecting anyone.

"No," I said as I pulled my keys out of my pants pocket and searched the ring for my mailbox key.

"A lady with a big guy, one of those bodybuilder types, was here earlier looking for you. When I asked her for a name and if she wanted to wait, well, she just kinda huffed out of here."

"She didn't leave a name or a message or anything?" I asked, thinking this sounded like the pair Ms. Gladys had seen in the office.

"No, sir. I asked her at least three times. I didn't know what I was going to do if you had been here. What was I going to say when I called you up? 'You have a lady and a goon waiting for you'?"

"That's strange," I said, frowning. "You sure it wasn't Celia, the young lady who works with me?"

"No, I remember Celia."

"I guess if it's important she'll be back," I said, and headed toward the mailroom right off the lobby.

"I hope I'm not here. That lady's attitude was scary," Reggie said.

I paused, remembering my final conversation with Griffin, but then I shook my head and said, "Nah," telling myself to stop trippin', because I didn't have money for a bodyguard.

I grabbed my mail, rang for the elevator, and before I stepped inside, thoughts of the mystery lady, her goon, and Griffin were gone.

CHAPTER TWENTY-SIX

"*What's* good, son?" spilled from my answering machine in a voice so deep and smooth it felt like I was being wrapped in silk. It was the voice of the one man I would have given more than three dates if only he'd let me.

"This is J. B., and I'm in your city and was calling to see if you wanted to hook up. Maybe we can meet at the ESPN Zone. I'm staying at the new Intercontinental on Peachtree. Call me there or on my cell. You got the number," he continued.

I picked up the phone and immediately called J. B., or John Basil Henderson, an ex–pro football player who was one of the most handsome men I'd ever kicked it with. He had the kind of good looks that would freeze my eyes, a chiseled body with skin the color of butterscotch and luminous slate-gray eyes that once you looked into, you'd never forget him. Throw in the fact that he was packing over ten inches and, well, I started to sweat just thinking about him.

I dialed his cell phone and got the voice mail after one ring. He was either on the other line or his phone was turned off. I didn't leave a message, but I quickly dialed the hotel and asked for Basil Henderson. Again, no answer, so I called his cell phone again and left a message telling him how I would love to see him. "Why not let me cook dinner for you?" I added that I had plans but would gladly cancel them. I guess I sounded eager, but I didn't care. Not only was Basil unbelievable in bed, but I enjoyed our conversations and just hanging with him. He was, Damien included, one of the most remarkable men I had met. But he was also the classic bisexual man, and the only thing I could hope for was that when he called me back tonight, he was the Basil I'd enjoyed the last time.

* * *

I called Celia. We'd planned to go to the bar at the Ritz-Carlton in Buckhead to drink champagne and eat a nice dinner to celebrate the big deal with Wal-Mart. Thanks to Celia's hard work, the retail giant had ordered 50,000 units a month for the next year, with an option to extend the deal to three years. Maybe my dream could come true and I could retire and concentrate on my music before I turned forty. Celia had mentioned that one of the VPs at Wal-Mart suggested I give them a call if I ever thought about selling my company. The interest from the largest retailer in the world was flattering.

This was my evening for answering machines. When I called Celia, I got her voice mail and was a bit relieved. I didn't want to hear the disappointment in her voice when I canceled our plans.

"Hey, Ms. Executive Salesperson of the Year, this is your boss. A real good friend of mine came into town unexpectedly and I need to take a rain check on the champagne and dinner. Maybe we can get together on Sunday after church and go back to the Ritz-Carlton? But if you got somebody else you want to take tonight, then go ahead and just put it on your expense account. Hey, why don't you just do a nice dinner at Bluepoint or Morton's Steakhouse? It's on me. See you tomorrow."

I walked into my closet to find something to wear for the evening. I didn't want to look like I was dressed up, but I didn't want to wear something too baggy. I wanted Basil to know that the body he hadn't seen in over five years was still tight.

I decided on some white linen drawstring pants that weren't too formal, and if I wore the right type of underwear and shirt, Basil would get the message.

I laid the pants on my bed and picked out white Lycra boxer briefs and a matching T-shirt styled like the classic wife-beater. I went into the dining room and pulled out three vanilla-scented candles and placed them in the window of my bedroom.

Just as I was getting ready to take a long, relaxing bath, the phone rang; my heart raced with the hope that it was Basil. I looked at the caller ID and saw it was the concierge of my building. Did Basil get my message and just come over without calling?

"Hello."

"Sorry to bother you, Mr. Greer, but there's a Miss Cunningham and a gentleman here to see you," Reggie said in a whispered tone.

"Who?"

"The lady . . . I mean, Miss Cunningham and a gentle-men."

"Reggie, I'm not expecting her. Would you please tell her to leave a number and I will get in contact with her later. I have other plans," I said. Whoever Miss Cunning-ham is, she can wait, I decided as I grabbed my clothes and headed to the bathroom. I lit the candles that were on my vanity and put in my *Isley Brothers Greatest Hits* CD in the small stereo I kept in my bathroom. The only thing miss-ing was something to sip on in the bathroom while I soaked the tension of the day out of my body and prepared for what I hoped for and needed: an evening of uninterrupted passion.

*   *   *

I had removed the last piece of the flaky, pink salmon from the grill and placed it next to a medium-well-cooked steak when the phone rang. I rushed with the platter from the patio to the kitchen. Since I didn't know what Basil's taste buds were leaning toward, I prepared both surf and turf.

"Hello," I said.

"Mr. Greer. This is Reggie again. I have a Basil Hen-derson down here to see you. Should I send him up?"

"Yes, Reggie, do that."

"Will do. Oh, yeah, I should tell you that creepy lady and the Rock look-alike weren't too happy when I wouldn't let them up. Be sure to watch your back, 'cause those two are strange," Reggie said.

"Thanks for the heads-up, Reggie, but I ain't scared." It wasn't that I was taking their visit lightly, but right now I was only worried about getting the salad made and the twice-baked potatoes golden brown.

"Mr. Henderson is on his way up."

"Thank you."

I quickly uncorked a bottle of red and then another bottle of white wine and pulled down four wineglasses from the cabinet. Just as I placed the white wine in the fridge, the doorbell rang. I raced to the bathroom and sprayed some of my Burberry cologne on my chest and behind my ears. I moved quickly to the front, took a deep breath, and then swung the door open.

"What's up, dude?" I said as I reached toward Basil and gave him the traditional brotherman hug.

"What's shaking, fam?" Basil hugged me back, and my body began to warm when I pressed against his well-muscled chest. Basil did not disappoint. He looked even better than I had remembered.

"Come on in. I'm so glad you took me up on my offer," I said.

"It smells damn good in here. You got the place looking nice. I should look in this building before I decide on a place," he said.

"You're moving here?" I wondered if I sounded as anxious as I felt. It would be great to have Basil in Atlanta. My three-date rule would be history.

"Thinking about getting a little place here but haven't quite decided. You know, I have a lot of clients down here, and there are lots of prospects here, with Georgia Tech and University of Georgia at Athens," Basil said.

"Come on into the dining room," I said.

"I'm following you, son."

"What would you like to drink?"

"Got any Chardonnay?"

"I just opened a bottle," I said. "Dude, I was so glad to hear from you. How long has it been?"

"I'm sorry. You know I've been busy. But I haven't forgotten about you. How's the card business?"

"Business is good. My assistant just closed a big deal with Wal-Mart. Maybe now I can roll like you," I said.

"And you know it," Basil said as he gave me a slap on the hand in support.

"So you're still in the sports management game?"

"Yeah,—son, you know, right now it pays the bills. But I'm always looking out for the next opportunity. I'm still thinking about giving acting a shot," Basil said.

"You know how long I've been wanting to put you and that beautiful body on a card or calendar? Either one. Now that we're all over the world, I could make you a big star," I said.

"Man, if niggas and bitches see this body on a card, they would run out of trees trying to keep up with the paper demand," Basil said. I noticed he hadn't lost an ounce of his macho bravado.

"So why don't we see if we can make that happen?"

"Now, Chauncey, you ain't got enough money to make that happen, son. The world needs to see this body on a big screen." Basil laughed.

I laughed with him. "So how many clients do you have?"

"I got six and I hope to sign a couple this year," Basil said.

"Any big ones, like Michael Vick or Kobe Bryant?"

"I would take Vick in a heartbeat, but you couldn't pay me enough to rep Kobe 'The King' Bryant."

"Are you ready to eat?" I asked as I took another good look at him over my wineglass. He was dressed like a model. The navy blue pleated slacks fit just right. Not so tight where you could see everything, but not so baggy either, so you could still tell there was a pair of powerful thighs underneath. The pink polo highlighted his arms so they looked like baseball bats stuffed with grapefruits.

"You know it. Starvin' like Marvin, son," Basil said.

*   *   *

Over dinner, Basil told me how he really loved being a father. He told me his little girl, Talley, was almost six years old and that was another reason he was looking to move to Atlanta, where the girl's mother was relocating. I didn't ask if he was still seeing her, but I got the distinct feeling that he was seeing someone, because a couple of times when he mentioned his travels, he slipped and said "we." It didn't matter to me, and secretly I hoped he was involved with a woman, because it made my chances better. Whoever she was, she couldn't do what I could do, and both Basil and I knew that.

After our third glass of wine we finished dinner, and as Brandy's new CD played in the background I showed Basil some of the latest cards and calendars we'd done. As our conversation continued and as the evening wore on, I felt my linen pants slipping down like the material had a mind of its own. Maybe my pants were trying to tell me it was time to make my move, or to put something else on.

"Basil, just hang out here for a moment. I don't know why I decided to wear these pants tonight. They pick up everything," I said as I brushed off some invisible lint, "I'll be back in a few."

"Sounds good to me," he said.

Did that mean he was looking forward to my return?

I went into my bedroom and pulled off not only the linen pants but my underwear as well. It was getting late, and if I was going to get the night of passion I needed, it had to start soon.

I kept on my T-shirt and put on a pair of cobalt-blue and gray cashmere sweatpants I'd bought at Saks. They cost almost $500, but when I put them on against my naked ass, it felt like money well spent. I loved the way they hung on my body. Surely, this outfit would remind Basil of what he was missing.

When I walked back into my office, Basil was looking at a *Vanity Fair* I had on the coffee table. Then he found some information I'd printed off the computer about Damien and Grayson.

"What are you reading?" I asked.

"About this preacher dude in Denver," Basil said.

"Oh, don't waste your time," I said as I sat on the sofa.

"Dude sounds like one of them crazy white politicians, and his wife looks oddly familiar."

"Do you know her?"

"It's hard to tell from this picture. Do you know her?"

"I know him," I said bitterly.

"Oh, it's like that," Basil said.

"That was a long time ago."

"What happened?"

I gave Basil the brief *TV Guide* version of my relationship with Damien and was relieved when he changed the subject.

"So you never told me you were a singer."

"When I met you, I was trying to forget that I was. But lately I realize it's a God-given talent and I'm trying to get back in the game," I said.

"How's it going?"

"Slow motion, but I won't give up."

"That's wassup."

"So what have you been doing with your life?"

"Well, there have been a lot of changes in my life."

"Like what?"

"Chauncey, I know you and me don't see each other that often, but you cool peoples. I knew that when I first met you. It's also the reason I didn't kick it that much with you, because I liked you so much. You know, back in the day, I think I fucked dudes hard because I was trying to get the desire out of my system. I didn't like any of the dudes or the chicks that I got down with, so when I had sex I tried to knock the bottom out. I know better now. For me it's about making love to someone you love," Basil said.

My knees weakened. Was he talking about me? Was he going to put it to me? Were my prayers going to be answered? What had I done in my life to be so lucky? I started to move toward him, ready to give him a kiss, when I remembered he didn't really like to kiss. Still, I was hopeful that had changed as well, and decided to wait a few minutes and see if he would make a move.

"So have you ever been in love with a woman?"

"Yes," I said quickly. I told him about Giselle, whom I had met in a bank when I was trying to get a loan for my company. I told him how not only did she make sure I got the loan but she directed me to seminars in Atlanta and Athens on how to conduct a small business, and she also convinced me to start attending church again. I told Basil how she was so kind and made me feel comfortable around her. And how I came close to slipping just once while I was dating her until I ran into old boy at the gym. I explained that I thought she was some angel on earth who offered me a magic potion to get over my desires. Ever since Damien had left me, I had prayed for God to take away my carnal desires for men. I thought Giselle was the answer.

"So what happened to her?"

"She wanted to get married. I wanted to marry her, but before I allowed her to accept my proposal, I was honest with her about my relationship with Damien and that I continued to have affairs with men after him."

"I bet old girl couldn't deal with that, huh."

"She was devastated. I kept telling her that I was changed and I hadn't cheated on her, but that wasn't really the truth. You know how we men view one-night stands."

"And that's how it should be. Women be tripping. They all say they want the truth, but when you give it to them straight up, they either don't hear you or they run for cover. Never tell a female everywhere you been and everybody you done. Feel me?" Basil had a serious look on his face, like he was giving me information I needed to survive.

"I hear you, Basil." Now was the time to jump him. He was feeling thoughtful and vulnerable.

As I moved toward him, I started to loosen the drawstring on my sweatpants so that by the time I reached him they would be around my ankles.

"So do you think you'll ever hear from dude?" Basil asked. He wanted to talk more, so I tightened the drawstring again. I looked at the clock on my desk and saw that it was 11:45. I would give it fifteen more minutes before I made my move.

"I've called him, but he hasn't returned my calls," I said.

"But you could blow old boy out the water if you came forward and told your story. The Democrats would show you much love," Basil said.

"You think I should do that?" I asked, wondering if Basil's position on outing people had changed.

"Naw, dude. I know you not that type of nigga. That's why I could hang with you and talk with you. I'm just saying old boy should be careful when he's running for office. No offense, but you probably ain't the only heart he's broke.

Today niggas going all Catholic and shit. Confessing everything in books and magazines. Every time you turn on the television, there is some brother telling his business on how he's kicking it with the hardheads. I still keep my shit on the low, even if I'm dealing with someone I trust completely," Basil said.

"So you're seeing someone?"

"Yes."

"Are you happy?"

"Very. Never felt like this," Basil said.

I didn't know if I believed him or not. I saw myself walking toward him with my sweats dragging around my ankles. I was going to press my body against his and take his large hands and have them cup my ass and then rub my chest. I would touch his beautiful full ass and lay my head on his massive chest as I grabbed his piece. I knew this man and how to make him beg.

But then I looked at him and he looked like he was in another place. A smile lingered on his face and I knew I wanted what he had: somebody who loved me the way I loved him.

CHAPTER TWENTY-SEVEN

"*Here* it is," Celia said as she handed me a leather folder. A huge smile covered her face and she twisted her body like a giddy schoolgirl.

"I didn't think I was ever going to get this. So this is going to make me rich," I said. I pulled out the contract, read the first line, and then flipped to page seven, where I glanced at the signed names of two Wal-Mart executives. All that was missing was my signature.

"When you sign it, I'll fax a copy to Christy at Wal-Mart and make sure it goes out this evening via Federal Express," Celia said, still grinning.

"Cool. I'll look it over and get it back to you."

"Fabulous." As she headed toward the door, she twirled around as if a handsome young man was spinning her in an elegant ballroom.

"You sure seem happy," I said.

"Why shouldn't I be? This is a perfect day. I know it's clickish, but has the sky ever been bluer?"

"You mean cliché?"

"Whatever."

"I hadn't noticed. What did you do last night?"

"I took your advice."

"What advice?"

"To have a nice dinner on you—and that's what I did. I went to Morton's and threw down on a perfectly cooked rib-eye steak, baked potato, and creamed spinach. I even forgot about my diet and ordered this chocolate-cake-and-ice-cream thing they have. It was off the chain," Celia said.

"That's great. I'm glad you enjoyed yourself."

"It was a wonderful evening." She almost sang the words.

"Who'd you go with?" I asked as I placed the contract down on my desk. I thought about my evening with Basil and how it hadn't turned out like I'd planned, and I hoped she'd had better luck.

"Marvin," Celia said quickly.

I raised my eyebrows and gave her a *did I hear you right?* glance. Celia returned a sly yet unsure grin.

"I thought you had a restraining order against him," I said, my voice harsher than I planned.

"I did, but he apologized," Celia said quickly. "Then he sent me these beautiful red roses. Four dozen. Can you believe that? I had never seen that many roses at one time. Four dozen."

"So you feel safe with him now?" I asked, trying to keep the judgment out of my voice. How could a woman as smart as Celia be so dumb when it came to men?

"Marvin is harmless, and I think he's finally realized

how much he loves me." Celia leaned against my door with her arms behind her back in full swoon effect. She giggled like a preteen girl who has just received her first *Will you go with me?* note.

"If you say so." I'd had enough of this conversation. I opened my desk drawer, looking for my calculator. I wanted to see what the Wal-Mart deal was going to do for my monthly budget.

"May I take the afternoon off?"

"What?"

"Marvin wants to take me to Piedmont Park for a picnic, and I don't have much going on," Celia explained.

"What about Federal Express? Who's going to call them? We need to get this back to Wal-Mart ASAP."

"If you get it signed before noon, then I can drop it off. Otherwise, there's a drop box in the lobby of the building," Celia said.

"I don't know if I can read the entire thing before lunch, and I need to have my lawyer look over it," I said. I knew I was acting helpless, but it wasn't just Federal Express I was worried about. I was concerned about Celia and how her new love life was going to affect her work. Already she was taking off early. I guess I took everything she did for granted.

"Okay. If you need me, I'll just tell him we can do it another time," Celia said sadly.

I felt guilty. "Go ahead. Take the afternoon off. I'll manage somehow. Maybe I'll get my lawyer's assistant or Ms. Gladys to send it out."

"Are you sure?"

"Yes. Go ahead," I said. When I saw her unsure expression, I added, "Have a great time."

"Thank you, Chauncey. Thank you so much."

Celia opened the door and I called her name. She turned around with a smile so big, it looked like she was wearing those candy lips I used to wear and eat when I was a kid.

"Promise me you'll be careful," I said.

"I promise."

Back in my office, I began to scan the contract but then stopped. I went into my wallet and pulled out the card Pastor Kenneth had given me. For a long moment, I stared at the name and phone number in the corner, then picked up the phone. After I dialed, the telephone rang a couple of times before a female voice answered.

"*Starting Over*. Lucy Simpson."

"Lucy?"

"Yes, this is Lucy."

"My name is Chauncey Greer. My minister, Kenneth Davis, gave me your number and suggested I give you a call."

"Oh, yes. The singer. You have a wonderful voice. I'm so glad I was there when you sang. You had that little church rocking."

I smiled and eased my shoulders into a relaxed position. It wasn't until that moment that I realized how stiff I'd been.

"Thank you. That's very nice of you to say."

"It's the truth. Thanks for calling me. I think we might be able to help each other out."

"I hope so."

"Have you seen the show *Starting Over?*"

I didn't recognize the name of the show on her card, nor did it sound familiar when she said it. "No, I can't say that I have."

Starting Over was a daytime reality show where real women, with the assistance of life coaches, tried to restart their lives in front of the camera. Lucy further explained that up to six women from different backgrounds lived in a house together and the life coaches worked to help them achieve their new goals. It sounded like an interesting show, but I didn't know where I could fit in unless they were getting ready to go coed.

"So how do you see us working together?" I asked.

"We have a young lady entering the house next season, and her goal is to resume her recording career. She had a hit CD a couple of years back, and I was thinking that maybe you could write some songs for her, and perhaps the two of you could even do a duet. You would get a lot of publicity on the show, and we have some connections with the record company that will be producing her CD."

"Can she sing?" I was already thinking of a song I'd written that would be perfect for a female voice.

"Yes, she's pretty good. She's been on Broadway, and her album went double platinum."

"Double platinum. That's pretty impressive," I said, wondering why someone like that would be on a reality show. "What's her name? Maybe I've heard of her."

"Yancey Braxton. We call her the declining diva." Lucy laughed.

"Why?"

"Well, she's sort of a prima donna. No one has told her that she's no longer a star."

"Oh, I see. Where's the show taped?"

"In Los Angeles this season. Last year we were in Chicago. We're still scouting locations around Atlanta for next season."

I paused for a moment. It was not what I expected, but it could be fun, and help me start my recording career. I didn't know how popular the show was, but if a couple hundred thousand watched it, that could help me when my CD came out. "What do I need to do?"

"Since I'm executive producer, all you have to say is you want to do it, and we'll get started."

"Count me in," I said, smiling at myself for being such a hypocrite. I'd told myself I would never do one of those reality shows like *Survivor*, *American Idol*, or *The Apprentice*. I had thought if I was ever in love again it might be nice to be on *The Amazing Race*. And if I was being totally honest, I would jump at the chance to be on *American Idol*, but I was much too old.

"Cool. Let me get your contact information and I'll set up a meeting with you and Yancey B."

I gave her what she needed and she promised to give me a call in a couple of days. I thanked her, and when I hung up, I smiled. I remembered Yancey B's hit single *Any Way the Wind Blows*. Celia was right. Today was a perfect day.

*   *   *

A couple of hours later, I placed the contract on my desk and rubbed my eyes. I'd reviewed each page twice. As I reached for the contract again, there was a knock on my door.

"Come in."

Ms. Gladys stuck her head inside my door and whispered, "That lady is out here to see you. She dresses nice, but I get a bad vibe from this heifer."

"What?" I frowned.

"Should I call security?"

"I need to figure out who this woman is."

"She got that goon with her. Should I get my Mace out of my purse?"

"No, I can handle this, Ms. Gladys." I turned the contract facedown, got up from my desk, and walked out to the foyer. I noticed the back of a woman talking to a handsome, but mean-looking, bald-headed light-skinned brother.

"May I help you?" I asked.

The woman turned around, and sister's face was beat. I mean, her makeup and hair were flawless on her toasted-croissant-brown skin. The petite woman stood no more than five feet and one or two inches, but her posture—shoulders back, head held high—gave her the stature of one much taller. I gave her a quick once-over. Her hair was perfectly coiffed into a French roll, an appropriate style for the navy blue knit suit she wore. The knee-length skirt and matching jacket fit as if it had been tailored to her slender body. From the gleam of her black pumps to the glitter of the diamond bracelet that graced her small wrist, this woman oozed money and confidence.

"Are you Chauncey Greer?" she asked, but before I could answer she said, "But of course you are."

I squinted slightly as I stared at her face. She looked familiar. Then, suddenly, I remembered. It was the woman from the Web site. The woman sitting next to Damien in the picture. The woman who was identified as Damien's wife.

"I'm Chauncey," I said.

"I need to speak with you," she said. It was a command, not a request.

I crossed my arms in front of me. "Do you mind telling me what this is about?"

"Not out here. Do you have a private office in here?" she asked as she looked around with disdain. The man standing next to her gave me a steely stare.

"Who are you?" I asked, not letting on that I knew who she was.

"I'm Grayson Upchurch, and it doesn't matter who he is," she said, motioning to the man behind her. "Let's just call him protection. Now, can we go into your office?"

"Not until you tell me what this is about," I said.

She half-grinned. "Oh, don't be so coy. You people always try to be so clever," she said.

You people. I couldn't remember ever being referred to as "you people" by a member of my own race.

"Look, Ms. Upchurch, unless you can give me a reason why I should talk to you, then I'm going to ask you to leave," I said forcefully. She looked sideways toward the big dummy. He opened the black leather jacket he was wearing and looked down. I could see the shiny silver head of what I was convinced was a gun. I didn't want to panic, but I didn't want to set myself up for harm, either. I could see the front page of the *Atlanta Journal-Constitution* with the headline "Preacher's Wife Shoots and Kills Husband's Ex-Boyfriend."

"I'll speak with you, Ms. Upchurch, but your friend will have to stay out here," I said. I was going to get that bitch in my office, lock the door, and call security.

"That's a very wise decision," she said as she walked through my door and I followed. Once I got inside, I locked the door and said, "Tell me, just what was that little stunt with the bodyguard and the gun?"

"Why in the hell are you calling my husband?" she asked, ignoring my words.

I paused for a moment. "Are you talking about Damien?"

"So you do know who I am." She gave me a piercing stare, as if she thought I would back away. "I knew you were playing that clever queen thing. You gay boys can be so bitchy." Without an invitation, she sat in one of the black-and-white chairs that was facing my desk. If the gun didn't stun me, then certainly Grayson referring to me as a queen and gay boy did.

"I recognized you from the Web site and I called because I needed to talk to Damien," I said.

"About what?"

"That's between the two of us."

She raised her eyebrows. "There is no *us* when it comes to Bishop Upchurch. I'm the only *us* in his life," she said firmly as she crossed one of her very shapely legs over the other.

"Did Damien get my message?" I asked, finally taking my seat.

"Do you think I'm a fool? I know who you are and I know all about your little sordid events with my husband."

Sordid events, I thought. Obviously, Damien hadn't told her everything about our relationship.

"I guess you didn't hear me. Did Damien—or should I say the bishop—get my message?" I asked in a tone that let her know I wasn't backing down.

"And I guess you didn't hear me," she responded, letting me know she was willing to go toe-to-toe. "I screen all of the bishop's calls. I knew it was only a matter of time before you would pop up."

"I didn't pop anywhere. I just thought Damien should know our paths might cross again when he shows up in Atlanta," I said.

Her eyes thinned to slits. "The bishop doesn't have time for people like you from his past. He is busy doing the Lord's work, helping our community, and being the head of our household. When he wins the seat in the Senate, it will only be a matter of time before we'll be residing on Pennsylvania Avenue. All this talk about Bayrock Obba and his wife being next in line for the presidency is bullcrap." Obba? I knew Grayson Upchurch was much too intelligent not to know the correct name of one of the fastest-rising black politicians, Barack Obama. She had to be just dissing the man. But I said nothing, allowing her rampage to continue.

"I told Damien people from his past would start to pop up and halt our . . . I mean his dreams."

I glanced at her for a long time and wondered if she was for real. Frustration began to boil inside of me, and I wondered why I was even having a conversation with this crazy bitch. After a few moments of disorienting silence, I finally spoke.

"The Damien I knew was never interested in politics," I said. I started to say women also, but I resisted.

"The Damien you knew is dead. Bishop Upchurch was called by the Lord to spread his word and to let people know that we must band together against the homosexual agenda—that sick agenda of asking for special rights against discrimination and getting married. I mean, how crazy is that?" Grayson said in a crisp voice that was both elegant and commanding. "Finally, the Republicans have an issue black folks can understand. We don't believe in that gay crap."

I took a moment before I said, "Can you answer something for me?"

"Maybe," she said coolly.

"Why the bodyguard with the gun? Are you trying to scare me?"

"There is no need for that." She shook her head. "I just wanted to find out what you want. Is it money, or are you delusional and think that Damien might still be interested in someone like you?"

I smiled. "Sounds like you're worried, and I don't need a dime from you or Damien."

Grayson looked around my office. "Well, it looks like you're doing okay, but you could do better, I'm sure." She directed her glance back at me. "The bishop and I have some supporters who might be willing to make a donation to you, your business, or to whomever, if we can get a signed document from you stating that you will never talk about Damien in public or private."

I laughed at her. Even if I'd been willing to go along with her pitiful scheme, that would never work. "In case you didn't know, Damien and I grew up in a very small town. If you do make it to the White House, or wherever, I'm going to show up in any investigation. They will definitely do background checks. Everyone in Greenwood knows that Damien and I were good friends."

"But they don't know about the sick relationship you talked him into," she sneered.

"I guess Damien didn't tell you everything," I said sarcastically.

"Damien didn't have to tell me. I've seen everything in the box he kept. All your letters and cards. I mean, if it wasn't so against God's will, I might even have reason to be a bit jealous." Grayson pulled out a checkbook and an aqua-blue pen. "Now, how much will it take to make you disappear again?"

My eyes widened at her audacity. "There is nothing about me that's for sale, so if that's what you came for, then I think this conversation is over."

She sighed as if she couldn't believe my words, "You really need to think about what I'm offering you."

"This conversation is over," I said as I stood and moved toward the door.

Grayson stared at me for a moment, put the checkbook and pen back into her purse, and stood. She straightened her skirt. Creases formed in her forehead as she frowned and said, "This conversation may be over, but we're not. If I were you, I'd be careful about where I went and who I talked to."

"So I should watch my back?" I said, remembering Griffin's words.

"You said it, not me."

And then Grayson walked out of my office, slipping past me like she was the Queen of Sheba.

*　　*　　*

Later that evening, I stood on my patio and listened to the soft sound of rain as it dropped down on Atlanta. The rain always made me reflective and today was no different. I was thinking about how Damien and I used to enjoy not only watching and listening to the rain but walking in it as well. I wondered how Damien wound up marrying a woman like Grayson. Didn't he realize how manipulative and conniving she was? I thought of something I'd felt when Damien exited my life: maybe true love was too much to ever expect as a black gay man.

The raindrops started to fall more heavily and I decided to go back into the house. When I stepped inside I heard the phone ring. I walked over and looked at the caller identification and saw *private caller* displayed. I started not to pick it up but thought it might be Damien calling to apologize for his wife's actions.

"Hello."

"Chauncey."

For a moment I was startled but surprised by the sound of his voice.

"Basil, what's going on? I didn't think I'd be hearing from you so soon," I said.

"I discovered some information that you might find interesting," he said.

"About what?"

"Your preacher and his wife. I thought she looked familiar and so I called a couple of my boyz from college. Grayson was a student, or at least she was enrolled at Miami when I went to school," Basil said.

"So did you know her?"

"Naw, not really, but a bunch of my boyz—you know, my teammates—knew her in how shall we say, the biblical sense. She was a real football groupie and used to have a reputation for being able to roll a perfect joint. That's why I said she was 'enrolled' in school. One of my boyz told me she stayed on her back most of the time and higher than the friendly skies," Basil said.

"That's interesting," I said, suddenly hoping "The Queen" would make another visit to my office and I could drop some of my newfound knowledge on her.

"So if you want old boy back then maybe you should share that information with him," Basil suggested.

I started laughing and said, "That's what you thought, Basil? That I want Damien back? No way."

"Well, you didn't see the look in your eyes that I saw when you were talking about him. I know niggas like him—and me, for that matter. We never really change."

"If we're talking about looks, what about the one I saw in your eyes when you were talking about being in love? Which, by the way, you didn't say if it was a man or a female."

There was silence over the phone.

"Basil, are you still there?"

"Yeah, you got me on that one. Is it important whether or not it's a male or female?"

"Not really, but I do want to know. I miss our sessions, and I'd be lying if I didn't say I was bothered by you not tryin' to hit this when we saw each other," I said.

"I feel you and I kinda got that. It's hard trying to change your ways when you an old dog like me. But it's a dude. Somebody I've known for a long time. He almost died about three years ago, and it woke me up and made me realize how much I loved him."

"I'm happy for you and it gives me a little hope," I said.

"Now don't be going picking out china for us. I ain't about that gay marriage thing. And this is the hardest thing I've done because Raymond, that's his name, told me when we hooked up it had to just be him or nothing at all. I get tempted sometimes, and I want to kick it with another woman or a dude, but I don't want to fuck this up," Basil said.

"I'm happy for you, Basil. Thanks for sharing that."

"Thanks, man, and I'm hopeful that you'll find love soon as well."

"Thank you," I said as tears welled up in my eyes. Maybe hopeful wasn't a bad thing to be.

CHAPTER TWENTY-EIGHT

"*You* know, these women are getting out of control. I can't believe Damien's wife came looking for you," Skylar said.

"Yeah, it's been a few days, and I'm still not over the shock," I said, wishing that I'd never brought up the topic.

I was over at Skylar's house grilling some steaks. My hope was to hear some more of his Tank story and not talk about Grayson and Damien Upchurch.

"I need to send you to Skylar's School of How to Deal with Crazy Bitches—the crash course," Skylar said, pointing at me. "So you won't have to put up with that stuff. One time my man's baby mama came to my house, and I guarantee you it's the last visit she paid."

Knowing there was a story there, and that it would change the subject, I asked him what had happened. Skylar made martinis for the both of us and sat at the bar while I seasoned the steaks.

"I was seeing this guy—Thurston, I think was his name.

Anyway, he used to always come to my house late at night and then leave early in the morning. He came at least twice a week. He was a cop, and I actually met him when he was giving me a ticket. You think blondes are the only ones who can flirt their way out of a ticket?" Skylar laughed as he took a sip of his drink.

"Anyhow, he told me he had a baby's mama, but that didn't bother me. It wasn't like I was trying to fall in love." Skylar paused, then added, "Although he was fine. Lean, but muscular, and he was packing over ten inches thick. Why is it that skinny boys have the biggest dicks?"

"That's just a myth," I said as I covered the steaks with aluminum foil and suddenly wished I had cooked at my house. It was an unusually warm evening for early October, and I bet I could have gotten away with cooking outside.

"Yeah, he was tight," Skylar said in between sips of his martini. "Sometimes he would wear his uniform and bring his gun so I could play with it."

I shook my head. "You're one sick puppy."

"Yeah, you're probably right. This was when I first moved to the ATL and I was just staying in a regular working-girl-type apartment over in midtown where all the kids lived. It was right off Peachtree, near the MARTA and where that Margaret house is."

"Margaret house? What are you talking about?"

"Who is the bitch that wrote *Gone with the Wind*? Never read the book, but loved, loved, loved the movie," Skylar said.

"Her name was Margaret Mitchell." I placed some sliced mushrooms in a skillet of sizzling olive oil.

"The point I'm trying to make is that it was easy to just walk up and knock on my door. So one day I hear a knock and I open the door without looking out, and there's this two-tone-hair, bad-dye-job, big-earring, gum-chewing sister standing in front of me with her eyes going in different directions, looking like that female character Jamie Foxx used to play on *In Living Color*."

"Ugly Wanda?"

"Yeah, her. Maybe not that ugly. So I thought she must be selling human hair from China, the way she was looking. I asked her how I could help her. She looked at me like dog shit, then had the nerve to ask me who I was. I told her my name, and I asked who she was, while she stood there trying to look over my shoulder and see inside my starter palace. The bitch might have been trying to rob me, so while I was looking at her, I was trying to remember where I put my gun."

"You had a gun?"

"Child, I keep a gun. Ain't nobody gonna try and punk me because of the way I look and act. I will beat a bitch or a nigga down and then shoot their ass," Skylar said.

"So what did she say?"

"Told me her name was Tamieka or LaSheika. You know the names. I asked her again how I could help her, and she said she wanted to know why Thurston had been seen leaving my apartment several times."

My face stretched with surprise. "Did you tell her?"

"I asked her who she was, and she told me she was Thurston's baby's mama. Then she got up in my face and asked me again what he was doing at my house. I didn't like her stance, so I told her he was coming to my place because I suck dick better than she did. Then I asked her if she had any more questions."

"You are a fool," I said, shaking my head, "What did she say?"

"Her eyes bucked out like she was shocked. She asked me if I was a cake boy. I asked her what was that, and she said a low-life faggot. I told her she should ask her alleged boyfriend," Skylar said, laughing.

I scooped up the mushrooms, whose aroma was overwhelming the area near the stove, and poured them into a bowl. My back was to Skylar, and when I turned around and saw him fixing himself another drink, I finally took the first sip of mine.

"I bet she was mad at you," I said.

Skylar waved his hand in the air. "The bitch told me she should smack the shit out of me, and I told her to bring it but if she put her grimy hands on my face she better kill me, 'cause I didn't mind slashing a bitch like her."

"You wouldn't have hit a woman, Skylar, would you?" I asked, wondering why I was surprised. I didn't put one thing past my best friend when something came between him and a man.

"Why the fuck not? If any bitch comes for me, I'm going to treat them like a dude. I tell you, if Damien's wife had come in my space trying to get in my business, she would have been with me about ten seconds before she would be in the corner licking her wounds."

"What did the girl do?" I asked, bringing the story back. I still didn't want to talk about Damien or his wife.

"She could tell by the look in my eyes that I wasn't playing, and the bitch scurried from my door. I never heard from her again."

"What happened to Thurston?"

"I guess the bitch learned how to suck dick, 'cause I didn't hear from him, either." Skylar laughed as he took a sip from martini number two.

*   *   *

One too many cocktails caused Skylar to crawl up on his sofa and fall asleep right after dinner, so I didn't get my Tank story. I came home, took a bath, watched *Will & Grace* and my favorite Atlanta newscaster, Monica Kaufman, and prepared for bed.

Just as I was getting ready to turn off the light, the phone rang. *Private* scrolled across the display, and since several people I loved, like Skylar, had private numbers, I picked it up. After I said "Hello," I knew I'd made a mistake.

"What kind of stunt are you pulling?" the familiar female voice demanded.

"What?"

"This is Mrs. Upchurch, and I want to know why you didn't tell me you were singing at Damien's sermon. You're up to something, and I won't stand for it. Is that why you've been trying to get in touch with my husband? Did I not make it clear that he's not on your team anymore? My husband is on God's team," she said, her voice tight. I started to say, "Like you were on the University of Miami's team," but I thought I would save that little piece of information for later.

"Then there shouldn't be any problems. Good night," I said. I hung up the phone before she could utter another threat.

I turned out the light and clicked off the television. Just as I was starting my nightly prayer, the phone rang again. But this time I turned the ringer off by pressing the Do Not Disturb button on my phone. When I got into bed, I sighed and enjoyed a smile of satisfaction. I knew I would sleep well. Just as I knew that Grayson Upchurch wouldn't— women with secrets like hers probably don't sleep much at all.

CHAPTER TWENTY-NINE

It was around 10 A.M. and I was worried. Celia hadn't come into the office, nor had she called, and this was not like her.

I picked up the phone and dialed her cell number. After a couple of rings, Celia answered. I was relieved and upset at the same time.

"Celia, where are you?"

"I'm at home. Didn't you get my message?"

"What message?"

"I called your house early this morning and left you a message telling you I wasn't feeling well," Celia said.

I remembered my phone call from Grayson last night and turning off my ringer.

"What's the matter?" I softened my voice.

There was a brief silence over the line.

"Celia, did you hear me? What's wrong?"

"Female problems."

Okay, I thought. *She has stepped over the friendship-sharing line once again.*

"Is there anything I can do?" I asked, praying that she wouldn't ask me to pick up some type of feminine products.

"No, I'll be all right. Is there anything you need for me to do from home? I have my laptop with me."

"No, just take care of yourself. I'll see you tomorrow."

"Okay, but if you need to reach me, I'll be here."

"Cool."

I pushed down the button without placing the receiver back and dialed my home number. When I heard my voice, I pressed the star key and then my secret code. The automated voice announced I had six messages.

The first message was from the previous night, another threat from Grayson: "I wonder what a God-fearing company like Wal-Mart would do if they found out they were doing business with a sodomite?" I quickly erased the message, wondering why this "good" Christian woman was worried about my sex life and, more important, how the fuck she knew about Wal-Mart.

The next call, time-stamped a couple of minutes later, was a hang-up that I assumed was Grayson.

There was a message from Jonathan asking for a couple of dollars so he could come and hear me sing. There was no mention of his family.

Next was a call from Vincent asking me if I would consider singing a solo at the Day of Absence service, and one from Pastor Kenneth inquiring about the contract. Finally, I heard Celia's message. She sounded like she was crying. What was that about? She must have been sicker than she was telling me, I thought.

I hung up the phone and tried to return to the prose that I was working on for some new cards. But I couldn't get two thoughts out of my mind. I wondered just how long Grayson Upchurch was going to harass me before I could no longer remain a southern gentleman. Obviously, Damien hadn't told her everything about me, because I could be tougher on women than Skylar when I needed to be.

But Celia was another thing. It wasn't the fact that she had called in sick that had me worried; nor was it her tears that didn't sound like just female problems. I shook my head, pushing my concerns about the Upchurches and Celia aside as I turned back to my computer, determined to finish at least one card before the day was over. Maybe I could come up with a card just for Celia conveying how much her friendship meant to me.

*   *   *

The day ended with my completing two inspirational cards and a few lines on the personalized one for Celia. I tried to reach Skylar and invite him to dinner, but I got his answering machine. Just as I was getting ready to leave, Ms. Gladys stuck her head in the door and told me a Vincent Young was on the line for me.

"Thank you, Ms. Gladys. Did you talk to Celia today?"

"Just briefly. She told me she wasn't feeling well, but I don't know if I believe that."

"What do you think it is?" I asked.

"If I was a betting woman, which I'm not because gambling is unchristian-like, I'd say man problems."

"You think so?"

"Let's see how she acts tomorrow. You better take your call. I'll lock up," Ms. Gladys said.

"You have a nice evening."

"You too, baby."

When Ms. Gladys closed the door, I picked up the phone and sat back down.

"Sorry to keep you waiting, Vincent. I was going to call you when I got home."

"That's cool. I know you're busy. I just wanted to give you a little update on the Day of Absence. We have participants from over ten churches now. Only problem now is space. The hotel ballroom might not be big enough to hold everybody," Vincent said.

"Have you thought of alternative spots?"

"Someone suggested we try one of the colleges at the AU center."

"I hope you're not thinking about Morehouse," I said.

"Are you crazy? They would laugh us out of Atlanta," Vincent said.

"What about doing an outside service at Centennial Park?" I suggested.

"Never know what the weather is going to be like even if we had tents. I'm going to check with the Fox and Civic Center, but they may be out of our budget. Have you decided if you're going to be able to sing?"

"I talked to Pastor Kenneth and he called about the contract, so I know a decision is near."

"I really hope you decide against singing there, Chauncey,

not because I want you to sing at our service, but this Upchurch man and his wife really scare me. Did you see them on CNN last night?"

"They were on CNN?"

"Yes."

"What for?"

"They have been arranging protests against some high schools in the Denver area that have Gay-Straight Alliance groups. They were talking about the need to save children from the gay agenda. It was just so sad to see supposedly educated black people sounding like such stupid haters. If I closed my eyes and just listened, I would have thought I was listening to some Klansmen. We need to show them that Atlanta ain't that type of city."

"Are you serious?" I said, shaking my head. I couldn't believe Damien and his wife were going after young people.

"I wish it wasn't so," Vincent said.

"What would you do if I talked to Pastor Kenneth and was able to get him to reconsider having the Upchurches speak at Abundant Joy?" I asked. I really didn't want to see Abundant Joy separated over this issue.

"I don't think it could hurt. You know how I feel about Pastor Kenneth and Sister Vivian, but I think they like publicity and making money—they can rake in some serious cash from this concert. You know how he's always talking about building a new church home."

"So you think it's about money?" I didn't say it, but I doubted Vincent's words. Pastor Kenneth had never seemed to be one of those money-hungry pastors. But then I thought about how happy he'd been the Sunday when all the gay people stuffed the offering plate.

"When it comes to a lot of these black preachers, it's always about money, and with President Bush and his faith-based initiatives, well, that's all Bush needed to get these ministers to sing his tune."

"Can you give me forty-eight hours to give you an answer?"

"Sure."

"Thank you. I'll give you a call."

There was a small silence, and I wondered if we had been disconnected; then I heard Vincent's voice once more. "Pray on it, Chauncey. God will send you the right answer," he said.

"I know," I said.

*   *   *

After my chat with Vincent, I knew tomorrow had to be decision day and I didn't have one. So I did the one final thing that I knew would help. I turned off all the things in my house that made sounds. I turned off the television and stereo and unplugged the clocks. I went into the kitchen and the bathroom to make sure there was no water dripping. Then I turned off all the lights.

Finally, I stripped down to my birthday suit (I know that sounds crazy, but I felt purer when I prayed in the nude) and got on my knees on the right side of my bed. I began to pray.

"Father, Lord God, I come to You in need of an answer.

Father, first of all, I want to thank You for waking me up this morning and watching over me today. I thank You for all the blessings You've given me. My family, my friends, my business, and the gift of song. Father, You know I've had a lot on my mind the last couple of weeks, and I need some type of sign as to what You want me to do. I know I will always fall short in Your sight, but You know my heart and that I try. I want to sing the praises of Your love for me and all Your children. Father, do You want me to sing at the revival when You know I'm in conflict about the message Bishop Damien will bring and what it will do to my spirit? What it will do to my soul? Should I sing at the Day of Absence services, where people who believe and love You will be holding up Your name in praise?"

I paused, took a deep breath, and continued my prayer. *"Father, I know I don't always do what I know You would want me to do, but I'm trying. I ask You for strength when I make the decision and to not look back. Wherever I end up on Sunday, God, I ask that You be with me, holding me. Father, please be with all the people who are involved and remind us that nothing that we do is important unless we put You first.*

"Forgive me for my sins and thank You for Your blessings and thank You for loving me despite my faults. Amen."

I stayed on my knees for a while longer, resting in the silence. I knew God was there; I knew he heard me. Finally, I climbed into bed, letting the softness of my sheets caress my naked body. I closed my eyes and waited for God and sleep to take over.

CHAPTER THIRTY

Morning dawned with a spitting rain, but at least I had my answer. It had come to me in a small voice. I got out of bed and called Pastor Kenneth's secretary and made an appointment to see him that evening.

While I was dressing, I thought about the decision I'd made. It was still on my mind as I drove to the office. But when I opened my office door and heard Ms. Gladys singing, "*Jesus on the main line. Tell him what you want. Oh,*" I smiled even more.

"Good morning, Ms. Gladys. Is Celia in her office?"

"Not yet, but there is somebody in your office," she said with a shrug.

"Who?" I quizzed.

"That girl," she said, rolling her eyes.

"What girl?"

"Celia's friend."

"Lontray?"

She slid her glasses down the bridge of her nose and

stared at me over the top of them. Then she removed her glasses before she said, "Yeah, *her*," losing her diction.

I walked toward my office wondering what Lontray was doing in my office and why Celia wasn't in yet. I took a deep breath and prepared myself for another round of Lontray's flirting.

When I walked into my office, Lontray was standing by the wall against the large window, studying my framed diplomas.

"So you got two degrees, huh? I knew you were a smart man," she said.

"What's good, Lontray?"

"I'm good." She smiled. "When are you going to invite me to church again?"

"Where's Celia?" I asked, ignoring the question about church.

"She's at home. Have you seen her lately?"

"Not for a couple of days. Is this why you're at my office so early this morning?"

"First of all, Celia don't know I'm here, but I figured you're a little more than just her boss. Even though she be frontin', I think she is feelin' you."

Where is this coming from? I wondered. My relationship with Celia had always been professional, and although I never felt the need to discuss my sexuality, I wouldn't have been surprised if Celia knew at the very least that I was bisexual.

"My relationship with Celia is strictly professional," I said.

"So you saying I might have a chance if I go out and get me a couple of degrees? I hear you can get them online now. Is that true?"

"I think so, but what's going on with Celia?"

"What did she tell you?"

"She said something about female problems."

"Hmmph. Whatever. Female problems my ass," Lontray said as she rolled her eyes and took a seat in one of the chairs facing my desk.

"Then what's wrong with her, Lontray? And speed it up, because I've got a busy day," I said.

"You ain't trying to get rid of me, are you? I think you be frontin', too, and you really trying to git with this," she said, motioning toward her upper body.

"Lontray!" I yelled. I didn't have time to play her games today.

"Don't be hollering at me. I just think you should know that Celia's female problems are really Marvin problems."

"What?"

"Yeah, Marvin be playing Ike Turner on her head," she said, moving her hands as if she were playing a drum.

"He's beating her?" This was my worst fear for any woman.

"You didn't hear it from me, but yes," Lontray said.

"How long has this been going on?"

"Hell, ever since she met the nigga. That's why she left his ass in the first place, but then he started sweet-talking her. Then the nigga went off when he thought he had her back. I told her she was going to be a lifetime member in the battered women's shelter if she didn't leave that nigga alone."

I moved toward the door, hoping Lontray would get the hint that I wanted her to leave.

"Thanks, Lontray. I'll see what I can do."

"If it was me, I would just call the po-po on the nigga. I know you a big dude yourself with all them muscles, but Marvin . . . that nigga bowed up, so I'd think twice before getting in the ring with him," Lontray said.

She got up and started walking toward the door. Lontray opened it and then looked back at me and said, "You want my digits in case you need some backup?" Then she winked at me, but I didn't respond. She gave me a final smile before she sashayed past Ms. Gladys's desk and out of the office.

*　*　*

I waited until I was alone with Ms. Gladys before I shared what Lontray had told me. But Ms. Gladys didn't seem a bit surprised.

"I told you it was man problems. You didn't notice how Celia was wearing more makeup than she usually do a couple of weeks ago?"

"No," I said, shaking my head and wondering what makeup had to do with this.

"That's men folks for you. When I first started working here, I used to notice how Celia didn't wear no makeup. She's a real pretty girl, but all of us women, even the beauties, need a little help. A little lipstick and eye shadow ain't never hurt nobody. I was beginning to wonder if she was one of them funny women, but I know Celia ain't like that. You can tell that girl like her some men from the way she wear her skirts, and she told me she once paid twenty-five dollars for a pair of panties," Ms. Gladys said. "What kind of craziness is that?"

"If it's true and Marvin is hitting her, what do you think I should do?"

Ms. Gladys looked at me for a long moment, pulled her large black leather purse from under her desk, and said, "You don't need to do nothing. This is Mama's work. I'll take care of Miss Celia."

"What are you going to do?"

"That will be between Celia and me, but I will need the rest of the morning off. You can manage on your own for a couple hours, can't you?"

"Yes, I think I can. I have a meeting with my pastor tonight, so I'll be fine."

"Well, you tell that preacher man to pray for our girl Celia. It's hard getting a bad man out of your system so a good one can come in."

I started to tell Ms. Gladys, "I hear ya talking," but I only said, "Okay."

CHAPTER THIRTY-ONE

Even though I was firm with my decision, I was a little nervous when I opened the door to Pastor Kenneth's office. He was reading his Bible, and I laughed to myself when he stood up to greet me. Pastor Kenneth had on rust-colored suit pants, a white shirt, and a skinny tie that matched his slacks. I loved the fact that I had a minister who wasn't worried about the latest fashion and took pride in being from the country.

"Brother Chauncey. Come on in, sir. I hope your lawyer found our contract fair," he said as he extended his hand and pointed to a chair across from his desk.

"Good evening, Pastor Kenneth. Thanks for seeing me."

"No problem. I always got time for my members. Have a seat."

I sat down and placed both of my hands on the edge of his desk, one on top of the other.

"So you got the contract?" Pastor Kenneth asked.

"That's what I need to speak to you about. . . ." I paused for a few seconds and then I just blurted out, "I can't do it."

"Brother Chauncey, come on now. Do you want more money?"

"No, Pastor. This has nothing to do with money," I said. I removed my hands from the desk, leaned back in the tight-fitting leather chair, and rested my hands on my thighs.

"What is it, then? I've dealt with agents and lawyers before. Is it your agent, or have you signed with a record label and they won't let you do it? Oh, by the way, I understand you talked with Lucy. Was that a good contact?"

"Yes, sir, it was. I haven't met with the singer she wanted me to meet with yet, but I have an appointment set up. Thanks again."

"No problem. Now back to the revival. You know, this puts us in a tight spot with the event being only a couple of weeks away. It will be hard to get a singer of your caliber at this late date."

"I know, and I'm really sorry. But I've prayed and prayed on this, and I think I'm doing the right thing."

"Well, Brother Chauncey, if you've prayed on it and you feel like this is the answer that God has given you, then we will have to live with it. Doesn't mean we like it, but the Good Lord doesn't always give us what we want."

"I feel pretty strongly about it," I said.

"If it's not too personal, would you mind sharing with me why you can't do it? I mean, did I do something? Did Sister Vivian or any member of my deacon board do anything to offend you?"

"No, sir. Everyone has treated me wonderfully. But I would like to ask you something."

"Sure. Ask me anything."

"Why Bishop Upchurch?"

"What do you mean?"

"Why have him speak? I visited his Web site, and some of his views on things are very extreme," I said.

"Bishop Upchurch and his wife, Grayson, are good, upstanding Christian people. I don't agree with everything he says in some of his speeches, but he's preaching the Word. I think we need to hear people like him, not only in the pulpit but in the Senate as well. We're losing a generation of our youth because they don't hear the message Bishop Upchurch and Sister Grayson are trying to spread."

"So even though you don't believe in everything he says, you think it's okay for them to come and preach their hate to our congregation?" I asked angrily. I'd expected more from Pastor Kenneth. I didn't want him telling me that I needed to hear the word of Damien and Grayson on how I lived my life.

"I don't see it as hate, and neither does Sister Vivian. These are good people. I ask that you sit down with him and talk over some of his views before you make a final decision," Pastor Kenneth said.

"Meet with him?"

"Yes. I mean, we can make it happen this evening. Bishop Upchurch is in town speaking at Morehouse, and he's going to come by and share a meal with me. It would be perfect timing if you'd join us and express to him your feelings, as you've done with me."

"I don't think I can do that," I said firmly.

"Why not, Brother Chauncey? You've always struck me as a fair brother. Put your questions to Bishop Upchurch. Give the man a chance," Pastor Kenneth pleaded.

I wanted to tell him that I'd already given Damien Upchurch a chance and had gotten nothing but heartbreak for my efforts.

"I think I'll pass on that opportunity. But I would like for you to ask him a question, and if you don't mind, I'd like you to answer it as well," I said, and then paused to make sure he heard my query.

"Sure. What is it?"

"Ask him where black gay and lesbian people go who believe in God with all their heart when we're not welcome in our churches. Not only in Denver and Atlanta, but all over this country. Ask him where we go to be nurtured and express our faith. Where do we go for forgiveness? Do we put our faith in a box like some of our people used to do with their money because they didn't trust the bank?"

"That's a very valid question, Brother Chauncey. Do you want me to answer it?"

"I would."

"It's sad to say, Brother Chauncey, but the church is like the world. You would think that in church everyone would be loving and accepting, but that's not the case. There are churches in this country that wouldn't want you or me because of the color of our skin. They go to school and work with us, but only because they have to. In a church, just like a country club, they can choose their membership."

"I understand that, but it still doesn't explain how black

churches can exclude a certain segment of our community because of something we do in private."

"You think being black stops us from being prejudiced? I know far more black bigots than I do white ones."

"That still doesn't answer my question. Where do we go?"

"Do you feel comfortable at Abundant Joy? Has anyone ever said anything unkind toward you?"

"I love Abundant Joy, but by bringing Bishop Upchurch I sense a dangerous change occurring that I've experienced at other churches. Before you know it, we will be another megachurch harboring hate," I said.

"Bishop Upchurch is coming because I asked him to come. We have to provide a forum for all voices. I'm not saying I agree with him, but we need people of all backgrounds and opinions in the church and the Senate. If Abundant Joy does become bigger, the center point will be God, His grace, and His mercy. I know that applies to all His children."

"I hope you're right, Pastor Kenneth. Still, I think it's best that I sit out the bishop's visit, and hopefully return to the church I love after he's gone."

"I don't agree with you, but I respect your right to make that decision. I still say you should come to dinner and sit down with Bishop Upchurch and get to know this man of God."

I was very angry but I didn't respond. I was tempted to say I had already explored all the sides of Damien Upchurch I was interested in.

"He's going to be here any minute. It's not too late," Pastor Kenneth said.

"What?"

"Bishop Upchurch is due any minute."

"Damien? I mean, Bishop Upchurch is coming here?" I stammered.

Pastor Kenneth looked at his watch and said, "Yes, but it looks like he's running a little late."

I stood up quickly and felt a desire to run from Pastor Kenneth's office. I felt sweat forming around my neck and rolling down the center of my chest like lava. I had to get out.

"Sorry, Pastor. I have other plans. Enjoy your dinner," I said as I moved quickly from his office and down the hallway toward the parking lot.

*   *   *

I walked out into an ordinary fall night, and just before I reached my car I saw the profile of a man getting out of a limo. Even though it was dark, the lampposts covering the parking lots provided enough light for me to see that it was Damien. He was punching his fingers into a gadget that looked like a Palm Pilot or a BlackBerry.

I stood still and felt my heart thudding in my chest. He put the gadget in the jacket pocket of his suit and turned to look toward the church. Just as I was deciding whether or not to call out his name, he turned his head toward me and our eyes met. I remained silent and still as he walked toward me. Seconds later, he was standing so close to me I could tell the flavor of his toothpaste.

"Chauncey, is that really you?" Damien asked.

"Yeah, it's me," I stammered.

"What are you doing here?"

"Leaving," I said softly.

"Is this Abundant Joy?"

"Yes."

"Do you work here?"

"I attend church here, but of course you know that," I said.

"How would I know that?"

"Didn't you get my messages?"

"What messages?"

"Damien, I called you several times and left several messages."

"I never got them," Damien said.

"Well, certainly Grayson told you I called."

"How do you know my wife?"

"I guess you could say she was stalking me for a minute and then we finally met," I said.

Damien had a puzzled look on his face like he didn't know what I was talking about.

"You met Grayson?"

"She didn't tell you?" I asked. *So much for that perfect marriage*, I thought.

"I don't understand what's going on. What are you doing at Abundant Joy?"

"I go to church here. I just told you that," I said.

"So you know Pastor Kenneth and Sister Vivian?"

"Yes, and I understand you're having dinner with him," I said.

Damien looked at his watch and said, "Yes, but I'm already late. Would you like to sit in my limo a few minutes and catch up?"

"Catch up?"

"Yeah, I want to show you pictures of my kids and let you know what I've been up to."

"I visited your Web site. I heard you on Frank and Wanda. So I know what you've been up to," I said bitterly. I moved slightly back from Damien, because I didn't know if I wanted to kiss him or punch him in the mouth.

"So you know about all the good work I've been doing with my ministry," Damien said. His voice gave off an air of authority that he'd had even as a teenager.

"Good work? Is that what you call your hate-speak?"

"You think the scriptures are wrong?" Damien asked.

"Don't tell me about scriptures. I've read the Bible, too. Answer me this, Damien: if we're to take every word of the Bible literally, then should we use a gun or knife to kill our neighbors who work on Sunday? And if you read Leviticus it also talks about *where* we should buy our slaves and that we shouldn't eat shellfish."

Damien peered at me like he was trying to figure out where I was coming from, and then he said sadly, "I guess you weren't able to get rid of those homosexual demons. I guess my praying has been in vain."

I shook my head and said, "You just don't get it, Damien."

I started toward my car, and Damien called my name. I was close enough to place the key in the lock, but instead I looked back toward him as tears rolled down my face.

"Chauncey, it broke my heart to break yours."

I started to shout out that a real man of God would never allow my heart to be broken. Instead, I got into my car and drove off as the tears continued to paint my face.

CHAPTER THIRTY-TWO

I didn't know if I was dealing with a has-been diva or a wannabe diva. But either way, I had definitely wandered into divaland.

I glanced at my watch. I'd been waiting for more than an hour. I signaled to the waiter to bring me the check for the glass of wine I'd had. Just as I stood to leave, a thin woman with a long golden weave, oversized Jackie O–type sunglasses, and a navy cashmere cape swept into Justin's. She looked like a Hollywood star trying to avoid the paparazzi.

She posed as if she were a model and peered over the top of her glasses. Her eyes scanned the lunch crowd, and when her glance finally rested on me, I nodded and she sauntered over to the table.

"Yancey Braxton," she announced, and held out her hand toward me.

I stood and took her hand in mine. "I'm Chauncey Greer. Nice to meet you." As she sat down, I decided I was right. This woman certainly thought she was a diva—emphasis on *thought*.

"Well," she began as she sat, "I understand that you're dying to work with me."

I raised my eyebrows and wondered who had told her that. I'd never heard of this woman before Lucy mentioned her. But I decided not to respond to her statement. I'd just go along with it—for the moment—to see how this conversation played out. "I'm looking forward to this project," was all I said. That at least was true. I was looking forward to getting back into recording music. If working with Yancey Braxton would help me obtain my goal, then I was all for it.

She said, "Lucy told me that you write music." Before I could respond, Yancey continued, "You know, I wrote many of the songs for my multiplatinum album. It went platinum within just weeks, but no one was surprised. My song 'Any Way the Wind Blows' was number one on the pop, R & B, and dance charts. My record label said that I had the pipes of Whitney Houston, the range of Mariah Carey, the soul of Aretha Franklin, and the class of Nancy Wilson."

I was dumbfounded to watch this woman's hands glide through the air as she compared herself to some of the best singers of our time.

"I was a huge recording artist, and the plan was for my agent to turn me into a big screen star. That was my next move. I was going to be huge," she said. She spoke a little loudly for my taste. I noticed the way some of the customers around us stopped their conversations to glance at Yancey. But she seemed oblivious to everyone else in the world. She acted as if God had created this planet—and its inhabitants—just for her.

"Everyone said that my CD was the best CD released in the nineties. I was in *People* magazine."

It took everything within me not to ask Yancey why, if she was so good, she had only one CD. But Lucy had filled me in enough, and I wasn't out here trying to hurt anyone's feelings.

"I knew that it was good. I was better than any singer out there at the time, male or female."

I couldn't help it anymore. "So you were that good and stopped singing?" I asked innocently.

She shrugged. "I had a small string of bad luck," Yancey said. Those were the first words she spoke softly. Her fingers trailed through her weave. "But now it's time. I'm about to make a major comeback," she said, perking back up. "And you can't have a comeback if you don't leave first." She smiled to herself. "Besides I need to do this before Whitney and Mariah wake up."

"I guess so," I said, keeping my voice lower and hoping she would take the hint.

"And that's where you come in." She leaned forward, her elbows on the table. "Okay, so this is what I want you to do. Lucy tells me that you sing a little?"

I crossed my legs and leaned back in the chair. "I do more than a little singing. I also write music. Lucy told me that I'd be writing with you and we'd be singing together."

Her laugh was so loud, the people at the table next to us stopped eating to watch her. "Oh, no!" Her hands flailed through the air as if she were erasing my words. "I don't need you to write anything. Weren't you listening to me?

I told you, I wrote most of the songs for my multiplatinum album."

Okay, I thought. *She has one more time to speak to me like this.*

"I certainly don't need you to do any writing. And as far as singing, I'm the lead," she said, pointing to her chest. "All I'll need from you is a little backup."

My eyes narrowed. "That's not the way this project was explained to me."

"Well, Lucy got it wrong," she said, peeking at me over her sunglasses. "This is how we're going to do it."

I sat for just a moment longer, then stood and dropped a ten-dollar bill onto the table. "You know what, Yancey? It seems that you don't need me. Why don't you write that song, sing that song, and make your big comeback. And may God bless you in your struggle. Now I'm going to leave so your comeback can begin."

Her mouth opened into a wide O, as if no one had ever spoken to her that way. Well, it was about time, I thought as I zigzagged my way through the maze of tables. Before I stepped outside, I took a final look back into the restaurant and laughed. Yancey was still sitting in her seat, as if she couldn't move.

I shook my head. If working with Yancey Braxton was what I needed to make my big splash, then I would just keep peddling my cards.

* * *

"My, my, what a busy week you've had. Turning down one of my favorite ex-divas, Yancey B, and running into the love of your life. Are you going to try and talk to Damien, and are you sure you want to turn down Yancey B?" Skylar asked, as he placed a pair of chopsticks next to a half-empty plate of shrimp chow mein.

We were both finishing up at P. F. Chang's and I'd spent most of dinner telling him about meeting with Yancey B and my brief run-in with Damien.

"I hope that's the last of Damien and as far as Yancey whatsherface I'm sure I made the right call," I said as I took the last bite of the honey shrimp dish I'd craved at least once a week.

"I doubt if that is the last you will see or hear from Damien. I just have a feeling about you two," Skylar said.

"I just want all of this over. I want my life to be normal again." I sighed.

"What's normal besides a city in Illinois?" Skylar laughed.

"You might be right," I said.

The waiter brought us the check, along with two fortune cookies, and I swiftly grabbed the check and one of the cookies. I pulled out my Bank of America Visa card and placed it on the brown tray.

"So you think you're slick, don't cha?" Skylar said.

"What?" I raised my eyebrows, pretending not to know what he was talking about.

"This was supposed to be my treat."

"That's okay. You get it next time," I said.

I cracked open my fortune cookie and Skylar opened the other. My fortune said: *"Your Life will soon be filled with spiritual and material wealth."* I read it aloud to Skylar and then asked him what his said.

"Drop it like it's hot. Drop it like it's hot," he sang and laughed.

"You're a fool."

"But that's why you love me."

"I guess so. When am I going to get part three of the story?" I asked.

Skylar paused, then said, "The last part is real sad. Are you ready for it?"

"Sad?"

"Not *Imitation of Life* sad," Skylar said. "Looking back on it now, it's more *Jerry Springer*–like, funny and crazy."

"I think I can handle it. I need to laugh."

"Then let's order an after dinner drink and I'll sing for my supper," Skylar said.

"You can have a drink, but I'll just have some tea."

"Whatever," Skylar said, as he waved, motioning to the waiter.

The waiter returned with my credit card, and Skylar ordered a cognac while I requested green tea. The waiter grimaced, realizing we weren't quite ready to leave the coveted booth in the corner of the dimly lit, but busy restaurant.

"So last time we left this saga you and Tank were quite the couple," I said, urging Skylar to start the finale of his love story.

He smiled. "Yes, we were happy for a little while. Whenever we were together Tank treated me like a princess. He was protective of me and always asked if any of the boys at school were trying to get with me. It tickled me to death when he acted jealous. I used to fib and tell him that some boys had asked me out but that almost backfired."

"How so?"

"Well one time I told him one of the star players on our football team left in my locker a note and a picture of himself only wearing shoulder pads and a jock strap. It wasn't a total fabrication because a third-string guy on my team did try to get with me but he knew me as Skylar, the boy."

"What happened?"

"Tank knew the player I'd lied about. It turned out they played basketball against each other on an AAU team. Tank knew where he lived and had his phone number, so he called him and asked him why he was trying to hit on his girl. The boy, whose name I forgot, told him he must be smoking some weed laced with crack because he didn't know what Tank was talking about, nor did he know any girl named Skylar."

"What did you say?" I asked, trying to imagine how Skylar could possibly have wiggled his way out of that situation.

"I told him the guy was saying that because he knew Tank could fight and he was probably scared to death. When Tank asked more questions, I silenced him with a kiss," Skylar said.

"So that was it? He didn't find out?"

"Oh, he found out all right, but just not then," Skylar said.

The waiter brought our drinks and then asked, "Will there be anything else or can I bring you *another* check?"

Skylar looked at him with eyebrows arched. "I know you're not trying to give us a funky attitude with as much money as my friend and I usually spend in this overpriced joint. So just take your ass to your little corner and leave us alone. We're discussing grown folks business."

The waiter rolled his eyes at Skylar, and walked away.

"I hope you ain't expecting a tip, bitch," Skylar yelled. A middle-aged couple sitting at the table across from our booth stopped their chopsticks in midair. They stared at Skylar.

"Keep your eyes and ears over there in your booth because you don't want to deal with me," Skylar said to them.

I knew I had to jump in before this got out of control. "Come on, Sky. Leave those nice people alone. Just finish your story," I urged, trying to change his focus.

"People don't know who they're fucking with. I can go back to my ghetto roots in a heartbeat," he said.

This was one of those times when I wondered why Skylar used his words to threaten people before they had the chance to pass judgment on him. I'd seen him do it many times over the years, and at first I thought it was cute. But I didn't like seeing Skylar being mean to people, especially women who usually were the victims of his venom.

"I know, Skylar, but tell me the story. So how did Tank find out you were a guy?"

"I'm getting there. I know I'm making light of this now, Chauncey, but this was a very painful episode of my life. In a lot of ways it would determine how I would handle relationships with not only lovers or potential boyfriends but my relationship with my family as well," Skylar said seriously.

"I'm listening."

"You know how I told you how I envied the relationship you had with your mother and father."

"Yes," I said. I thought back to how when I first met Skylar I noticed he never talked about his parents. When I asked him about it he told me when he'd finished high school his parents had gotten a divorce and he really didn't talk to them that much. He told me neither one of his parents could deal with his sexuality and the fact that Skylar was so comfortable with it. He said both had remarried and that the new stepparents didn't want Skylar around because they had younger kids and thought he'd molest them or something.

"I didn't quite tell you the entire story about my split with my parents. They're both homophobic; my mom married an asshole, and my father married a manic bitch but what I didn't tell you was that I ran away from home before I graduated from high school because they wanted to have me committed," Skylar said.

"That's sad," I said. "But what does that have to do with Tank? I'm sure every parent of a gay son or daughter thinks some kind of medical intervention will make their child heterosexual," I said.

"You're right about that. But what happened was my mother found out about me and Tank and embarrassed the hell out of me. Sometimes when I think back on that day I feel like I have hives all over my body, and all I want to do is rip off all my clothes and dive in a cold, deep ocean," Skylar said.

"How did she find out?"

"It was the first time that I gave in to Tank's request about coming to my house. I know it was stupid, but it was easier for me to get into my outfit. My sister's room was so frilly and pink and I can't tell you how many times I'd dreamed of making out with Tank on her canopy bed. So one evening when I knew my parents were at my sister's dance recital I acted like I was sick. When the coast was clear I called Tank and he came over faster than an express subway train. I showed him around my house, and I'd taken down all the pictures of the boy Skylar. When I took him into my sister's room and he took a look at the bed, well, he got harder than a block of cement. I don't know if it was the room or the bubble gum pink miniskirt I was wearing," Skylar said. He paused and took a slow sip of his drink and then continued.

"It was the most magical evening or time I'd had with Tank. He just kissed me so gently and rubbed on my thighs and it was the first and only time he told me he loved me. Nobody had ever told me that they loved me," Skylar said softly.

"Not even your parents?" I asked.

"If they did I don't remember. So the answer to that question would be no."

"So on the day Tank told you he loved you he found out you weren't a girl?"

Skylar didn't answer right away. Instead he took the final sip of his drink, looked at me with sad eyes and said, "Yes."

"I know this is painful for you but talking about it might help," I said.

"I lost track of time and my parents came home sooner than I'd expected. I sent Tank out through the front door and he bumped into my mother. My parent's usually parked the car in the back carport and came in through the kitchen door. To this day I don't know why that woman was coming through the front door. When she came in and saw me slightly disheveled in my sister's clothes and her best church wig, well, she just freaked. She screamed at me and called me all kinds of sissy boy and then told me to put on my clothes and then she dashed out of the door running like she was Flo Jo. About ten minutes later she returned with Tank in tow and demanded that I 'tell em.'"

"What did you do?"

"What could I do? I just stood there embarrassed beyond my wildest dreams crying like a baby as Tank looked at me silent as a deaf mute. When I wouldn't say anything my mother pulled down my undergarments and screamed at Tank, 'Look he got the same thing as you!'"

"What did Tank do?"

"Even though he was a dark-skinned guy, it was as though all the color drained from his body and the look of love I had experienced earlier turned into pure disgust. He ran from my living room, and my mother and I never saw him again," Skylar said sadly.

"Were you ever afraid he might try and hurt you?" I asked, thinking of the movie *Boys Don't Cry*. Hilary Swank won an Academy Award for playing a girl who lived her life as a boy and who was killed when some other boys found out.

"No, I was never afraid he would hurt me. Despite everything I knew Tank loved me and would never hurt me."

"Is that when your parents tried to put you in the hospital?"

"They did everything they could to make me feel like I was the lowest of the low. They took me to school and told the principal and teachers what I'd done."

"Why did they do that?"

"Said they wanted to make sure I hadn't pulled the same thing with any of my other male classmates. Of course the teachers told me everything would be kept in confidence and off of my permanent record, but somebody blabbed and a couple of days later the whispering and giggles started. Boys and girls started calling me Miss Skylar."

"What did you do?"

"I took a knife to school and dared anybody to fuck with me. Of course that got me suspended. I went home, packed up my shit, including my Mama's best wig and I booked for New York City."

"So do you have any contact with your parents now?"

"Maybe once or twice a year when I send them a card or leave them a message. I do that to let them know that

I'm still alive and that my spirit is stronger than ever," Skylar said boldly.

"What happened to Tank?"

"He went to Ohio State on a wrestling scholarship, and I understand after he graduated he married and moved to Youngstown, Ohio, where his wife is from. I heard he has four kids. All boys."

"That's a sad, sad story," I said as I touched the top of Skylar's hand, which felt as warm as the sun.

He looked at me with tears hovering in the corner of his eyes and said, "But thank goodness a bitch like me can survive sad stories."

CHAPTER THIRTY-THREE

It was two days before the Day of Absence. I was doing a test run of an oyster pie I'd seen on Paula Deen's home cooking show on the Food Network. I was preparing it for my family when they arrived, but the smell alone teased my taste buds so much that I had to try it out.

Just as I was getting ready to take a bite of the piping-hot concoction, the phone rang. I put the spoon down on the stove and picked up the receiver. I hoped it was Skylar, because I hadn't spoken to him in a couple of days. I wanted to remind him of the service on Sunday and see if he would come by and sample my new dish.

"Hello," I said, still thinking about the pie.

"Chauncey," the familiar voice said. It wasn't Skylar. I was shocked and surprised that it was Damien.

"Why are you calling me?" I demanded.

"We need to talk. Pastor Kenneth told me you weren't going to sing at the revival. He told me what a great singer you are, but I already knew that. When he mentioned

Reunion, I told him I was a fan of your music and I wanted to try and convince you to sing," Damien replied.

"So he didn't remember you from the group?" I asked.

"I don't think so. You didn't tell him, did you?"

"He doesn't even know I know you," I said. Where was this conversation going?

"I'm sorry about the other night, but I would like to talk to you," Damien said.

"I'm listening."

"In person," he said.

"For what?" I asked. I didn't think I could stand to be in Damien's presence again. The scene in the parking lot left me disgusted, especially the part about him praying for me.

"There are just some things I've been wanting to say for so long. I don't like this gulf between us. I want to be your friend."

"So you can save my soul? I don't need friends like that. Thanks, but no thanks."

"So you're still angry with me?"

"You mean after twenty years? Like I said the other night—"

Before I could finish Damien interrupted me. In a voice that was soft yet masculine, smooth but still deep, he said, "It was never my intention to hurt you."

I listened as Damien told me how he was conflicted but knew what we were doing was wrong and that God had a better plan for him. He said a part of him wanted to spend the rest of his life with me, but he knew we'd never be totally happy together. His words made me feel just as I did twenty years ago when we would stay up talking late at night.

"How did you know then that we wouldn't be happy?" I asked as I took a seat on the bar stool.

"Chauncey," Damien continued, "what we had was special and it was love, but we would have faced so many obstacles. We were getting careless, and it would have ruined both of our futures."

"So instead you decided to ruin mine," I said.

"It looks like your life has been okay. You seem happy."

"How would you know that?" I screamed. It always bothered me when people made assumptions about other people's happiness.

"I don't. Look, maybe our meeting isn't such a good idea. I just wanted you to know that I never lied to you about the way I felt about you. The feelings we had were real."

I stared out at my terrace in a heartsick silence. A strange sense of vindication surged through me. I hadn't been wrong. There had been such a powerful connection between Damien and me, a time when I felt we would always be dreaming the same dream.

"Chauncey? Are you still there?"

I came out of my trance and said, "I'm here."

"I never meant to hurt you. I'm sorry. That's what I wanted to say," Damien said. His voice was gentle and low.

My eyes were moist with regret, and I said, "I'm sorry,

too." I hung up the phone and tried to prevent what I knew would happen next. *Don't start crying,* I told myself. *Don't be a punk ass, too.* But I couldn't, and tears began flooding down my cheeks. I didn't know if they were tears of sorrow or simply relief to know finally that I hadn't given my love in vain.

CHAPTER THIRTY-FOUR

The lot was already full when I pulled up to the hotel where the Day of Absence service would take place. I stopped in front of the lobby to let Mama, Daddy, and Belinda get out. Jonathan stayed in the car with me as I drove slowly through the spaces trying to find an empty one.

The weekend had already gone better than I ever expected. My parents had arrived the previous afternoon. I knew Belinda was coming with them, but when Jonathan walked through the door, I'd been totally surprised. My little brother looked good—although I suspected he was still having problems. His recent calls for money troubled me. I was excited, though, when he told me he was thinking about going to community college.

Last night had been perfect. After I served my oyster pie for lunch, Mama kicked me out of my own kitchen and took over. When she was finished, the table was covered with fried chicken, macaroni and cheese, collard greens, and a sweet potato pie. It almost felt like Thanksgiving and Christmas rolled into one.

We sat at my dining room table like the family we'd been so long ago. No spouses, no nieces and nephews—just the five Greers. We talked and laughed like we used to. But now we teased Mama and Daddy about turning into the Traveling Grands.

Throughout dinner, I looked for signs of disappointment from my parents. Not so much from Mama—I knew she'd love me no matter what. But I wasn't so sure about how my father felt. When they arrived, I had told them why I wasn't singing at the revival. Mama had said she understood, while my father remained quiet.

But last night, there were no signs of distress from my father, and that pleased me. It made me think that my entire family had finally accepted me the way I am.

I parked the car in the back of the hotel and then strolled to the front with Jonathan.

"So how are you doing, baby brother?" I asked as I put my arms around him.

"I'm doing okay. And yourself?"

"I'm a little nervous," I said.

"You'll be fine. Nobody can sing like you, dawg."

I gave him a sly smile and said, "It's not my singing I'm worried about."

As soon as we walked into the lobby, I could feel it. The air was charged—electric with excitement. I shook hands with many of the members I recognized from church and a few I'd met at the planning meetings.

I was looking around for the rest of my family when my eyes landed on a familiar sight. From the look on his face he was just as surprised to see me as I was him. It was Phillip Hicks, the handsome brother who'd caused us a good amount of aggravation when his printer failed and he couldn't deliver our cards on time.

"How're you doing, Chauncey?" he asked.

"I'm doing great," I said. Jonathan had spotted my parents and went to get them.

"I'm a little surprised to see you here," Phillip said.

"I could say the same thing about you," I said.

Phillip put his hands in front of his chest like he was defending himself and said, "Oh no, I'm not gay or bi. I'm strictly clitty but I'm here supporting my younger brother. He's gay and he asked me to come, and I didn't see any harm. Feel me?"

"I feel you. How's business?"

"Better."

"Sorry we couldn't work things out. I owe you an apology. I was pretty tough on you," I said.

"That's all right. I needed somebody to tell me to get my stuff together. It's funny, but I was going to call Celia and ask if you were still upset with me. I wanted to tell you I would be dropping off a check for half of what I owe you," Phillip said.

"That would've been a nice surprise, but I'll tell you what I'd like you to do," I said.

"What?"

"Why don't you make a check out to an AIDS charity?" I said. I didn't understand why I suddenly trusted Phillip but something about him told me he'd come through.

"I'll do that. Thank you, Chauncey, and maybe we'll get to do business again in the future," Phillip said as he extended his hand.

I shook his hand and wished him well as I finally made eye contact with my parents.

Right before I reached my family I bumped into Vincent.

"Are you ready?" Vincent asked.

"I think so. Hey, come meet my parents."

"Sure."

Before we stepped into the ballroom, I introduced my family to Vincent.

"Your son can really sing," Vincent said to my beaming parents.

"We're very proud of him" was all Mama said.

I turned around and spotted Skylar, who was wearing a church-inappropriate short red jacket and white pants so tight you could see the brand of underwear he was wearing.

"Skylar, you made it," I said as I gave him a hug.

He whispered, "I had to hear you sing again and to see if Jesus was going to blow up this place with all these sissies up in here trying to praise Him. I guess we'll soon find out if He hates us or not."

"You're crazy. Come on and say hello to my mama and them," I said. I smiled to myself as I thought, you could take the gay boy out of the club, but it didn't mean he would change his style just because he was going to worship.

After Skylar and my family exchanged pleasantries, we

walked into the ballroom, which was already filled with church members and their guests. I led my parents, siblings, and Skylar to their reserved seats in the first row and sat down with them.

I couldn't believe the turnout. There had to be over a thousand people in the ballroom. I thought back to when we'd come up with the idea for the Day of Absence service at Bruce Maxwell's house. It felt good to know that no matter how many people spoke out against us, there was still enough support and agreement that Damien's and his wife's messages were dangerous. Now tears felt close, but I held them at bay.

The service started. There were several speakers before the guest minister took the podium. Someone read a message from noted minister and professor Michael Eric Dyson, who sent his heartfelt regrets that he had a previous engagement but he wished us a wonderful service and commended us for speaking out against homophobia in the black church. Professor Dyson was heterosexual and was the first choice of the committee as the featured speaker, mostly because of his stance in support of gay and lesbian Christians in many of his popular books.

The committee had invited Keith Boykin, a handsome, openly gay writer and lecturer from New York. Boykin spoke eloquently about having the courage to speak out against people like Bishop Damien. He talked about formerly gay ministers and the self-loathing of gay men who go to these churches and support them by tithing. He closed by reminding the packed audience that "the bigger the saint, the greater the sin." He left the stage to thunderous applause.

Following Keith, several people offered personal testimonies about how important their faith was to them and how they still took pride in being gay. I was surprised when Vincent stood up and talked about once being sent to an ex–gay clinic by one of his music directors at a former church. It sounded like they'd admitted him into some type of asylum where he would be released only after he renounced his homosexuality.

"Well, you can see it didn't take," Vincent said as he snapped his fingers in the air. He went on to challenge the crowd to make our lives not about sex but about love. He shared that even though he still had carnal desires he'd decided to remain celibate until he found the right man.

After the entire congregation sang "The Center of My Joy," Bishop Dale Thornton, the guest minister from Detroit, took his place at the makeshift pulpit with a huge smile on his face.

The bishop told us a little about his background. He had led one of the largest churches in Michigan and had his own television show and a series of bestselling inspirational DVDs.

Bishop Thornton had sparked a national debate in the battle between AIDS activists and the church when he started an AIDS ministry. Almost half of his congregation had left the church in protest.

But that didn't stop the Bishop, and he'd appeared on several national talk shows admonishing the black church on its position on AIDS and gay people. His *Leave No Soul Behind* campaign became the mantra of black gay activists around the country.

The Bishop and his wife had recently moved their ministry to nearby Marietta, Georgia, and while I hadn't visited his church, I'd heard great things about his passion and preaching.

I nodded along as I listened to Bishop Thornton. His words touched my heart. He talked about forgiveness and how God's love never leaves us. In his message he used the words of nonjudgment he'd once heard in a sermon from Billy Graham. Billy Graham had been one of his heroes ever since he had refused to preach to a segregated audience in his boyhood town of Little Rock, Arkansas. To give us hope, the Bishop used the example of how much things had changed in terms of race relations not only in the South but all over the country. He prayed that he could live to see the day when our difference in sexual orientation would not be chastised but celebrated. He challenged the black church to stop acting like the KKK and to take their noses out of the sand when it came to admitting we had gay brothers and sisters who loved God as much as the grandmother who took care of everybody in the church. He said that all of us fell short of the perfection we thought God expected from us, but that He loved us and offered us forgiveness no matter who we were. I needed to hear that. That God loved me. I did love God. No matter what my orientation, no matter what sins I committed, God loved me.

My eyes looked to my parents, and my mother smiled. My father stayed stiff, without a smile on his face. I knew some of this had to make him uncomfortable, but still, I was thrilled that my father had gotten to that place where he could support me and my life.

"And now I'd like to introduce one of our very own." I hadn't even noticed that Vincent now stood at the podium. "You know, the first time we heard this brother sing," Vincent said, "he turned the church out."

A few amens rang out throughout the room.

Vincent continued, "And I know he'll do the same for us today. Join me in welcoming Brother Chauncey Greer."

The crowd applauded as I stood. I took slow steps to the microphone and then nodded my head slightly so the guy who was working the audio in the back knew I was ready for him to begin the track. I looked out into the crowd, but I couldn't help looking at my family. They were all beaming at me—even my father, and that by itself was enough to make me cry. But there would be time for that later. I closed my eyes, took a deep breath, waited for the prelude to end, and then opened my mouth. After the first verse, I could feel and hear the crowd stirring.

I looked at my family again and all I could see was my mother. Tears were already tracking down her cheeks, and I couldn't look at her anymore. So I focused on people I didn't know and sang on.

"If God is dead, what makes life . . ."

The words flowed from the depths of my soul. I was singing with every inch of my heart and soul for this Day of Absence. I was singing for all the gay men and women who had been victimized. I was singing for my family. I was singing for Skylar. But most of all, I was singing for God.

Letting Him know how much I loved Him. How much I wanted to please Him. How much I hoped that He was pleased with me.

"I can see Him moving through the trees . . ."

As I prepared to sing the last note, I leaned back slightly and let it all out.

For a few seconds after I finished, there was silence. And then a mighty applause filled the ballroom. Everyone stood to their feet, clapping, cheering, and shouting.

With my eyes closed, I raised my hands to the Lord and was no longer able to hold back my own tears. When I opened my eyes, I looked at my family—and every single one of them, Skylar, too, was standing, and clapping, and cheering, and crying.

Minutes passed before I was able to move. My legs were shaky as I walked back to my seat. I slumped into the pew and into my mother's arms as our tears of joy flowed uncontrollably.

CHAPTER THIRTY-FIVE

My parents left Atlanta happy that they'd come to hear me sing, but they didn't say much about the service. Mama smiled as we walked back to the car and said, "Well, that sure was something, wasn't it?" None of us responded; we just smiled at each other. Right before they left, my daddy commented on how well Vincent played the organ. He said, "That young man had the organ sounding like New Orleans jazz. I didn't know whether to pull out my Bible or a shot of good bourbon."

After they left, I made a salad out of some of Mom's left-over fried chicken and enjoyed it with a glass of strawberry lemonade Belinda had made. Just as I got ready to go to bed, the phone rang. Before I picked it up, I wondered how Damien's sermon had gone and if he and his wife were still in town. I looked at the caller ID and recognized Vincent's number.

"Hello."

"Chauncey, this is Vincent."

"Hey, Vincent, I was thinking about you earlier. My

daddy loved the way you played today. You had the old man tapping his feet," I said.

"Thank you, but you were the star. You sang up in that make-believe church. I was calling to thank you. You really made the service soar," Vincent said.

"Thanks, Vincent. That's so nice of you, but you didn't have to say that."

"You got a minute for a little gossip?"

"Gossip?"

"Well, I heard the bishop and his wife packed them in over at the service, but we were missed. I heard the choir didn't have nothing but women and three men, who all sang baritone. They didn't have enough ushers, and a couple of deacons who normally lead praise service were missing, too, but we know where they were," Vincent said, and laughed.

"So I guess we made our point," I said.

"Yes, I think we did."

"Did you hear anything about Damien—I mean Bishop Upchurch's sermon?"

"You know, I had a couple spies there. I heard he mentioned something about the controversy but that he wasn't going to stop because he felt he was doing God's work and sometimes it meant speaking out on unpopular topics. I understand he was mild compared to his missus."

"She preached?"

"My source said she had all the sisters shouting and amening. Talked about how unnatural homosexuality is and that gay people were responsible for the last days approaching. She had all the sisters stand and shout, 'The down low is low down.'"

"Sounds like a mess," I said.

"A hot mess, if you ask me," Vincent said.

"Well, I hope they're good and gone."

"I'm sure that's not the last we'll hear from him. I understand that he's twenty points ahead in his race, and I bet he plans to use the Senate as a bully pulpit against us."

"I'm tired of talking about the Upchurches. I wanted to ask you something."

"Holla."

"How tough is it being celibate?"

"Not tough at all. It ain't like I hadn't had my time in low places doing mess I know I didn't have no business doing. Put things in my mouth, well, I won't go there," Vincent said.

I was glad, because I was thinking he was getting pretty close to the share line.

"But don't you miss having sex? And feeling another human being next to you?"

"I miss it, but I'm not living like a monk. You can have somebody sleep with you and not do the do. I just try and live my life without drama and in a way God might smile on. If He wants someone in my life He will send him," Vincent said.

"What if He sends you a woman?" I asked.

Vincent let out a loud scream and said, "Honey, God knows me and He ain't gonna do something crazy like that. Haven't you heard? My God is a smart God."

I felt myself starting to laugh, so I thanked Vincent and said, "Good night."

* * *

A couple of days after the Day of Absence service, I was on my way to fulfilling my dreams. I was headed into the studio to record an eclectic CD, a collection of music that would include not only some R & B cuts but some inspirational ones as well. I was going to do it my way. I hired Big John, one of the top producers in the industry, who had come to the Day of Absence service at the hotel with his gay sister.

I checked my messages before leaving home. The first message was from an organization called AIDS Atlanta thanking me for the donation that had been made in my name by Phillip. He was truly growing and changing. There was one from Pastor Kenneth saying he wanted to talk to me and he also wanted me to sing at a surprise birthday party he was planning for his wife. It was good to hear his voice, and I decided to call him later to tell him I would be honored.

The next message startled me. It was Damien. He sound hurried: "Chauncey, you don't have to call me back, but there are some people out there trying to ruin my ministry and my campaign. They might try and use you to do it. Please don't let them. Try and remember the good times we shared."

I quickly erased his message and smiled to myself as I thought my good times were only beginning.

CHAPTER THIRTY-SIX

It was a lovely late-October evening, the time of year when cool wind held the faint hint of fall and the days slid slowly one into another. I was just entering my building from the parking garage after a four-hour recording session that I thought went really well. I was looking forward to having a drink, taking a warm bath, and listening to the tracks I'd laid down.

I went to the mailroom and found my box filled with bills and advertisements. When I walked into the lobby, I noticed a tall black man with his back toward me looking out of the window. Heading toward the elevator, I suddenly heard Reggie, the doorman, call out my name.

I turned and said, "You called me, Reggie?"

"Yes, Mr. Greer. That gentleman has been waiting for you for a couple of hours."

"Who?"

"Him," Reggie said as he pointed to the guy looking out the window.

I walked toward the window, and as I got closer I recognized the profile. He was wearing a camel-brown trench coat, but I knew I had seen him with much less on. It was Griffin.

"What are you doing here?" I asked.

Griffin turned around, and his eyes were the size of cookies. He looked like he was on drugs or something.

"Chauncey, I've been waiting to talk to you," Griffin said. His voice was full of urgency and distress.

"What do you want with me?"

"Can we go up to your place to talk?"

"What is this about, Griffin?"

"I think we need to talk in private," he said.

At first I was hesitant, and I thought about the last time we'd been together and how he'd given me the weird warning that turned out to be about Grayson Upchurch. I wondered if that's what this visit was about.

"Ten minutes," I said as I turned and started toward the elevator.

We rode up in silence. No small talk. No eye contact. I just watched the light hit the numbers on each floor as we went up.

A few moments later, I was turning the key to my apartment and could feel Griffin's breath on the back of my neck as we entered the dark residence.

I hit the light switch and laid my keys and mail on the counter without looking in Griffin's direction. I took off the lightweight jacket I was wearing and then turned around to face Griffin, whose eyes were still large.

I didn't offer him a drink or suggest that he take off his coat. I wanted him to have his say and get the fuck out of my apartment.

"So what do you need to talk to me about?"

"Someone is out to get you," he said softly.

I'd had enough, so I yelled, "Nigga, don't come here with that shit again. I don't have time to play games. If you're talking about Grayson, then don't worry. Is that who hired you the last time?"

"Sorta."

"What the fuck does that mean?"

"You've been talking to Damien, haven't you?"

"Who I talk to is my damn business." How did he know Damien, and how did he know we'd spoken?

"Chauncey, listen to me. Grayson doesn't play and she's on the warpath. She tracks everything Damien does. It's really out of control now, and I don't think this time she's going to just threaten you. If she thinks there's any way you might talk to the media before the election, she'll do anything to stop you."

"I can talk to whoever I want to, and her threats don't scare me. Now, if that's what you came to tell me, then you've wasted your time. I've got work to do," I said as I moved toward the door.

"Maybe you should talk to the media, and soon. That way if something happens to you the story will be out there."

"So what are you now, a model slash public relations guru?"

"I know Grayson Upchurch very well."

"What does she have over you? Why would you be her flunky?"

Griffin paused for a moment and then said something that shocked me. "Grayson is my sister."

Now my eyes were as big as his.

"What? Did you say Grayson is your sister? What kinda sick shit is this? She sent her brother here to fuck me, then find out information on me?"

"That wasn't work, and what she has over me is money. She's the executor of my father's will and, well, I had some financial problems and some bad investments and a boyfriend who was there during the good times but was gone once I ran out of money. Grayson sent some guy named Charles down here to seduce you, but I guess he wasn't your type. So she told me she'd help me with my debts if I came and found out if you were still involved with Damien."

"So if she's your sister, why are you down here warning me? What about your money?"

"She double-crossed me, and I know Grayson—she wants that Senate seat and she'll do anything to make sure it happens. I did my part, and the bitch gave me a check that wouldn't even pay for my dog groomer," he said.

"You don't look like you're doing so badly," I replied, noticing the yellow plaid Burberry cashmere scarf I'd seen in Saks Fifth Avenue. I knew for a fact it cost over two hundred dollars.

"I do what I do, and even my sister should know better than to fuck me," he said firmly.

I wanted to say, "I hear you talking," but I didn't respond

with words. I just looked at him directly in the eyes, search-ing for a preview of his plan.

"So do you want me to tell you what I think you should do?" Griffin asked.

I remained silent for a few more seconds, and then I said, "I'm listening."

"There is a producer I know over at CNN with *Larry King Live*. They want to do an interview with you the evening before the election. They would black out your face and distort your voice—all you'd have to do is to say you had an affair with Damien."

"Now, why would I want to do that?"

"Because I know someone in Denver who'd pay you a pretty penny for that interview."

"I don't want that kind of money."

"You don't have to take the money, but think how that would force Grayson and her cronies to leave you alone."

"What do you have to gain from this?"

"A little finder's fee from the state Democratic Party and payback," he said with a smile.

"I don't think so," I said as I moved toward the door again.

Griffin touched my arm and said, "Then if you don't do it for me, think about all the people you'd be helping if we made sure Damien was not elected. You know how he feels about men like us. If this comes out, there's no way the peo-ple in Colorado will send him to Washington."

"So I guess you don't like Damien," I said.

"Let's just say I think he's a snake in the grass, and if he outlives my sister then it will be him and not me spending my father's money. Besides, I'm not so certain he's given up men."

"What makes you say that?"

"I have my reasons. Starting with Charles. I mean, Grayson could have LoJacks built into Damien's suits, but he'd still do what he wanted. He's a man."

So Damien was still saving souls with the personal touch like he'd done with me. I knew he hadn't given up dudes. Once you sleep with and make love with another man the way Damien had with me, you never forget it. And no amount of pussy or money can change that. But why did he have to hurt people along the way?

"What do you want me to do?"

"Call this lady," Griffin said as he handed me a card with the name Lauren Masterson on it. "Just tell her your name and that you're calling about Bishop Upchurch. She will take it from there."

I stared at the card and then at Griffin and said, "I'm not sure I'm going to do this."

"Think about it. Grayson and Damien have to be stopped, and it's in your power to stop them," Griffin said firmly.

I continued to stare at the card and tapped it against the palm of my hand. I was so deep in thought that I didn't see or hear Griffin as he left my house.

CHAPTER THIRTY-SEVEN

After a meal of rib-eye steaks, fries, and salad, Skylar slouched in the big leather chair right off the dining room and sighed. "I feel like a fat woman who just closed down an all-you-can-eat buffet," he said.

"You did eat a lot for you. You getting a head start on your winter weight gain?" I asked.

"I don't gain weight," Skylar snapped.

I put the last of the plates in the dishwasher and stretched my arms toward the sky. I'd worked out before Skylar came over for dinner and my muscles were stiff and cold. I'd put off my workouts in recent weeks and now I was paying for it.

I wanted a drink, but instead I got a bottle of water from the fridge as the phone rang.

"Hello."

"*Please hold on for a message from the Republican Party,*" an automated voice announced.

"I don't think so," I said as I hung up the phone.

"You got any red wine?" Skylar asked.

"Check the bar. The maid and butler are gone for today," I said.

"Who was that?"

"Who?"

"On the phone."

"Somebody from the Republican Party with a message begging for my vote. Do you know where you vote on Tuesday?"

"I'm not voting," Skylar said as he headed toward the bar.

"What. Why not?"

"Is Jesse or Al running?"

"No."

"Is Bill Clinton running?"

"He can't run."

"What about Hillary?"

"For the Senate in New York."

"Then I ain't voting," Skylar said as he poured himself a glass of wine.

"Come on, Skylar, you've got to vote. If Bush gets to put two people on the Supreme Court, we might not have the right to vote," I said.

"Bush or whoever that woodlike man is he's running against—my little vote won't make a bit of difference."

"You gonna vote," I said sternly.

"Let's go out," Skylar said.

"Where?"

"To a club. Let's go look at some boys with slinging dicks," Skylar said.

"You know I'm not going to a club. Why even waste your breath?"

The phone rang again.

"Let me get it," Skylar said.

Before I could respond, Skylar picked up my phone and said, "Greer residence. How may I serve you?"

"Skylar, give me that phone," I said.

"Yes, he is. May I tell him who's calling? Who? A Mr. Gains from CNN. What is this regarding?" Skylar asked in a voice that sounded like it belonged to the perfect girl Friday.

"Skylar, give me that phone," I said as I snatched the phone from his ear. I rolled my eyes at him, put the phone to my ear, and said, "Hello."

"Mr. Greer, this is Terrence Gains, a senior producer at CNN for *Larry King Live*. I got your number from Griffin. He told me you had some information that we are interested in. Can I meet with you tomorrow morning to discuss this?"

"What do you want to discuss?"

Mr. Gains told me they were doing an exposé on Damien and wanted to interview me about our relationship. I told them that I wasn't sure I wanted to do that. I wasn't ready to air my dirty drawers in public.

"Mr. Greer, this is very important. The election is only a few days away, and don't you think the voters of Colorado need to know everything about the man who might be their next senator?"

"I don't know if that's up to me."

"Will you just meet with me? There are ways we could do this without you being identified," he said.

"Give me your number and I will give you a call in the morning."

I took the number and jotted it down, and when I hung up the phone I looked at Skylar and said, "The world just got more bizarre." I told him about the phone conversation with the producer, and Skylar's eyes perked up.

"Oh, this is so exciting. You're going to be a celebrity like Monica what's-her-name," he said as he clapped his hands gleefully.

"I'm not going to do it," I said.

"Oh yes, you are. That man messed all over you, and now you got a chance to get back at him. Better yet, let the world know who this gay-basher really is."

"I'm through with it, Skylar."

"Isn't this just as important as me voting?"

"One has nothing to do with the other," I said.

Skylar grabbed both of my wrists and looked me dead in the eyes and said in a serious tone I'd never heard him use, "Chauncey, you've got to do this. The hate the kids hear in churches and political organizations leads to violence against people like you and me. You got to do it. By telling your truths, it will make all these haters with less-than-perfect backgrounds reconsider who they trampled on. Do it for that young girl in Newark who got killed because she was a lesbian. Think about Matthew Shepard. Do it for me. If you do this I promise I'll vote, even though I'm just going to write in Reverend Al."

I didn't answer Skylar. I just looked straight ahead and rested my eyes on the painting over my buffet. Could telling what I knew about Damien make a difference in the world?

Did I have the courage to do it?

CHAPTER THIRTY-EIGHT

I walked into my office a little past nine to the aroma of Ms. Gladys's cinnamon rolls. Her back was facing me, and it looked like she was placing more icing on the calorie-laden delicacies. When she turned around, I realized I'd made the right decision the night before. I'd met with the producers of CNN and agreed to tell my story as long as my face wasn't shown and my voice was distorted. The producer was so excited, I thought she was going to kiss me. She said they would start their promos immediately, and we agreed to do the interview later in the evening.

"Good morning, Chauncey," she said with a smile. Ms. Gladys was wearing a cotton-candy-pink sweater with a blue *W* button on one side and a red *Purdue for Governor* button on the other.

"Good morning, Ms. Gladys. Did you make cinnamon rolls?"

"Can't you smell them?"

"I sure can. May I have one with some coffee?"

"Sure. Celia has already had one and a little smidgen of a second one. You running a little late this morning?"

"Yeah, I had a meeting downtown. So Celia is in her office?"

"Yes, she told me to tell her when you got in. Said she had to talk to you about something. I can tell you whatever it is, it's weighing heavy on her mind. That young girl got stress marks all over her forehead," Ms. Gladys said.

"Tell her I can see her whenever she's ready."

"Will do."

I walked into my office and looked out of the huge picture window onto the city. Would my life change after this evening, and would the truth about our relationship finally hurt Damien like it had hurt me?

A part of me wanted to call him and tell him what I was going to do, but I figured Grayson would intercept the call and he'd be taken out like a boxer's sucker punch. I wondered if this would hurt my planned music career, but told myself I didn't want fans who would be offended by my truth.

Ms. Gladys came in with coffee and a cinnamon roll. This time when I saw the buttons she was wearing, I couldn't resist asking her a question.

"Ms. Gladys, I would have taken you as a Democrat. Are you sure your minister wants you to vote Republican?"

"That's what God wants."

"How can you be sure?" I asked.

"Because of what the Democrats stand for. You know

they take us black folks for granted—welfare, support of abortion, and gay marriage. All those things are against God's will," she said.

"How do you know that?"

"Because it says so in the Bible."

"Ms. Gladys, with all due respect, in Ephesians 6 it says, 'Slaves be obedient to your masters.' Do you believe that?"

"All I believe is that George W. is a God-fearing man who my God wants to be president, and so I'm going to vote for him and do my part. I guess you think that other guy is better. We elect him and we'll have another Sodom and Gomorrah."

I decided this conversation was going nowhere. Ms. Gladys wouldn't believe me even if I showed her in Ezekiel 16 that God never mentions homosexuality in his list of Sodom's sins. When people like Ms. Gladys and her church made up their minds, there was no easy way to make them change their opinions. All I could do was stuff the cinnamon roll down my throat and hope it prevented me from speaking until Ms. Gladys was out of my office.

* * *

A few moments later, Celia came in with a sour look on her face.

"You look like I feel," I said as I glanced up from a notepad where I'd absently scribbled *Sodom*.

"What's the matter with you?" Celia asked as she took a seat.

"Just kinda bummed out at Ms. Gladys for being a Bush supporter."

"Yeah, I was surprised, too, but there are a lot of black church folks voting for him," Celia said.

"Are you voting tomorrow?"

"I guess."

"Celia, you've got to vote."

"Yeah, I know."

"What's bothering you? Marvin hasn't been bothering you, has he?"

"Not lately."

"Gladys said you needed to speak with me about something."

Celia cleared her throat and looked around my office and then said, "I've been offered a job, and I'm thinking about taking it."

"A job. Where?" I asked. I didn't know if this was a ploy to get more money or if Celia was serious. I'd never known her to be that type of person. I didn't know how I could run my company without Celia.

"Wal-Mart has offered me a marketing manager's position. I would be working with their card and calendar section. I would be responsible for over ten states," Celia said.

"Is this about money? Because if it is, we can talk about a raise. I mean, I was going to give you a bonus for the Wal-Mart deal."

"No, it's not about money. They have offered me a ten

percent increase, but I know you're fair and would match it. This is more about me needing a change," Celia said.

"A change?"

"Yes. Chauncey, you see, the job would require me to move to Bentonville, Arkansas. I need to get out of Atlanta."

"Bentonville, Arkansas? Celia, please, how long do you think you're going to last in Arkansas?" I asked.

"Well, Tulsa, Kansas City, and Dallas are all within driving distance," she said.

"Celia, don't let Marvin run you out of the city. You're stronger than that," I said.

Celia was silent for a moment, and then she looked at me with doe eyes and said, "No, I'm not. If I stay here, I know I'll end up back in his arms. And one day when he slaps me, he might not stop," she said mournfully.

I moved from behind my desk and went over to Celia and put my arms around her like a big brother. At first I heard her sniffles, which soon turned into out-and-out boo-hooing.

I wanted to think of something I could tell her that would make her feel better, but I couldn't, so I said what my mother used to tell me and my siblings when we cried buckets of tears: "Let it out, baby. God can't fill the Mississippi River every day."

*   *   *

As the day came to an end, Celia walked into my office with her face freshly made up and a trace of a smile.

"How you doing, Celia?" I asked.

"Much better. Thank you," she said.

"For what?"

"Being there," Celia said.

"And you know I'll always be here for you. Even if you're in Bentonville, Arkansas," I said.

"Maybe that won't happen. I talked to Ms. Gladys and I think I'm going to stick it out here. I mean, if I still have a job," Celia said.

"You'll have a job as long as I'm around," I said.

"Good. I think I can handle this situation and I'm not letting Marvin or any man run me out of the city I love," Celia said forcefully.

"I know you can do it."

"That's right, I'm a strong black woman like my mama and Ms. Gladys. I'm not running, and I might even go back to that church of yours and find me a husband."

I started to laugh and tell her maybe she should try the nightclub Twist, but instead I hugged her and whispered, "I'm so very proud to know you."

CHAPTER THIRTY-NINE

I needed to show courage.

I needed to tell the truth.

I looked at Ms. Masterson and said, "Okay, let's do this."

"Wonderful, Mr. Greer! You've made the right decision. Let me tell Mr. King and the director. I will be back to get you in five minutes."

I looked at my watch. It was 8:30 P.M. in Atlanta, 5:30 in Denver on the eve of Election Day, with the presidential race still in doubt. I wondered if the Colorado Senate race would be in doubt after I sat down with Larry King.

I pulled out my cell phone and started to call my sister to tell her to turn her television to CNN, but then I remembered she didn't have cable because she thought it was bad for her children. I didn't think of calling my parents, because I didn't know how they would react. Anyway, I was certain that someone in Mississippi would see me and call and tell them.

I walked over to the table of food and picked up a bottle of water. The green room was now empty. As I opened the bottle, my cell phone rang. I looked at the display and saw a 303 number flash on the screen.

"Hello."

"Chauncey. Where are you?"

"Damien. What are you doing calling me?"

"Where are you?" he repeated.

"In Atlanta. Where are you?"

"I'm getting ready to make a speech."

"So what can I do for you, Damien?"

"Chauncey, please tell me what I just heard isn't true."

"That depends on what you heard."

"That you're going on *Larry King* to talk about our relationship."

"What relationship? According to you, we never had a relationship," I snapped.

"So it's not true."

"Oh, I'm going on *Larry King* in a few minutes. I'm already here at the studio. *But don't you worry*—I'm telling my truth. Not the one you've convinced yourself of."

"Chauncey, please don't do this. Remember when I told you someone was out to get me?"

"Yeah."

"I found out who it is, and they're using you."

"What are you talking about?"

"It's my wife, Grayson, and her brother. They've set you up to expose me. Please don't do the show," he implored.

"Damien, you're not making sense. Your wife's already planning for you to move into the White House. Why would she want to set you up? I thought you guys were so in *love*."

"I'm still in shock, but one of my campaign workers confessed to being a part of the plan. Listen to me. Please don't do the show. Walk out of that studio and I promise to call you later and explain. I will make this up."

"You sound like a crazy man. I've got a show to do," I said.

Just as I was getting ready to hang up, Damien said, "Chauncey, if I ever meant anything to you, please don't do this to me."

"Good-bye, Damien."

I hung up my cell phone and turned the power off. I looked out of the green room door for Lauren Masterson. There was no one in the hallway. What was going on? Just as I turned to go back into the room, I noticed three people coming through an off-white metal door. Even though I was about a hundred feet from them, I recognized them immediately. Grayson and Griffin were talking to Lauren Masterson and didn't even notice me. I slipped back into the room. I pulled out my cell phone, powered it on, and dialed the number Damien had called me from moments earlier. After the first ring, it went immediately into voice mail.

"Damien, call me right back," I said.

As I clicked my phone off, Lauren walked back into the room with a mic pack.

"Are you ready?"

"Lauren, what's going on?"

"What do you mean? We're ready to do the show. Are you nervous? That's okay and it's normal."

"What are Grayson Upchurch and her brother doing here?"

Lauren's face went from pale to crimson. She nervously messed with her earphones, looked down at her clipboard and then up at me.

"What are you talking about?"

"I just saw you with Grayson and her brother. What's going on?"

"Oh, you must be mistaken. Those were some guests for another show," she said nervously. What was going on, and why was this lady telling me a bald-faced lie? She then pushed the mic pack into my hand and instructed me to put it in my wallet pocket.

"They will attach the mic once we're on set."

"I don't need this," I said.

"What?"

"I'm not doing the show," I said.

"Not this again. I thought you had made up your mind," she said.

"I've made up my mind. Get your story somewhere else," I said. I walked out of the green room and down the hallway.

Lauren followed me, yelling, "You can't do this to me."

I walked swiftly past the door where I'd seen Grayson and Griffin walk in. I was tempted to look in and tell them their plan had failed, but instead I continued down the hall until I was standing in front of a bank of elevators. I pushed the down button and pulled out my cell phone again to try and reach Damien.

Just as the elevator arrived and I was getting ready to step on, I turned and saw Grayson and Griffin running toward me, with Lauren a few paces behind. They didn't look happy.

"Come back here, you faggot," Grayson screamed.

"My, my, such language for a minister's wife," I said.

"Grayson, stop it," Griffin said. "There are cameras and recording devices all over this place."

"I'm not letting him get away with this," Grayson said. "Come back here and go and tell the world my husband is a booty packer. Force him to resign so I can take his place on the ticket."

"If you do this, there could be a lot of money in it," Griffin said in a hushed tone.

"I told you I'm not interested in dirty money," I said.

Griffin moved close to me, pulled my arm, and whispered, "Then we'll make sure nothing happens to you."

I jerked my arm back, pushed him, and shouted, "Mutherfucker, your punk ass don't scare me."

I pushed the down button again. I looked over at Grayson, who was crying and cussing at Lauren at the same time.

"Make him do it, you silly bitch. Make him stay and do the interview."

When the elevator opened, I looked back at the three stooges and shook my head in disgust.

* * *

About an hour later, I nursed a naked glass of brandy in the dimness of my living room. I had intended to put on some music and light some candles, but the silence was comforting, like a thick cloud of air covering me and everything around me.

I thought about how close I'd come to finally hurting Damien like he'd hurt me. Then I realized something profound. My life was broken. Had been broken so long ago. And I thought of all the dreams I'd prevented from entering my head because of a failed youthful relationship that never really had a chance.

How would my life have been if I'd taken the time to mourn the end of my relationship with Damien for a couple of months and then gotten back on the horse called love? Where would I be in that life? Would I be looking into the glowing eyes of love instead of stale darkness?

I noticed there was only a sip of brandy left in my glass, and when I got up to refill the glass, the phone rang. Without even looking at the caller identification, I knew who was calling me.

"Hello."

"Chauncey, thank you," Damien said. There was a surprising gentleness in his voice.

"For what? I didn't do anything for you," I said.

"Well, I guess it's not so much what you did as much as what you *didn't* do. I can't tell you how relieved I was when I realized you weren't going to be on *Larry King Live*," Damien said.

"So you never told me why your wife was trying to call you out," I said.

"It's pretty hard to believe."

"I have an active imagination. Give me a try."

"Grayson was trying to get back at me," Damien said soberly.

"For what?"

"Over an alleged affair."

"With who?"

"One of my campaign consultants."

"Male or female?"

"Does it matter?"

"Answer the question, Damien," I demanded.

"A young man name Charles who worked as a consultant for me. He's the one who put me in contact with your minister for the revival."

"So was it true?"

"What?"

"Damn it, Damien, stop playing games!"

"No, it wasn't true."

"Are you sure?"

"Yes."

"Then what's the truth?"

There was silence for a moment, and then Damien started to talk again. "The truth is God is not finished with me yet and I allowed my homosexual demons to take over one night."

"It's not about some fucking demons, Damien. It's about the fact that you're still attracted to men."

"Let me finish."

"Damien, do you understand that when you use terms like 'homosexual demons' it's hurtful and mean-spirited to people trying to live their lives the best they know how?"

"I didn't mean to hurt you."

"Which time?" I snapped.

"I had a one-night stand with the person you know as Griffin, and when I didn't want to do it again he tried to blackmail me. He arranged for Charles to come into my life. Charles and I had a relationship that wasn't sexual, but Griffin convinced Grayson that we were having an affair. He used some of the information about me that he knew from our one-time fling."

"What did he tell her? About the diamond-shaped birthmark on your dick?"

"Something like that."

"So if you are so much in love, you couldn't tell your wife the truth? Don't you worship a God that's forgiving?"

"It's more complicated than that."

"I'm sure it is, but I'm getting ready for bed. I have to vote tomorrow."

"Okay. Thanks again, even though you don't know how much you helped me. If there is there anything I can do, let me know."

Suddenly, I knew what I wanted.

"There is something you can do for me, Damien."

"What?"

"You can tell me the truth."

"About what?"

"Tell me the truth right now about us. Did our relationship mean anything to you other than sex?"

"It was more than just sex. I mean, the sex was great, but I really, really loved you."

For a moment, his words rendered me speechless. How I'd longed to hear Damien say something like that again.

"Chauncey, are you still there?"

"I'm still here. There is something else I want you to do for me."

"What?"

"I want you to stop all your hate speech against gay people. Pick on somebody else from your bully pulpit."

"My supporters would never let me do that," he said.

"Then I will have to do what I have to do," I said.

"What do you mean?"

"I mean, if I hear you speaking out against your own kind again, then I will release the tape to the press."

"What tape?"

"The tape you and I just made. You're getting ready to enter the Senate, so you should be a little smarter. You never know when somebody might be taping your conversation. Remember that the first time a lobbyist offers you money in a brown paper bag. Remember, Damien, I will be watching and listening. It's totally up to you."

"Chauncey, you didn't," Damien yelled.

"I'm still taping," I said.

"Can we talk about this?"

"You have a good night," I said.

"When will I hear from you again?" Damien asked.

"When you least expect it," I said as I hung up the phone with a smile as wide as the Mississippi Delta.

I decided against another drink, so I turned off the lights and headed toward my bedroom. A peaceful tenderness had come over me, and I was thinking about what I was going to say to God when I got on my knees to pray.

There was so much I wanted to ask for when the rest of my life started the next morning. But first I had to ask for forgiveness. For being gay? Naw, not that. For lying to a future U.S. senator about a taping that never happened.

Election Day came. The city felt unusually quiet on a brilliant, sun-washed day. I walked the three blocks from my home to the middle school where I voted. It was a beautiful pink-red building with cobblestone sidewalks surrounded by towering oak trees. I felt a nervous energy flooding through me as I walked into the building like it was the first time I'd voted. Somehow today felt different. Like I was going to be a part of something special and when I placed my ballot in the box I felt relief. No matter what happened I'd let my voice be heard. I told myself it was okay for me to keep my memories of Damien for myself and not become the activist Skylar wanted.

I was finally ready for some me time and I was going to use it being the person God created me to be. A man who was happy with himself and who he was and happy with life.

When I got to my office I was welcomed with the marvelous smell of food. Ms. Gladys had turned the outer office into a southern buffet. I looked at the table and saw fried

chicken, collard greens, and potato salad. Ms. Gladys herself was taking a piping-hot waffle out of the waffle iron.

"Good morning, Chauncey. I hope you're hungry," Ms.
Gladys said.

"I am, but what's going on? Is it somebody's birthday?"
I asked.

"Not really, but it is a special day," she said.

"What? Election Day?"

"That, too, but today is a special day because the good
Lord woke me up this morning, he woke you up, and I know
he woke Celia up because we had prayer this morning over
the phone. Now isn't that something to celebrate?"

"Yes, it is," I said.

"Today might be the day when one or all of us do or
start something special that can change the world or somebody's life," she said. "Now I'm going to make you a plate
and bring it into your office. You want pecans on your
waffle?"

"Yes, Ms. Gladys, I'd like that," I said.

When I sat down at my desk I thought about Ms. Gladys
and what a gem she was. Then I noticed the card of one of
the producers who'd offered to help produce my CD. I
decided at that moment that I couldn't wait or depend on
some record company to come and sign me up. God had
given me my talent but it was up to me to make it happen.
Today was that day.

Just as I picked up the phone and was getting ready to
dial the number, Ms. Gladys walked in with a plate of delicious food. She put a placemat on my desk followed by the

plate, and I noticed Ms. Gladys wearing a button that said, *Vote Democratic.*

"Ms. Gladys, what's that?" I asked as I pointed to the large red-and-white button.

"Now, Chauncey, I know you can read," Ms. Gladys said.

"But what happened to what God and your minister wanted you to do?"

"I think my minister was sending me the wrong signals, so I might be joining you at that little church of yours."

"So you had a change of heart?" I asked.

"You could say that, but more than anything I got a message from above. Last night I had a dream. I dream all the time but I don't always remember them. But this one was loud and clear. My husband asked me what was my fool behind doing voting for someone I didn't believe in, and I don't know if he meant the President or that minister of mine, so I'm kicking them both to the curb. My husband also told me that my sons were coming home soon, clean and sober, so I needed to get ready to be a mother again. I told him I was already being a mother to you and Celia."

"That's right," I said.

"My mother was in the dream too, looking just as beautiful and feisty as ever. Guess what she said to me?"

"What?" I asked.

"If the shoes fit, they yours."

E. LYNN HARRIS is a former IBM computer sales executive and a graduate of the University of Arkansas at Fayetteville. He is the author of eight novels: *A Love of My Own*, *Any Way the Wind Blows*, *Not a Day Goes By*, *Abide with Me*, *If This World Were Mine*, *And This Too Shall Pass*, *Just As I Am*, *Invisible Life*, and the memoir *What Becomes of the Brokenhearted*. *Just As I Am*, *Any Way the Wind Blows*, and *A Love of My Own* were named Novel of the Year by the Blackboard African American bestsellers, Inc. *If This World Were Mine* won the James Baldwin Award for Literary Excellence. In 2000, 2001, and 2002, Harris was named one of the fifty-five "Most Intriguing African Americans" by *Ebony* and inducted into the Arkansas Black Hall of Fame. In 2002, Harris was included in *Savoy* magazine's "100 Leaders and Heroes in Black America." His memoir was given a Lambda Literary Bridge Builders Award. Harris divides his time between Atlanta, Georgia, and Fayetteville, Arkansas. He is currently writer-in-residence and visiting professor at the University of Arkansas at Fayetteville.